M000197104

HIGH STAKES TRIAL

HIGH STAKES TRIAL

WASHINGTON VAMPIRES (MAGICAL WASHINGTON) - BOOK 3

MINDY KLASKY

ALSO BY MINDY KLASKY

You can always find a complete, up-to-date list of Mindy's books (including books in other genres) on her website.

The Washington Vampires Series (Magical Washington)

Fright Court

Law and Murder

High Stakes Trial

The Washington Witches Series (Magical Washington)

Girl's Guide to Witchcraft

Sorcery and the Single Girl

Magic and the Modern Girl

Single Witch's Survival Guide

Joy of Witchcraft

The Washington Warders Series (Magical Washington)

The Library, the Witch, and the Warder

The Washington Medical Series (Magical Washington)

The Witch Doctor Is In

Fae's Anatomy

The Lady Doctor Is In

Copyright © 2019 by Mindy Klasky

All rights reserved.

No part of this book may be reproduced in any form or by any electronic or mechanical means, including information storage and retrieval systems, without written permission from the author, except for the use of brief quotations in a book review.

This is a work of fiction. Any references to historical events, real people, or real locales are used fictitiously. Other names, characters, places, and incidents are products of the author's imagination, and any resemblance to actual events or locales or persons, living or dead, is entirely coincidental.

Cover design by Dreams2Media

Published by Book View Café Publishing Cooperative
P.O. Box 1624, Cedar Crest, NM 87008-1624
www.bookviewcafe.com

ISBN 978-1-61138-808-4

Discover other titles by Mindy Klasky at www.mindyklasky.com

042519mkm

1

I, *Sarah Anderson, do solemnly swear that I will strangle the sadist who invented Take Your Child to Work Day.*

After all, I was a sphinx. My ancestors were bred to strangle criminals in the earliest days of Egyptian civilization. And I couldn't think of a criminal in the history of the Eastern Empire who was more deserving of execution than the torturer who thought up Take Your Child to Work Day.

Exhibit 1 for my exoneration: The word "your." I wasn't the parent of any child. In fact, given the shambles of my love-life, I wasn't likely ever to *become* a parent.

Exhibit 2: The word "child." Children accompanying beloved parents to stimulating days at offices in the mundane world were human boys and girls. But the children visiting my workplace included one griffin, a centaur, a basilisk, a sylph, and a cat shifter. It was hard enough for adult imperials to mind their manners when that many imperial races were thrust together in close quarters. I'd already separated the obligate carnivores from the prey species three times, and my chances of maintaining the peace for the rest of the night were low.

Exhibit 3: The word "day." I worked for the Eastern Empire *Night* Court. We were open at *night*, when well-behaved children were snug in their jammies, tucked into bed, their slumbering minds filled with sweet dreams. Children who were forced to stay awake hours past their bedtimes, wearing uncomfortable grown-up clothes, and listening to incomprehensible legal mumbo-jumbo were most decidedly *not* well-behaved children.

But as clerk of court, I was a devoted team player, intent on making Washington DC safe for imperial and mundane citizens alike. Especially when we had a new judge on the bench. In fact, Elizabeth Finch was the first new judge in twenty years.

I, um, killed the last one.

Sure, as a sphinx I was supposed to *protect* vampires, not kill them. Protecting vampires was literally in my DNA. But when paranormal push had come to supernatural shove, the best protection I could offer Judge Robert DuBois was giving him the coup de grâce, releasing him after a magical battle where those of us on the side of right and justice had come up short.

Very short.

Ten months later, I was still recovering from the emotional and physical fallout of that fight. Sphinxes weren't sure what to make of me because I'd murdered a vampire I was sworn to protect. Vampires didn't trust me either because, well, ditto.

I had to prove I was a team player. So, when Judge Finch personally asked me to manage the court's Take Your Child to Work Day, er, night, festivities, I reluctantly agreed.

Of course, I hadn't taken into account how long it would take the kids to clear court security. Since last June, we'd been functioning at Security Level Orange—limited access through a secret underground entrance, heightened restrictions on the metal detectors, hand inspection of all bags larger than a standard briefcase, and regular full-court searches by bomb-sniffing wolf shifters.

All of the adults who worked at the court had grown used to the routine. We called it Security Theater, an elaborate charade intended to make us forget that Maurice Richardson—the most vicious criminal mastermind of the vampire world—had been on the loose for ten months. Judge DuBois's unfortunate demise had resulted in a mistrial in the case that was supposed to put Richardson behind silver for the rest of his unnatural life.

We adults were used to the hurry-up-and-wait of court security, but the kids were restless even before I rounded them up for a fun night of wholesome, educational, workplace-based activities.

It didn't help that we needed to stay in hiding for the first four hours of night court, the time when humans frequented the hallways and Judge Finch heard mundane cases. I kept the kids isolated in a dusty supply room down a long, deserted corridor, far from the actual courtroom and any chance we'd be spotted by mortals.

Twisting the hematite bracelet on my left wrist, I fought the urge to straighten the shelves around me. The clutter of partially used notepads jangled in my mind like out-of-tune violins. The plastic bin that held a jumbled pile of pasteboard folders made my palms itch.

But if I started organizing the supply closet, I'd never get the kids to settle down. Instead, I tapped the face of my coral signet ring, trying to reassure my sphinx brain that a little disorder had never killed anyone. Yet.

With desperate good cheer, I handed out word-search puzzles, explaining to the kids that they were going to find fun terms related to the case Judge Finch was hearing that night. As they dutifully started to circle letters, I told them about plaintiffs and defendants, doing my best to make land-use litigation sound engaging. *Easement*, I said brightly, helping them pick out letters on the diagonal. *Laches. Estoppel.*

Why the hell weren't these kids visiting some *other* parent's workplace?

Using a fresh box of sixty-four crayons that I'd snagged from the local drugstore, we colored the court's logo—an ornately carved sword that pinned down a sheaf of parchment.

I dumped a huge bin of Legos (thank you, Amazon Prime)

onto the table, and each kid built something related to the courthouse—the judge's massive bench, a gavel, a fragile scale of
justice. That activity met its untimely end when the cat shifter
started rigging an electric chair.

After a refreshing snack break of cookies and juice, I handed
out workbooks ruthlessly cadged from a computer site: "What I
Want to be When I Grow Up." I passed out pencils and
watched the kids complete their scaled-down version of the
Myers-Briggs personality test.

It wasn't my fault the centaur came back with "meatpacker"
as his primary job focus. It only took half an hour to get him to
stop sobbing when he realized exactly where packed meat came
from. (How many meatpacking plants even existed these days?)

The sylph wasn't thrilled with the recommendation that she
pursue a career in nuclear power reactors. And I couldn't begin
to explain to the griffin that "ballerina" was never going to fly,
not for a mountain spirit who already clocked in at more than
two hundred pounds.

So much for the workbooks.

"Okay, kids," I said, glancing with relief at the clock on the
wall. "It's time to head into the courtroom. But before we go,
what is Judge Finch's number three rule?" We'd rehearsed them
every hour, on the hour.

"No talking to humans!" shouted the cat shifter, loud
enough that any human within a five-hundred-yard radius could
easily hear.

I nodded before I prompted, "And Judge Finch's number
two rule?"

"No harming other imperials," recited the sylph, with a
sweet smile that almost made me miss the hungry looks the
shifter directed toward the centaur foal.

I smiled encouragement at all the kids, hoping my own calm
demeanor would still the savage beasts. "And Judge Finch's
number one rule, the most important one of all?"

"No speaking out loud while court is in session," the basilisk hissed.

Well, I'd indoctrinated them as much as possible. Still, my heart pounded with misgiving as I led my ragtag army down the hall to the courtroom. I was just about to open the heavy oak doors when the centaur clutched the crotch of his pants, shifting from foot to foot and whinnying an all-too-familiar song of need.

"Time for a pit-stop, kids," I announced, making a detour to the restrooms. It only took fifteen minutes to get my motley army pottied, zipped, and hands-washed before we reached the courtroom's massive oak doors.

"Remember, everyone," I whispered, exaggerating the words by raising my eyebrows. I set a finger on my lips, and five earnest heads nodded. I eased the door open, and my charges slipped inside.

Judge Finch glanced up as we settled on the back bench. She still manifested her human form, the mien she wore to handle human cases before midnight. Her shoulders sloped beneath her black robes. When she blinked, her muddy brown eyes watered. Her hair was frizzy, a tragic victim of Washington DC's legendary humidity, even though it was only late April.

Before she settled her gaze on me, her eyes flickered to the clock at the back of the courtroom. Shrugging, I tried to think of a discreet way to tell her we'd been unavoidably delayed by various calls of nature. She pursed her lips, carving lines on either side of her narrow mouth.

The skin on her hands looked powdery as she reached for the sleek steel carafe beside her gavel. Lifting a cut-crystal goblet, she poured precisely, taking care not to spill a drop. The liquid was dark, nearly black in the courtroom's fluorescent lights. A fine curl of steam rose from the surface.

As Judge Finch downed her cocktail of fresh blood, the basilisk bounced up and down and whispered, "Cool!" At the same time, the centaur began to tremble, his reaction violent enough that I was grateful his bladder was empty.

Judge Finch turned a cold smile toward my little group, her fangs clearly visible. My little centaur tossed his head, looking wildly from left to right.

"Ms. Anderson," the judge warned. "If you can't keep your charges quiet, I will be forced to take action myself."

Clearing the courtroom. She meant clearing the courtroom, sending all unnecessary imperials away as she adjudicated the stultifying case at hand.

But the glint in her vampire eye threatened more. And the tongue she flicked past her fangs only emphasized her power.

I—a sphinx, a strangler, a confident imperial citizen with full awareness of my rights—wasn't afraid. But the centaur child beside me began to keen, a high neigh of distress that echoed in the marble-walled courtroom.

I caught a flash of motion out of the corner of my eye. The cat-shifter brat, my direct boss's daughter, was rubbing her thumb over the nails of her right hand.

The centaur wasn't terrified by Judge Finch—at least not completely. The centaur was terrified because the cat shifter had raked her nails across his nape. Even now, a trio of bright red lines ripened on the centaur's trembling neck.

"Ms. Anderson!" Judge Finch bellowed. She didn't need to follow up with a direct command. I understood that I needed to get the kids out of the courtroom immediately.

Snatching the petrified centaur's hand, I pulled him to the aisle between the courtroom's hard wooden benches. With more whispers than should have been necessary, I got the other kids moving as well—the smug cat-shifter, the docile sylph, the stolid griffin.

The basilisk brat held his place. "What?" he said, in response to my jutted chin and glare. "You said we could watch Judge Finch!"

"I've got treats, back in my office," I wheedled. When that

did nothing, I tried, "I've got special secret agent pens for everyone." Bupkis. I brought out the big guns. "We can play on the computer!"

All five kids fell in line without further hesitation.

So that's how we ended up back in my office, with three more hours of Take Your Child to Hell left to endure. My emergency Valrhona chocolate bar was broken into six portions—even though the kids didn't have the good sense to recognize superior confectionery when it melted across their tongues.

I grabbed a handful of pens, the retractable ones, with Skilcraft embossed on their clips. "Here you go, kids. Secret agent pens. Each one will write for an entire mile of ink!"

That's what the box said, anyway. The griffin's broke the first time she set its point to paper.

That left the computer. And there was no way I was going to let anyone—much less a group of chocolate-sticky kids—use my office computer. That was common sense, not my obsessive-compulsive control-freak temperament shining through.

But the kids were supposed to see what a workplace was like, right? And my workplace involved handling massive amounts of information, new filings in a vast array of cases. And those filings were on my computer. So I hadn't really lied to them, back in the courtroom. They *were* going to get to play on my computer. Or, at least, to watch while *I* played.

Or, you know, got a tiny bit of work done on this evening of otherwise-wasted time. "Okay, everyone," I said. "Here's something most people never get to see! Here's how one of Judge Finch's cases starts!"

I sat in front of my computer and encouraged my five charges to gather around. Fighting the twinge in my gut as I broke up the order and precision of my desk alcove, I tilted my computer monitor so they could see the screen more clearly.

My fingers moved over the keyboard automatically, entering my password to access the Eastern Empire's secret court docu-

ments. I clicked on a flashing box to pull up the first filing
waiting for me to process.

"Oh, look, kids!" I pointed toward the bold-face title. "This
is an *indictment*. That's when a group of imperials just like you
gets together in a great big room. They're called the *grand jury*,
and their job is to listen to *witnesses* who all tell the truth about
something that happened. If the grand jury thinks a *crime* has
been committed, then a lawyer called the *prosecutor* files an
indictment, so Judge Finch can decide if the grand jury is right."

The kids nodded gravely.

The basilisk, son of a prosecutor, boasted, "My mom puts
lots of bad people in jail. They stay there years and years and
years."

There was no need for me to elaborate that some criminals'
stays were cut short by execution. The tear-stained centaur by
my right elbow might never sleep again. Instead, I scrolled down
a little further.

"Here we go!" I said, as if I'd just discovered a pirate king's
buried treasure. "This line says that the case is being heard in
the Night Court of the Eastern Empire."

The kids nodded, eyes wide.

I scrolled down again and pointed to *Clans of the Eastern
Empire*. "And this means the case is being brought on behalf of
every single one of us, because the Empire wants every citizen
to be safe and sound."

My audience caught its collective breath.

Smiling with confidence, pleased that I finally had everyone's attention, I turned back to the screen. "And the next part
says who the defendant is."

I paused a moment, adding to the drama for my dedicated
little audience. When I was certain they were clinging to every
word, I moved the cursor down, line by line. "The..." I said
teasingly.

Each child took a step closer. "Indictment..."

I felt them breathing against the back of my neck. "Is..."

Someone whined with impatience, and I bit back a smile, "Against…"

One last line. One dramatic reveal.

But my words froze in my throat. I couldn't make a sound. The screen glared at me, black letters on white, searing into the backs of my eyeballs: *Sarah J. Anderson, Sphinx.*

2

In my first moment of shock, I had a perfectly ignoble thought: I could delete the indictment.

One tap of my finger, and the document would disappear from my computer screen. I could pull up the next filing, maybe entertain the kids with a thrilling escheatment case. I could give them an exciting romp through the elements of a negligence claim. I could pull out all the stops, and we could explore the rule against perpetuities, as it applied to gargoyle appurtenances at National Cathedral.

Of course I couldn't destroy the indictment. Not really. I was an officer of the court. I was required to follow the letter of the law.

Plus, the prosecutor could refile with a handy tap of her own finger.

"Cool!" rumbled the griffin girl at my elbow. "Is there an indictment for all of us?"

"Yeah," chimed in the basilisk. "I wanna see *my* name on the computer!"

You will, I thought uncharitably. Juvie would get to know this kid before he was old enough to drive. I was certain of it.

My heart hammered. I couldn't draw a full breath. But I was still responsible for these imperial kids for the next three hours.

I slid open the paper drawer on my printer and pulled out a stack of clean white pages. Automatically, I tapped the paper twice on the long side, turned it, and tapped three times on the short side. My fingertips sensed the minute alignment as each sheet slipped into place. The cumulation of order relaxed the tiny muscles between my ribs, just enough that I could fill my lungs.

"You *will* see your names on the computer," I said, with all the fake good cheer of a nurse holding a foot-long hypodermic. "But first, you need to write your *own* indictments!"

The words sounded crazy, even to me. As soon as they were out my mouth, I pictured the kids proudly showing off their lists of crimes to their parents—not exactly the type of treasure to be stuck on refrigerator doors for all eternity.

I didn't care. I needed time to read my own indictment. So I handed each child a sheet of paper and ordered them to sit in a circle on the floor around my desk. "Okay, kids. I want you to make a list of all the rules you've broken in the past month. Rules at school. Rules at home. Everything you can think of. The longest list wins!"

They dove into the project with the enthusiasm of sparrows attacking a loaf of bread. I managed to wait a full minute before I opened the indictment that still glowed on my screen. My fingers shook as I scrolled down.

One count of murder in the first degree.

One count of murder in the second degree.

Murder in the third degree.

Manslaughter.

Assault.

Thirty-seven counts of revealing imperial secrets to mundane eyes.

I clutched my hematite bracelet, trying to slow my

rampaging heartbeat. I forced myself to take a deep breath, to hold it for a count of five, to exhale for a count of—

Before I could complete my calming regimen, the door to the clerk's office swung open. I pasted on an automatic smile, but froze when I saw an EBI officer, a gargoyle in full uniform.

The Empire Bureau of Investigation was the closest thing the Eastern Empire had to a police force. Their main focus was keeping our magical world secret from the humans around us, but they were also responsible for maintaining the peace and investigating open cases.

And they arrested imperials who'd been indicted for major crimes.

"Sarah Anderson?" the officer asked.

At the same time that the gargoyle unsnapped the handcuffs from his belt, the door behind me opened. I only had a moment to glance at the *Staff Only* sign before Angelique Wilson bounded into the room.

"Sarah!" my boss hissed, every fiber of her cat-shifter body trembling on high alert. The Acting Director of Security for the District of Columbia Night Court was clearly enraged.

"Mom!" shouted the shifter child who'd cut short our court-room stay. She ran to her mother's side, brandishing her handi-work. "Miss Sarah has us writing up 'dictments! Did I take three desserts from Geoffrey, or only two?"

"What in the name of Great Danes is this?" Angelique yowled. I wasn't certain if she meant her daughter's list of venial sins, the gargoyle's jangling handcuffs, or the printed indictment she brandished, my name shouting from the top of the page.

The kids looked confused. They had no way of knowing that Angelique routinely cleaned up her swear words by refer-encing the most vile creatures she could think of—dogs, of course. The larger the breed, the more violent her reaction. If we were starting with Great Danes, I was pretty much doomed.

"Sarah Anderson," the policeman repeated, choosing to

ignore all five staring kids *and* Angelique. "You are under arrest for the murder of Judge Robert DuBois."

He didn't need to read me my Miranda rights. Those were for humans.

"Please," I said. "I'm responsible for these children."

Angelique's fingers curled over her daughter's shoulder. "Absolutely not," She said. "You're not getting anywhere near these children. Not with a mastiff-loving indictment hanging over your head."

The EBI gargoyle looked almost as confused as the kids, but that didn't stop him from snapping his cuffs around my wrists. He was rougher than he needed to be, barely shoving my hematite bracelet out of the way.

"Angelique—" I said.

"Children," she interrupted, taking only a moment to shoot me a glare as sharp as her manicured fingernails. She pointed to the shredder beside the chronically malfunctioning copy machine. "I want every one of those lists destroyed. Hop, hop! What are you, Bassetts? Get a move on!"

The kids scurried over to the machine. I suspected this wasn't a good time to warn them against getting their fingers caught, but if anyone amputated a limb, Angelique would certainly add that to my list of crimes.

"Ms. Anderson," the gargoyle said.

"Angelique—" I tried one more time, even though I wasn't sure what I intended to say.

She turned her back on me.

My old boss, James Morton, would never have left me to the tender ministrations of a gargoyle with a badge. But James wasn't there. He hadn't been for ten months.

Officially, he was on sabbatical. But a handful of us sphinxes knew the truth: James had gone rogue. Wounded physically and psychically in the same battle where I'd been forced to dispatch Judge DuBois, James had disappeared from the Eastern Empire.

I'd looked for him. As a sphinx I *had* to. I had to make sure a vampire under my care was safe from harm.

But I'd tried harder than that. I'd tried like a woman who'd once drunk a vampire's blood. I'd tried like a woman who'd let a vampire drink from me. I'd tried like a woman who'd once truly *believed* that he and I could… that we had… that we were meant to…

But those days were over. I'd killed that relationship the instant I plunged an oak stake into Robert DuBois's chest.

"Let's go," the gargoyle said, pulling me back from my memories of that disastrous night.

As Angelique distributed a ream of clean paper to the gleefully shredding children just to keep them occupied, I grabbed my purse and let the policeman lead me downstairs to the processing room. We imperials hid our jail in subterranean chambers beneath the courthouse, the better to avoid prying human eyes.

At the booking desk, I handed over my personal possessions —my purse and my cell phone, my hematite bracelet and my coral ring. The jewelry formed my insignia, the physical focus for my sphinx powers. I felt more naked without them than if the bored gnome sergeant behind the desk had ordered me to strip off my clothes.

As I fretted, the disinterested earth spirit chomped on her gum, taking her time as she typed my personal information with two broad index fingers—name, address, date of birth. I tried not to shudder at the multiple typos that made their way into my record.

It took her three tries to get a clean set of my fingerprints, and that was *after* she removed my handcuffs. I stood beside the height markings on the wall while she took my mug shot. Holding a plaque with my case number, I looked straight ahead, then turned to the left and the right on command.

"Let's go," she said when my mortification was complete.

"Go where?"

"You want your phone call, don't you?"

I followed her down the hall, to an ancient wall-mounted telephone with a dial. I gave her a dubious glance, but she said, "Go ahead. I'll wait back here." She took an ostentatious step away and produced a nail file from her pocket. The rasping sound set my teeth on edge.

At least I knew who to call—Chris Gardner. He was the closest thing I had to a mentor as a sphinx. The closest thing I had to a boyfriend too. At least that's how I'd come to think of him in the intervening months since James's enraged departure.

As a former reporter for *The Washington Banner*—Chris had taken a buyout just last month—he knew more than his share about legal bureaucracy, imperial and mundane.

Plus, I had his phone number memorized.

I glanced up and down the hallway, but I couldn't see a clock. It had to be two, maybe three o'clock in the morning. Chris would be sound asleep beneath his navy blue comforter. He'd have his alarm set for six, so he could take his usual morning run.

I hoped he wasn't in the middle of an especially good dream.

Using my body to shield the phone from the gnome's sight, I dialed Chris's number. I don't know why I bothered to hide the outgoing call. The EBI probably monitored every word said on the line.

One ring. My throat constricted as I tried to think of how to reassure Chris, to ease his pounding adrenaline as he startled awake.

Two rings. My palms grew slick.

Three. My belly flipped, a nauseated little twist as I wondered why he wasn't picking up.

Four. I scrambled to compose a message, an explanation of what I needed, why I was calling in the dark hours before dawn.

"Chris," I said after the beep. "I don't know where you are. I don't know what's going on. There was a grand jury, about DuBois. I—You're my one call. I need—Chris? I—"

The machine cut off. I stared at the telephone handset, suddenly thinking of everything I *should* have told him, starting with details about the indictment. He'd need to know each individual count as he worked to get me a lawyer.

When I turned around, the gnome was eyeing me with pity. "Go on," she said, pushing her Juicy Fruit into the pocket of her cheek. "You can make another call."

"Really?"

"This is the real world, hon, not some TV show. You get a reasonable number of calls. And I'm pretty sure you've got a good reason to make another one."

"Thank you," I said, with real meaning.

But when I turned back to the phone, I realized I didn't actually know who else to call. A year ago, I would have reached out to James. But that was clearly impossible now. I was pretty certain he'd be first in line to lock me up. Maybe first in line to throw the switch on the electric chair, too.

My best friend—Allison Ward—was human. Plus, she wasn't talking to me. That was a disturbing trend among my acquaintances, I realized. But even if Allison and I had spent last weekend giggling over umbrella-topped drinks like besties, I could hardly ask her to spring me from a supernatural jail she knew nothing about.

I didn't have any family to speak of. My mother had died when I was still in college, and I'd never known my father. I was an only child, and I didn't have any aunts or uncles or cousins.

I did have a few imperial friends—the griffin bailiff in Judge Finch's courtroom. The sprite court reporter. But they were working upstairs. And asking them to track down a lawyer for me was beyond the limits of our working friendship.

What the hell was wrong with me? Why didn't I have a single person I could reach out to in the middle of this crisis?

And where the *hell* was Chris? Why wasn't he answering his phone in the middle of the night?

"Hon?" the gnome asked.

I shook my head, forcing myself to focus past the trembling that threatened to take over my limbs. "Th—" I started, but my voice broke. "Thank you," I said again. "I'll just wait for him to get my message."

The gnome shrugged. "It's your funeral."

I sincerely hoped it wouldn't come to that.

The gnome walked me to my cell. I closed my eyes as the door clanged shut. When I reluctantly opened them several minutes later, there wasn't a lot to see. A metal bed jutted from the wall, covered by a thin mattress. A toilet sat in the corner. Otherwise, the tiny room was empty.

I lay back on the mattress and closed my eyes, but I wasn't tired. This was still the middle of my working day. I was supposed to be awake for five, six, seven more hours.

Automatically, I reached for my hematite bracelet, my fingertips seeking its soothing touch. When I brushed bare skin, though, I shuddered. I couldn't squelch the reflex to twist my absent coral ring.

My sphinx brain craved order. It demanded simple, neat organization. Alas, the only thing to straighten inside my cell was the thin cotton sheet on the mattress. I pulled it into alignment, tucking in the corners with military precision.

After that, all I could do was pace. One, two, three, four, five steps to the front of the cell. Turn around, neatly, cleanly, with forced efficiency. One, two, three, four, five steps to the back. Turn again.

Over and over, I walked the length of the cell. The counting soothed my frazzled nerves. The rhythm began to unknot the tension in my shoulders.

As I walked, I assured myself that Chris would appear in the morning. Once he got my scrambled message, he'd figure out what to do. He had the resources to track down my indictment. He could find me an appropriate lawyer.

It would have to be a sphinx, of course. Essential fairness required imperials to be represented by lawyers of their own species. It wouldn't do to have a fire spirit representing a water elemental; the potential was too high for cases to be reversed on appeal due to inadequacy of counsel.

Chris was the Sun Lion, the strongest sphinx in the Eastern Empire. He'd been the Director of Archives since he was fourteen years old; there wasn't a sphinx in the continental United States he didn't know.

And so, I tried to relax as I paced. I tried to tell myself all would be well. I tried to believe this was all a terrible mistake and that Chris would make everything right in the morning.

But hours passed, and Chris didn't arrive. Guards walked down the line of cells, shoving trays of lumpy oatmeal and lukewarm coffee through the bars. Other guards picked up the untouched food. Prisoners called out, protesting injustice, demanding to be freed. A lucky few were taken from their cells, presumably escorted to private rooms where they could consult with lawyers.

Lunch came, a dried-out sandwich that might have been turkey. I left the tray untouched.

I was tired now, so tired. I'd walked a thousand miles, pacing my cell from end to end. I'd been awake for centuries.

I stumbled over to my bed. Facing the wall, I curled up on my thin mattress, pillowing my head on my arm. I closed my eyes and started counting by sevens, trying to trick my brain into forgetting where I was.

Finally, I slept.

∾

I woke sometime after sunset—at least that's what I gathered when a vampire guard strode through the cell block. Meekly, I asked if I could make a phone call. The vampire, though, wasn't as easy-going as the gnome had been. He ignored me and stalked away.

Sometime earlier in the evening, a dinner tray had been passed through the bars of my cell. I wasn't tempted by the gelatinous mass of something that might once have been stew.

Hours had passed since I'd tried to reach Chris. Would the guards have let him into the cellblock if he'd come to the courthouse? Maybe he was waiting in the courtroom upstairs. He might have tracked down a sphinx lawyer and, even now, they were sitting on a hard wooden bench, watching Judge Finch wrap up mundane court activities for the night.

But if he wasn't there…

Had Maurice Richardson gotten to him? The vampire had plenty of reasons to hate the Sun Lion.

I shook my head, trying to drive out graphic images of exactly what an enraged vampire could do to an unsuspecting sphinx.

Maybe I was fretting over nothing. Chris could be busy with some obscure sphinx business. He might even be facing his own legal challenge. He'd been present the night I executed Judge DuBois. Maybe he'd been indicted too.

He could have succumbed to something mundane. He could have been hit by a bus.

I spun out another dozen scenarios. In every single one, Chris lay dead or hurt or dying, and I was powerless to help him. I caught myself rocking back and forth on the edge of my metal bed, my arms folded around my belly as I struggled not to keen.

"Let's go," the vampire guard said, making more noise with his ring of keys than was strictly necessary.

"Go where?" I asked. Suddenly, I wasn't sure I ever wanted to step outside of my cell.

"Courtroom," the vampire said. I hoped he wasn't being paid by the word. "Arraignment."

"But I don't have a lawyer yet!"

"I don't make the rules."

But his suddenly expressed fangs made it perfectly clear he was willing to enforce them. I did my best to straighten my clothes, and I followed him upstairs to the courtroom.

Lawyer or not, it was time for me to answer to the imperial court.

3

E leanor Owens, the griffin bailiff, took over from the vampire, marching me into the courtroom and leaving me to stand alone beside the defendant's table. I craned my neck, trying to search the gallery for Chris even as I was reluctant to turn my back on the judge.

There were plenty of imperials in the seats; it was a busy night at the courthouse. But I didn't see a single sphinx—not Chris, not a lawyer he might have sent, no one.

A nervous dryad sat at the prosecutor's table, shuffling papers and running twig-like fingers through her tangled hair. Judge Finch peered down at both of us from the bench. She'd already transformed into her vampire persona.

"Counselor," she snapped, making the dryad jump. "Will you read the charges?"

The dryad cleared her throat and rattled her papers one more time. But then she recited the claims I'd seen in the indictment—murder in the first degree, second degree, third. Manslaughter. Assault and revealing imperial secrets. None of it had changed.

Judge Finch's eyes glowed like embers as she turned her

attention to me. I stood accused of killing a judge. Killing a *vampire* judge. Could I possibly trust her to treat me fairly?

Her voice was dangerously soft as she asked, "How do you plead to these charges, Sphinx Sarah Anderson?"

I wanted to protest. I wanted to demand a lawyer. I wanted to march out of the courtroom and back to my desk and pretend that none of this had ever happened. I wanted to know what had happened to Chris.

Instead, I stood up straight and looked the judge directly in the eye. "Not guilty, Your Honor."

Judge Finch pursed her lips, as if she tasted something bitter. "Very well, then. We'll docket your preliminary hearing for…" She flipped the massive pages of a calendar that nearly filled the desk in front of her. "For Wednesday, the first of May," she finally said. "Get a lawyer, Ms. Anderson. You're free to go until then."

Me? An accused murderer? Free to go? Wasn't I a threat to the community? Or a flight risk? Wasn't she supposed to demand an ungodly amount of money as bail? "E— Excuse me, Your Honor?"

"I'm releasing you on your own recognizance."

I nodded, too stunned to speak. I was through with bureaucratic restraints. I could find Chris. My steps grew faster as I reached the swinging gate that led to the gallery.

Only as I passed the first wooden bench filled with spectators did Judge Finch speak again. "Ms. Anderson!"

I turned back, dreading the authoritarian note in her voice. I suddenly knew I'd been right to fear justice in this courtroom. "Your Honor?" I asked, and as hard as I tried, I couldn't keep my voice from shaking.

She planted her hands on her desk and leaned forward. "You can pick up your personal possessions from the booking clerk downstairs. We only need to keep your insignia."

That was it—the sound of the other shoe dropping. My fingers automatically clutched my bare wrist. "Your Honor—"

She cut me off. "Or you could, of course, return to your cell."

No. No I couldn't. Not with freedom dangling so close. Not with my boyfriend lost and unaccounted for, somewhere beyond the courthouse walls. I stammered, "N— No, Your Honor."

Her nod was so minute I might have imagined it. "Very well, then. That's decided. And you might as well take the rest of the night off. Bailiff? Notify Acting Director Wilson that Ms. Anderson will be back at her desk on Monday night."

"Thank you, Your Honor," I said, my voice melting with relief.

Judge Finch had giveth and she had taketh away. On the one hand, I could avoid Angelique Wilson for another night. Short on sleep, long on anxiety for Chris, I wasn't sure I could stay silent for my boss's cock-eyed canine curses. On the other hand, my fingertips already itched at the thought of going without my insignia for five full days, until my preliminary hearing. Longer, if my eventual lawyer couldn't work out some satisfactory alternative arrangement.

But there was nothing to be done about that. My insignia guaranteed I wouldn't skip town, better than any dollar amount of bail. Gritting my teeth, I speed-walked to the booking desk. One short detour to grab my purse and phone, and I could find out what had happened to Chris.

I couldn't imagine what had motivated the judge's generous offer of a paid day off. But nearly four hours later, I understood.

The sympathetic gnome of the night before was no longer on duty. Instead, a bear shifter was processing new cases. I knew the calendar said it was late April, almost May. But watching the man behind the desk, I could almost believe he was still hibernating. He moved so slowly, my own exhausted joints ached.

It was a Friday, two nights shy of a full moon, and all sorts of imperial mischief had broken out. Three different EBI agents brought in new defendants. Each of them was processed before the bear shifter turned his attention to me.

The sky was softening to grey by the time I staggered out of the courthouse. I had my purse and my cell phone and a headache that threatened to make me see double. I was in no shape to take the subway, much less to walk. I summoned an Uber and gave the driver Chris's address.

Calling his name as I walked in the front door, I already knew he wasn't home. Not a light was on inside the house. No smell of fresh-brewed coffee wafted from the kitchen. *The Banner* had rested on the front doorstep, still inside its plastic sleeve.

Fighting a rush of foreboding, I climbed the stairs to the second floor. Chris's office was empty, his laptop missing from his immaculate desk. Across the hall, his king-size bed looked like a display model in some ultra-high-end department store. The bedspread hung in perfect folds, as if no one had ever slept there.

Doubling back to the kitchen, I walked over to the sink. A dessert plate rested on the counter, cookie crumbs littering its surface.

My stomach lurched.

In the ten months I'd been with Chris, I'd never seen him leave a plate on the counter. Sure, he ate cookies as a before-bed snack every night, three Lorna Doones, always taken out of the package and centered on a salad plate before he carried them to the table. After eating them, he washed the plate and placed it in the dishwasher. He sealed the bag of cookies. He wiped down the counter. Everything was in its place. Always.

The plate and crumbs were the equivalent of a burglar's rampage in anyone else's home. They shrieked of wrongness as much as slashed couch cushions, shattered drawers, or torn books strewn across the floor.

My phone was out of my pocket before I got to the sidewalk. It only took a moment to call another Uber, this time heading into Georgetown. Every traffic light sent a new surge of adrenaline through my exhausted body.

By the time I arrived at the Den, I expected to find a smoldering pile of ruins. Instead, I stared at a perfectly balanced red-brick façade behind a high stone wall. A familiar wrought-iron gate swung smoothly on its hinges as I entered from the side-walk. The scanner beside the entrance registered my retina. The front door glided open.

"Liam!" I gasped to the unflappable young sphinx behind the security desk. "Is Chris here?"

"Good morning, Ms. Anderson," the guard said.

I didn't have time for social niceties. "Where's Chris?"

"He's in a meeting, Ms. Anderson."

Not murdered by Richardson then. Not kidnapped without a trace. Not indicted. My relief was so intense my knees buckled, and I grabbed onto Liam's desk for balance.

"Mr. Gardner asked you to wait for him in the front study."

Wait for him... Then Chris had known I would show up. What the hell was going on?

But I'd been a sphinx for long enough that I recognized an order when I heard one, even if it was delivered politely. I headed down the hall.

The study was exactly as I'd last seen it. An overstuffed sofa sat between two armchairs. Fringed throw pillows filled the corners of the sofa, each turned to a precise angle. The brocade curtains were still drawn against the night.

I walked over and slipped a finger past the heavy silk. A watery beam of sunlight leaked through the sheers. The gravel courtyard beyond looked bleached.

My body twitched, resisting my need to wait patiently. I thought about rushing back to Liam, about demanding that he page Chris. But the Sun Lion had issued his command. I had to wait.

One times two is two, I thought, taking a deep breath and pressing my right thumb against its matching forefinger as I studied the immaculate courtyard. *Two times two is four.* I exhaled slowly and pressed my middle finger. *Four times two is eight.* Inhale.

Ring finger, bare of my coral ring. *Eight times two is sixteen.* Exhale. Pinky.

I counted off the series, forcing myself to slow down, to breathe in for five, out for five. In my exhausted state, the roof of my mouth began to buzz. My fingertips tingled.

Calm. Peace. Order.

The hell with that. I had just calculated 16,777,216 when the study door opened. I recognized Chris's presence without turning around—the sound of him or the scent, something about his very essence.

I heard him close the door. I felt him cross the carpet. And then his arms were around me, and his chest was pressed to my back, and his lips were warm against my temple.

I relaxed into the solid, steady strength of him, letting the curtain slip back into place. His arms tightened around me, pulling me close, keeping me safe.

This was the way I'd always felt around Chris. Even before I knew that he and I were sphinxes, that he lived his life with the same compulsions I did, that he understood the constant restless drive that pulsed in my blood...

Chris made me feel centered. He made me feel right.

"Where were you?" I asked, whispering the words to keep my voice from breaking.

Instead of answering, he spread his fingers across my belly. Warmth flowed through me, soft and sweet and comforting.

I turned within the circle of his arms, smiling when I saw his familiar chestnut curls. His eyes were more gold than brown behind their horn-rimmed glasses. He wore a crisp blue shirt and khakis with a crease that could have cut glass. He was calm and controlled and perfect. He was *Chris.*

I settled my lips on his. I meant the kiss to be something casual, a greeting, but he was the one who deepened it. His fingers tangled in my hair. He murmured my name against my throat. He did distracting things with the zipper on my skirt, and I wondered if he'd locked the study door when he'd come into the room.

"I was so worried," I said, pulling back just enough to settle my palm over his heart. "When I saw the plate on the counter…"

His fingers tightened around my waist. "The Pride called." The committee that managed all sphinxes in the Empire. "It was an emergency."

I should have heard the warning in his words. Instead, I continued with my own concern. "I called you too. I need a lawyer, a—"

Before I could say "sphinx", the door to the study swung open. A cadaver of a man walked in, looking like the love child of a stork and an oil derrick. Ronald Mortenson was a teacher at the Den and a member of the Pride. And he'd been one of my greatest critics from the first moment I entered the Georgetown mansion.

"Excellent!" he said to Chris, actually rubbing his hands together like a cartoon villain. "Then she already knows?"

"Knows what?" I asked.

Chris's face was pale. I suddenly realized how exhausted he looked.

No. Not exhausted.

Afraid.

I'd never seen Chris afraid.

I whirled on Ronald and repeated, "Knows what?"

I saw the instant he realized he'd spoken out of turn. His eyebrows peaked. He smirked at Chris, a wry smile that might have been an apology. Or maybe it was a reprimand.

"Knows what?" I repeated, trying not to panic.

Ronald finally answered my question, clearly relishing every single syllable. "You're banished, Sarah. Kicked out. You're excommunicated from the Den forever."

4

Rage. Hot as desert sand. Quick as a striking cobra.

One moment, I was a dazed sphinx, standing by a curtained window, trying to make sense of three simple sentences.

The next, I was a murderous weapon. My thoughts sped up until I couldn't parse them word by word. Every muscle in my body tensed. My vision *shifted*.

I wanted to destroy Ronald Mortenson, to crush his throat with a strangling grip.

Agriotis. The word came to me, my thoughts flying faster than my body could follow. I was suffused with the perfect rage of a sphinx, the bloodlust that had sustained my ancestors in brutal battle.

Agriotis. My fingers stiffened into a set of ten matched knives.

Agriotis. My legs flexed, my knees bent; I was ready to soar across the room.

Through my widened eyes, I saw that Chris's mouth was just beginning to open. His throat was only now beginning to vibrate around a syllable: *Sa—*. His lips pursed as he formed the rest of my name: *—rah*.

In that instant, I realized my rage wasn't reserved for

Ronald. I was furious with Chris, too. He'd known I was cast out before he'd entered the study. But rather than tell me, rather than give me a chance to prepare some sort of logical response, he'd allowed me to be disgraced in front of one of my greatest enemies in the Den.

Sekhmet's blood ran in my veins, making me a killer, urging me to destroy the sphinxes before me.

"*No!*" I cried, forcing the word past the crimson sand dune molten rage. I clapped my palm down on my wrist, where I should have worn my hematite bracelet.

But I'd lost my insignia. The court had taken it because I'd executed Judge DuBois.

That night, standing with Judge DuBois's blood literally on my hands, I'd vowed never to succumb to *agriotis* again. I knew the danger. I understood the cost. I'd promised myself and the Den that I would find a way for all sphinxes, everywhere, to be forever free from our blinding fury.

"No," I repeated, forcing my body to take a breath. I wouldn't use my power. I wouldn't use my force. Not today. Not here. Not against Ronald and Chris.

I glared at both of them, slower now, sane now. "No," I repeated a third time.

"Let's talk, Sarah," Chris said, his voice steady, as if he hadn't just faced down a murderous sphinx. He was even brave enough to take a step closer. "The Pride called an emergency meeting last night, the instant they heard about the indictment."

"That's impossible! *I* only found out when I filed the paperwork!"

"*The Inquirer* had a reporter outside the grand jury room."

Of course. *The Imperial Inquirer* was a newspaper, a daily that reported on Empire business. A sphinx accused of murdering a vampire judge—that was a big case. I'd probably made the front page.

"So you *knew* about the indictment?" I had to be sure.

"Within five minutes of it being issued," he said grimly.

"And you didn't tell me?" He'd been my one phone call. I'd *needed* him. And he hadn't thought to warn me of looming disaster.

"It isn't that simple," he said.

"What isn't simple? I've been accused of murder! Murder and a hell of a lot more. I called you because I need a lawyer so I don't go to jail for the rest of my natural life. I'm a sphinx. So I need a sphinx lawyer. I don't see anything complicated about that. I don't see—"

"You aren't necessarily a sphinx."

He caught me mid-tirade, literally knocking the breath from my lungs. I glanced from Chris to Ronald and back to Chris before I managed, "What?"

Chris's voice was impossibly gentle. "The Pride isn't convinced you're a sphinx."

Once again, ten months disappeared in the blink of an eye. I stood on the plaza in front of the Jefferson Memorial, staring at the spot where Judge DuBois had died. At the same time, with the impossibility of magic, I walked with Sekhmet, surveying an ancient battlefield.

Mother Sekhmet had shown me the truth that night. She'd told me my father was Sheut, not Ptah, like all the other sphinxes. Sheut—a shadowy figure so ancient he wasn't even recorded in the Den's archives.

I was special. I was different.

But ten months ago, Chris had promised me it didn't matter. The Pride had approved my belonging to the Den. I'd passed their tests. They'd accepted me.

"I don't understand," I said, even though I was terrified I understood perfectly well.

Ronald's lips pursed, as if he'd sucked on a lemon. "Really, Sarah. It's not complicated."

"Shut up!" I shouted. I didn't want to hear from Ronald. I wanted Chris to tell me the truth. I wanted him to explain how he'd known about the indictment, he'd known I'd been thrown out of the Den, and he'd still come into this room and found the time to *kiss* me, to make me think everything was all right, that I was safe and he was there for me, even though he'd *known* I was cast out.

I couldn't stay inside the Den, surrounded by sphinxes who thought I was a monster. Surrounded by creatures I longed to kill with the red-hot fury of barely restrained *agriotis*.

I scarcely registered Chris's chagrined expression as I pushed past him. I didn't bother to look at Ronald. Liam's face was a blur as I fled across the foyer. Somehow, I opened the front door and then the iron gate. I fled down the sidewalk, beneath the oak trees with their new yellow-green spring leaves.

I left the Den forever, and I walked.

I walked with the energy that could have shredded two adult male sphinxes. I walked with the determination to save myself, to spare my soul from the cost of *agriotis*. I walked from Georgetown to the National Mall, along the Potomac River, past the Lincoln Memorial, past the Washington Monument and the low, modern temples to knowledge, the Smithsonian.

I climbed Capitol Hill, and I skirted the Senate office buildings. I angled down side streets, automatically lifting my feet over broken sidewalks, maneuvering past scattered trashcans and recycling bins.

Each step burned a little more of my madness. Every footfall brought me back from the brink of *agriotis*. Each stride saved a little of my soul.

I could breathe again.

I could think again.

I could speak.

Ordinarily, after an *agriotis*-fueled battle, I would ground myself with food and drink. But having throttled my instincts, I didn't want the customary centering meal, no water or wine or the beer that had first been brewed to dull Mother Sekhmet's battle-lust.

I wanted the impossible. I wanted to be a sphinx, and I

wanted to be welcome at the Den, and I wanted to love Chris and marry Chris and bear Chris's normal, everyday, healthy sphinx children.

I wanted to belong.

I'd spent my entire life looking into groups from the outside. I'd never had the easy camaraderie of my peers, the simple grace to laugh at the right jokes, to cry over the right commercials, to feel simple, healthy rage at the correct slights.

I'd slipped from grade to grade in school without ever truly belonging. I'd weathered college with the same sense of disillusion. I'd started law school, believing I worked for some sort of common good, but I'd left after two years, confused and lonely and...empty.

I'd worked a series of meaningless jobs—collecting signatures for the Penguin Rescue Campaign, making overpriced fruit bowls at an artisanal juice bar, distributing free samples of drinkable yogurt at subway stations around town... None of it had mattered to me. None of it had been important—until I arrived at the District Court for the Eastern Empire.

That job—clerk of court—had fit me like a piece snapping into the center of a jigsaw puzzle. I understood it from the first moment I stepped behind my desk. I helped mundane customers and imperials alike. I brought order out of chaos. I was *good* at what I did. I belonged.

And now, all of that was being taken away from me. The indictment threatened my employment. The Pride had cast me out of the Den. I was alone. And I'd forgotten how much it hurt to be cut off from the rest of the world.

But my life before the Den hadn't been all bad. I hadn't been a total failure. I'd had a friend: Allison Ward.

Allison was my best friend—or she had been, before I ruined everything by putting the imperial world before her needs. After everything had fallen apart in June, when she accused me of choosing my job over her, I'd given her the space she'd demanded. I hadn't called. I hadn't stopped by with cupcakes from the Cake Walk bakery. I hadn't even acknowledged the birthday of Allison's daughter Nora, my one and only goddaughter.

I thought I was reconciled to the loss.

But obviously not—because now I was standing on the doorstep of Better Kids Now. Allison was the head lobbyist for the adoption non-profit.

I stared at the sign in front of the townhouse, with its bright logo of red, blue, green, and yellow—stylized children holding hands in a circle. Those children were happy. Those children belonged.

Ten months was long enough for a best-friend stalemate.

I climbed the steps and opened the plate glass door. A receptionist looked up from a neat desk in the front room. "May I help you?" she asked with a smile.

"I'm here to see Allison Ward." The instant I said the words, I knew they were *right*. They were the reason I'd walked halfway across the city.

"Is she expecting you?"

"No," I admitted, "But I'm a friend. Sarah Anderson."

The receptionist smiled again and gestured toward a padded armchair. "If you'll just have a seat, I'll see if Allison's available."

I sat.

Looking out the bow window at sunlight playing over the sidewalk, I smiled. It was a gorgeous spring day. The air was soft and warm. The sky was a deep blue.

The receptionist's voice was as bright as the sunshine outside. "Hello, Allison. There's a Ms. Sarah Anderson to see you. She says she doesn't have an appointment, but—"

A cloud skittered in front of the sun. The reception area was suddenly wreathed in cool blue light. I rubbed my arms, aware of a chill for the first time since I'd completed my cross-city marathon.

"Of course," the receptionist said. "No problem. No, no, I understand."

I stood as she hung up the phone.

"I'm sorry," she said, but she sounded angry rather than regretful. "Ms. Ward is in a meeting now."

Not *Allison* anymore. *Ms. Ward.* "She isn't in a meeting." I said, and the receptionist looked uneasy. "You were just talking to her."

My protest hardened something in the other woman. "Ms. Ward is unable to see you this morning."

I took out my phone. I could call Allison from here in the lobby. I could tell her I needed to see her, that we needed to talk.

The receptionist stood, setting her palm squarely on her desk. "Have a good morning," she said. Her tone cut off any possibility of further conversation.

I could press the issue. Even without my sphinx powers, without a hint of *agriotis*, I could push past the desk. I knew my way up the stairs, and down the hallway, into the office of the woman who'd been my best friend. I could insist that Allison finally hear my side of the story.

But that wasn't the friendship I wanted. I didn't want to force anyone to *let* me belong.

"If you could please tell *Ms. Ward* that I stopped by," I said, opting to preserve the charade that Allison was totally unaware of my presence.

"Of course," the receptionist said. She stayed on her feet.

Shaking my head, I retraced my steps. Through the door. Down the stairs. Out to the sidewalk.

From there, I looked up at the second-floor windows. Allison was staring down at me. Her hair was shorter than the last time I'd seen her. At this distance, it looked like she'd lost weight, or maybe that was just the ripples in the old glass between us.

I raised my hand, palm up, a stilted, stifled wave. She turned and looked over her shoulder, as if someone had called her name from the corridor outside her office. She stepped away from the window without waving back.

Suddenly, I was exhausted. My feet screamed in my practical office shoes, complaining bitterly about my miles-long hike. My right shoulder ached, as if my purse weighed a metric ton. My lungs hurt when I tried to take a deep breath.

I needed to sleep.

I didn't want to go to my own apartment. I still rented three rooms in the basement of a townhouse, just twenty minutes from the courthouse. Chris had walked me home just last week, after meeting me at the end of my shift.

We'd both been happy then, a little giddy with the scents of spring. He'd followed me down the stairs with a knowing smile on his face, and I'd led him back to my bedroom.

We hadn't made love. We'd *never* made love, not in the classic sense.

Much to my initial mortification, Chris was the one who'd first warned me about the dangers of sphinx nookie. We children of Sekhmet were a fertile bunch, he'd explained. And no one—especially not the Sun Lion of the Eastern Empire—wanted a bouncing baby... whatever the hell *I* was, to complicate matters.

Actual sex was off the menu.

But over the past ten months, Chris and I had come up with a quite a few satisfying alternatives. No. I'm not the type of girl who kisses and tells. Suffice to say, we found plenty to do in the sexy times department. Chris was a sensitive lover. A creative one, too.

I couldn't face the thought of lying in the bed I'd shared with him just five nights before. Not when he'd betrayed me to the Pride.

And I certainly wasn't going back to Chris's townhouse. I couldn't turn the perfect lock with my perfect key. I couldn't fold back the perfect bedspread with its perfect pleats. I couldn't wake to Chris's perfect understanding of everything that had gone wrong.

I walked a block, up to busy Pennsylvania Avenue. It took less than a minute to hail a cab. I couldn't use Uber, not to reach my current destination. I didn't want a computer record of where I'd gone.

I fought to stay awake as the taxi wove through city traffic. I would have given anything for the driver to drop me off on the doorstep of my goal.

Well, not anything.

I wouldn't risk the safety of a vampire.

The cab dropped me at the back entrance of the National Zoo. I paid in cash and added a fifteen percent tip—a perfectly ordinary transaction, nothing the driver would remember.

After waiting for ten minutes, scanning the road to make sure I hadn't been followed, I set off down one of the hiking trails that cut through Rock Creek Park. I wasn't wearing appropriate clothes, but there was nothing to be done about that. I compensated by looking over my shoulder at regular intervals. I took a bench at the intersection of two paths. I doubled back and picked up a different trail.

All the while, I fingered the keyring in my pocket. It held my house key and Chris's. But it held a third key too, a brass one with jagged teeth that pricked the pad of my thumb.

When I was ready to drop from exhaustion, I offered a quick prayer to Sekhmet that I'd avoided all detection, and then I headed for my true goal. I climbed a steep road that led out of the park. I walked past a row of townhouses with faux Tudor fronts.

The last one on the right was unremarkable. The lawn was slightly overgrown; its owner hadn't completed spring cleaning. A weathered sign next to the door said, "No Solicitation."

The brass key fit in the lock. It caught a little as it turned, but muscle memory came to the rescue. I pressed down slightly as I twisted.

"Hello?" I called softly, as I stepped into the entry hall of James Morton's sanctum. "Anyone home?"

I didn't call James's name, though. The sun was still high in the sky. If anything was awake inside that house, it wasn't a vampire.

No one answered. I hadn't really expected a reply. I closed the door and secured the deadbolt.

I was a sphinx, no matter what the Den said. Caution ran in my veins. I walked through each room on the ground floor, checking to make sure they were empty. I tested the metal shutters over the windows, the enclosures meant to keep out any hint of burning sunlight.

Upstairs, I found two empty bedrooms. A king-size bed stood inside the third. The linens were musty, but clean. The pillow smelled faintly of dust.

My eyes welled up at the sight of such luxury. I was tired enough to sleep in the middle of a hog wallow, with nothing but a gravestone for my head.

I kicked off my shoes and unzipped my skirt. As an afterthought, I freed my blouse from my waistband and reached beneath to unhook my bra.

I thought I would fall asleep before my eyes could close. But I had longer than that. I had enough time to make myself a promise.

I was going to find Sheut. I was going to learn the true identity of my father, how he was like a sphinx, how he was different. We'd be a club of two. And the Pride and its exclusive rules could be damned forever as I fought to exonerate my name with the Eastern Empire Night Court.

5

I woke up with a raging thirst, an equally intense need for the bathroom, and a hunger so intense it felt like nausea. It took me a moment to untangle my feet from the sheets, and then I had to fumble for my phone on the nightstand.

6:37 pm. On Monday evening. I'd slept the clock around, and then some.

And I had to get moving if I was going to scare up food for breakfast and get to the courthouse by the start of my shift. I was still employed by the Eastern Empire—at least for now—and I couldn't endanger my job by showing up late.

I scrambled for a light switch, then made my way down the hall to the bathroom. The toilet bowl was dry, but enough water remained in the tank to flush properly—no small relief. I found a scramble of clean towels in the linen closet. They looked like they'd been folded by a rabid raccoon with spatial relationship problems, but they smelled like fabric softener.

With a pang, I pictured James shoving those towels onto the shelves. Vampires weren't good at organizing information or things. I should be grateful he'd done his laundry before he disappeared.

I did my best to fashion a sponge bath with cold water and

no soap. My fingers had to take the place of serious hair care products, and I resigned myself to facing the long night of work without benefit of foundation, blush, or mascara. At least I had a lipstick in my purse.

I tucked my blouse into my skirt and slipped into my shoes before heading downstairs. Each step creaked like an old-fashioned haunted house. If anyone had come upstairs during the day, I would have heard them.

Looking around the dining room, I was blindsided by a sudden surge of memory. I could still recall my shock when James had trusted me with knowledge of his sanctum, his ultimate refuge against prying mundane eyes.

He and I had hidden here for nearly a week when we were trying to identify the creature who'd kidnapped Judge DuBois. We'd worked well together. We'd trusted each other.

Now I had no idea where he was. And I wasn't likely to see him anytime soon. The computer we'd used to search for Judge DuBois was long gone; James had removed it when he'd scoured all identifying information from his sanctum. I suspected the monitor was consigned to a trash heap somewhere. Given James's expertise in corporate security, the hard drive was probably shredded into metallic confetti.

What a waste. The computer was destroyed like so much else—James's career, Judge DuBois's legacy, the safety and security I'd once dreamed of at the Den...

Sighing, I headed toward the kitchen.

And I stopped dead in the doorway.

Breakfast sat on the counter. A plate held a scone—bacon, cheddar, and chive by appearance and scent. A small bowl was filled with soft butter. A larger one held strawberries, bright red, with perfect green caps. A carafe sat next to a mug.

"I stirred the coffee seven times."

Chris spoke from the far side of the kitchen, from the doorway that led to the laundry room.

After a pause, he added, "Good morning." He sounded almost natural, as if I'd responded to his initial greeting.

"Good morning," I finally said. "How long have you been here?"

He shrugged. Instead of answering my question, he waved me toward the food.

"Aren't you eating?" I asked, because that was easier than any of the other questions I had for him.

"I'm not hungry."

A polite woman would have said she wasn't hungry either. She would have insisted on sharing—some of the berries, at least, if not actually halving the scone. She would have found a second coffee cup and poured out some of the rich brew that was lightened by a generous pour of heavy cream.

I wasn't a polite woman. I was a starving woman. Sphinx. Whatever. I fell on the food like a ravening wolf.

Last June, I'd kept a vegetarian diet, with an eye toward taming James's most predatory instincts. But when one month of his absence had stretched to two, then three and four, I'd turned back to my preferred foods. After all, bacon *was* one of the four basic food groups.

I washed down the scone and fruit with two mugs of coffee. All the while, Chris watched from across the room. Only when I'd used my napkin to wipe stray crumbs from my lips did he finally say, "Sarah."

I heard the urgency in his voice, as if he wanted to add a thousand things but was barely holding himself back.

I couldn't think of anything to say, though, any response that wouldn't have been awkward. But I should have realized that "awkward" was just getting started. A longer, uglier pause stretched between us.

"I wanted—" he finally said.

At the same instant, I summoned some basic courtesy. "Thank you for break—"

We both stopped at the identical second. "Go on," he said.

"No, you," I said.

This was worse than a first date. Worse than the breathless calculation before a first kiss—would he or wouldn't he and do I have anything green stuck between my teeth? Worse than wondering if *this* was the night we ended up in bed, or *this* one, or *this* one.

He drew a deep breath and held it for a count of ten, and I knew he was calming himself through one of the rituals of order that made him a sphinx. By the time he spoke, my entire body was primed for his words. "You have to know I tried. Ronald read the *Inquirer* article, and he immediately called a private session for the Pride. By the time I got there, they'd already pulled a copy of the indictment from public records."

Public records. I'd tapped the keys that had made the indictment available for the sphinxes who'd wanted to destroy me. My voice shook as I said, "You should have told me. Not Ronald Mortenson. You should have told me the instant you entered the study."

"You're right."

I wasn't expecting that. A protest—sure. Maybe even a lie. But absolute, complete capitulation?

"That's it?" I asked. "You don't have anything else to say?"

"Of course I have a lot more to say. I wish this had never happened. I wish *The Inquirer* had given us a little more time. I wish I'd been able to stop the Pride—"

"You're the Sun Lion!" I couldn't scrub the bitterness from my protest.

"I'm still a sphinx," he said. "I'm subject to the Pride, just like every other sphinx."

"That's not true! You could issue a Command of the Hunt!" Like, the Pope speaking ex cathedra, the Sun Lion could be infallible. All he had to do was proclaim that I *was* a sphinx. I belonged in the Den. Ronald and every other member of the Pride would *have* to accept me.

Chris shook his head, his frown telling me he'd considered—and rejected—my demand. "Not for this," he said. "Not now."

"Why not?"

"Dammit, Sarah! Issuing a Command isn't like ordering breakfast! It's only been done six times in the entire history of the Eastern Empire."

"Seven is a perfectly good number."

He looked me in the eye. "I can't issue a Command just because I want to. Just because it would make my life easier. My life and the life of the woman I love."

Love.

Well, *that* took all the air out of the room. Chris had never said that before. We'd both avoided labels.

Part of me wanted to squeal like a teen-aged girl in a bad comedy. I wanted to make him repeat it. I wanted to call my best friend and replay every word of his confession, dissecting each individual syllable for tone and weight and meaning.

But my best friend wasn't talking to me. And I wasn't a teen-aged girl. And Chris and I were caught up in a far larger drama, threatened by a much greater problem than whether I was supposed to respond immediately with my own recitation of three little words.

I nodded, because it felt completely churlish not to acknowledge his statement in *some* way. But then I said, "I don't get it. Why is the Pride acting now? The indictment is a legal document, and now we know there's going to be a trial. But they've known about that night for months. Hell, they only *accepted* me into the Den after I…"

Killed Judge DuBois. After all this time, it should be easy for me to say the words. But they still stuck in my throat.

Chris hesitated, and for a moment I thought he wasn't going to let me off the emotional hook. I thought we *were* going to have to discuss love and labels and intentions and futures… All the things I wasn't sure I deserved.

He must have read my discomfort on my face, because he

twisted his lips into a frown. He shook his head, just a little, but he spread his palms on the center island between us.

"It's not about the killing," he said. "It's about what you did *after* the fact."

"What I—" But then the answer came to me. I'd *lived* the answer when I fled the Den the day before, when I'd consciously thrust down my *agriotis* and the urge to fight every living sphinx in the Georgetown mansion.

The Pride had banned me because I was determined to find a way to eliminate *agriotis* from our lives. I'd promised to search the archives, to study the Old Library, to find any scrap of information that would free sphinxes from the blinding, murderous rage that was embedded in our DNA.

I didn't want any other sphinx to feel the regret I felt. I didn't want a single one of Sekhmet's children to live with the guilt that burdened me every day. I wanted to eliminate *agriotis*.

But *agriotis* made us special. *Agriotis* made us different. *Agriotis* was our super-power, the thing that set us above all other imperials.

If I succeeded in my quest, sphinxes would be weaker.

And so the Pride had cast me out, rather than give me any protection, any resources I might require. And on some level, in some way, Chris agreed with them. At least, he wouldn't issue a Command against them.

But he wasn't abandoning me. He was here, in the kitchen of James's sanctum. He'd brought me breakfast. He was waiting, patiently, while I thought things through, while I measured out all the whys and the wherefores.

I sighed. "What do we do now?"

He released a breath I hadn't known he was holding. "Now, I drive you to work. And once you're there, you can start researching cases that will help your lawyer argue your defense."

"I don't have a lawyer," I reminded him, loading the words with frustration. Now that I was cast out from the Den, I wasn't going to have a lawyer. No sphinx in the Eastern Empire would dare to represent me.

"You do now," he said. "That is, if you'll accept the Sun Lion of the Eastern Empire in your corner."

I stared at him, shocked beyond words. "You?" I finally said.

"Okay. I don't actually have a law degree. But I watched a hell of a lot of trials, both mundane and imperial, while I worked the courthouse beat. And the court won't dare to throw me out."

The Sun Lion, sitting beside me at the defendant's table. Chris's presence wouldn't turn my case into an open-and-shut matter. But for the first time since I'd read the indictment, I felt a glimmer of hope.

Chris reached out. His fingers brushed my cheek as he tucked an errant lock of hair behind my ear. "I couldn't stop the Pride, Sarah. But I can do this for you. For us."

Love.

The word still hovered between us. Now I was totally supposed to say something. I was supposed to tell him how I felt. Instead, I turned my head and leaned into the warmth of his palm. I closed my eyes, searching for the perfect words.

When I didn't find them, I steadied myself with a deep breath. And I smiled when I met his gaze. "Let's go," I said. "Your client will only make her case worse if she's late to work."

He knew what I was doing. He understood all the things I wasn't saying. But he stepped back and let me lead the way to the garage and his waiting car. We didn't speak, all the way to the courthouse.

6

We may have been silent on the ride across town, but when we arrived at the courthouse, Chris pulled over to the curb, put the car into Park, and gave me a farewell kiss that sent my heart rate into the stratosphere. My lips still buzzed as I cleared Security Level Orange. Another move like that, and I'd be shouting my eternal love from the rooftops.

Or, as the case might be, from the clerk's office. Where it was just as well that I squelched my amorous enthusiasm, because a trio of mundane lawyers waited for me to open the door.

Like any established business, I had my "regulars." Davey Callahan, cheerful as ever while he patted his pockets looking for a pen, was ready to represent any human defendant in need of counsel. Eugene Roberts was making his weekly query about cases involving police brutality. Alicia Moran, her breath heavy with bourbon and Wint-O-Green LifeSavers, was prepared to file a sheaf of papers in a number of cases she was handling.

Their matters weren't complicated. Nothing was life-or-death. And the human lawyers who used the night court were friendly and good-hearted. They made me glad to come into the office each evening. Not least because—I had to be honest—

they tended to keep my cat-shifter boss from spending too much time on my side of the *Staff Only* door.

Eventually, though, the human lawyers had to go about their ordinary lives. I took advantage of the lull in the action to restore order to my desk.

Maybe the day clerk *tried* to be respectful of my work station. But every single night, I found at least one thing out of place. Tonight was a triple play. My stapler had been left at a haphazard angle, clearly the victim of a drive-by pounding. Someone had slipped a blue pen in among the black ones. The cord on my telephone was twisted around itself in one full loop.

As I twitched each violation back into order, I felt a little more peace settle over my mind. Disorder was like the hum of a leaf-blower in the distance. I wasn't always aware of what I was hearing until the far-away drone fell silent.

I glanced at the clock. Five minutes to midnight. I wasn't likely to see another mundane customer that night. I might as well start my real research. I could always key in the emergency code to bring up the human court's logo to cover whatever imperial business I had open.

I had two choices. I could start with the most dire charge against me: Murder. Or I could start with the greatest number of counts: Revealing imperial secrets to mundane eyes.

There were extenuating circumstances for both. The so-called murder had actually been a merciful coup de grâce. And since that was the charge that could result in me forfeiting my own life, I started my search there.

First, I looked for cases where sphinxes had been charged with murder. Apparently, though, the residents of the Den were preternaturally law-abiding. That, or they were better than I was at not getting caught.

In the history of the Eastern Empire Night Court, only one sphinx had been charged with murder. He'd been a member of the Pride in 1952. He'd gotten into deep debt supporting a naiad mistress, and his gnome banker had finally called in his markers. The sphinx had chosen murder over repayment. Along the way, he'd done his best to make it look like his mistress was the guilty party; he'd tried to free himself up to pursue a relationship with a centaur mare.

The case might make a great TV show on premium cable, but it hardly applied to my situation. Try as I might, I couldn't find any other murder cases involving sphinxes.

At least, that was, in the electronic files. Despite my best work over the past year, there were still loads of records that hadn't made it into the computer system. They were maintained in the Old Library, deep in the bowels of the courthouse.

I stood, pushing in my desk chair carefully, so that the arms lined up precisely beneath the computer keyboard and the five wheeled legs were perfectly centered beneath the desk. Obediently, I set the *I'll Be Back* clock on the office door, twisting the big hand to twelve and the little hand to two in the morning.

The courthouse's marble hallways felt colder than usual. My footsteps echoed louder than seemed strictly necessary as I made my way deeper into the building. One long corridor, and then another, around a bend, and past a quartet of long-empty offices. One last hallway, with the familiar door at the end calling to me.

By the time I set my thumb against the sleek, biometric lock, I was fighting an unexpected jolt of adrenaline. Descending flight after flight of stairs, I left behind the bare lightbulb on the landing, letting my eyes adjust to the dimness.

James had been the first person to show me the Old Library. He'd introduced me to the rare books, the disorganized records, and the detritus of a courthouse left to entropy for years.

He'd also shown me the Old Library's other assets—its boxing ring and gym mats, along with a collection of weapons that would make any museum proud.

I flexed my right arm, remembering how James had broken it. How he'd healed me with a second draught of his blood.

Then, James had let us into the Old Library with a heavy

cast-iron key. Now, a new electronic keypad protected the Eastern Empire's secrets.

I wiped my sweaty palms against my skirt and typed in my personal code. As I opened the door, I realized I was breathing deeply—not to calm myself, but rather to catch any hint of pine and snow that might remain on the air around me.

But James hadn't been near the courthouse for months. As much as my heart remembered the winter scent of him, my brain knew he was nowhere in the vicinity.

I had no reason to believe he was even still in DC. Swallowing hard, I fought against my twisty longing for a man who hated my guts.

I shouldn't even be thinking about James that way. Chris was my boyfriend now. Chris, who had stood by me after the chaos of Judge DuBois's death and who had brought me breakfast and who'd agreed to represent me in the courtroom upstairs.

The opening library door triggered automatic lights in the ceiling. I raised my chin and stepped inside, looking toward the deep blue gymnastics mats by force of habit. I even twisted my lips into a smile, grimly determined to set aside my memories of James.

An iron collar closed around my throat.

No, I realized, as my fingers automatically rose to tug at the constriction across my larynx. Not iron. Flesh. Bony flesh, determined to cut off my breathing.

I clawed at my attacker, trying to scratch my way to freedom. I succeeded only in ratcheting his grip tighter around my throat. *His* grip, I was certain, because I could feel coarse hairs under my fingertips—not the pelt of a shifter, but the flesh of a hairy man.

Or, rather, vampire.

The reek of my attacker scorched the roof of my mouth, rank body odor as heavy as soaked newspaper. Below that was a sweeter fug.

Blood. Enough to soak hair or clothing.

My attacker was a vampire, and he'd fed within the past hour. The stench was sharper, deeper, because my brain had been teasing me with memories of evergreen and ice. At least James had prepared me for this precise type of assault.

Rule one: Don't waste energy fighting a hopeless battle.

I stopped scrabbling at the hands around my neck. I wasn't going to get a purchase. I wasn't going to break free by brute force.

As if to reward my common sense, the vampire shifted his hands from my throat. I caught a single breath, short and sharp, and I opened my mouth to scream.

Rule two: Vampires are fast.

Faster than I could bellow a protest. Faster than I could twist my way to freedom. Faster than I could stagger toward the door and the stairs and safety.

He clamped a hand over my mouth, bruising my lips against my teeth and pressing his index finger—hard—beneath my nose. He threw his other arm across my throat, forcing my head against a chest that felt more like oak than muscle.

I jammed my elbow into his side, a single short arc made only slightly more effective by my effort to jackknife forward. Instinctively, I aimed for his lungs, deep inside the bony cage of his ribs.

Rule number three: Vampires don't breathe.

A human opponent would have grunted. He might even have loosened his grip as he gasped for his own breath. I could have pushed my advantage and stomped on his insole, twisting down and around.

But the creature behind me only jerked my neck to the side. I felt the cold slither of a fang against my jugular. Wet lips, slimy like refrigerated liver, slipped over the vein.

Even as bile rose in my bruised throat, I forced myself to relax against the vampire. I had no choice. I had to battle every instinct; my body wanted me to stay upright, to fight my way to the door, but I had to surprise my attacker. I had to put him off balance.

My ploy worked. His forearm loosened, just enough for me to turn *toward* him, moving farther into his embrace.

He was unsettled by the surprise motion, startled just enough that I could grab hold of the front of his shirt. Then, I let myself fall, allowing gravity to supplement my own spare weight.

Rule number four: Humans do better on the ground against vampire opponents.

He was stronger than I was. Faster, too. In an instant, he had me on my back, straddling my hips as he renewed his grip on my throat.

Despite his advantages, though, my attacker was poorly trained. As his right fingers closed around my throat, I clamped my left hand onto his wrist. Before he could pull his hand away, I reached across my body, clutching at his upper arm, just behind his elbow. I'd locked his right arm across two vulnerable joints, giving me a tiny advantage.

Shifting my knees and twisting like a fish on a line, I got my left foot against his hip. I knew how he'd respond; any opponent with greater weight and strength would simply flip me on to my belly and shove my face into the floor.

I didn't give him a chance. Instead, I summoned all my strength, raising my hips and sliding my knee behind his right shoulder. Fighting not to breathe too deeply of the stench that wafted from his cold, cold body, I tightened my right knee against his torso, squeezing as tightly as I could.

Now I controlled three of his joints—wrist, elbow, and shoulder. With whiplash speed, I dropped my hips, using his momentum to pull his forearm across my abs. Before he could regain his balance, I threw my left leg over his shoulder, crossing my ankles behind his back and securing him in a vise between my thighs.

I reinforced my advantage by circling my left arm around his neck, gripping his left shoulder and pulling him close. The motion crushed his arms between our bodies; he had no choice but to release his grip on my throat. Immediately, I squared up my hips, once again setting him off-balance.

With a final jackknife twist, I secured his body with my legs —my right wrapped around his waist, my left anchoring his vulnerable neck. His arm was hyper-extended beneath my right hand.

Vampires might be undead, but they weren't immune to the pain of broken bones. I pulled up sharply on his elbow, simultaneously using my legs to tamp down any consideration he had of escaping.

He grunted in pain, and I demanded, "Who sent you?"

He started to shake his head, but I shifted my weight, stretching his elbow to the breaking point.

"Who?" I shouted.

When he stayed silent, I dug in hard, not caring when the monster beneath me bellowed. I closed my fingers on his wrist in one last warning, pressing even harder against his over-extended elbow.

"For...the last...time," I panted. "Who?"

"Richardson!" he gasped just before I shattered his ulna.

Maurice Richardson.

A tiny corner of my rational brain actually expected as much. The courthouse had been poised for an attack by the vampire kingpin for months.

First things first. I had to learn how the enemy had gotten into the courthouse, so we could plug that hole and keep any other invader from breaching our defenses. I renewed my pressure on his arm. "How the hell did you get in here?"

I expected him to say he'd worked with other imperials. A harpy had spirited him through solid walls. A basilisk had frozen the security guards with his poisonous gaze. He'd bribed a gnome to build a new tunnel, delivering his weight in gold.

I never thought he'd force me to twist his arm even further. And I never imagined he would gasp, just before his elbow shattered: "Morton gave me the code!"

7

N o.
       James couldn't have anything to do with the animal
beneath me.

James would never sacrifice the safety of the courthouse, not after his years of honorable service as Director of Security.

James, the most moral vampire I'd ever met, would never work with Maurice Richardson, the most venal imperial east of the Mississippi.

Maurice Richardson had Turned James, over a hundred years ago. Richardson had *Impressed* him, stealing his free will.

A chill convulsed my spine. Had Richardson Impressed James again? Was that why James had kept his distance from the courthouse all these months? Why he'd kept his distance from me?

But James was far from the weak, newly-Turned vampire he'd been when Richardson had first taken possession of his will. James had become one of the strongest vampires in the Empire, in the world. And he knew Richardson's touch. He'd never be fooled into working with his enemy.

Which left one option: James was allied with Richardson voluntarily.

My belly twisting in revulsion—at the disgusting arm I gripped, at the thought of James betraying the court, at the thought of James *choosing* to join forces with Richardson—I released the enemy vampire, adding a quick kick to his kidney as I spun away.

I used my momentum to carry me over to the far wall. I'd handled the weapons there often enough to set my hand directly on the one I wanted: A silver dagger.

The blade was as long as my forearm. No self-respecting vampire would get near the double threat—a blade sharp enough to sever an artery fashioned out of a metal guaranteed to deliver third-degree burns.

By the time my enemy recovered his balance, I'd regained my position between him and the door. Balancing the knife lightly in my hand, I glanced around the library.

No files were out of place. None of the weapons had been disturbed. A faint whir, though, came from the ancient computer terminal on the far wall. Its monitor flickered, white letters rippling on a dusty black screen. I must have interrupted my attacker before he could locate the electronic resources he needed.

What the hell did James want in the Old Library?

That assumed, of course, that James had actually sent this sorry excuse for a vampire. I couldn't imagine him *talking* to the creature, much less entrusting a mission to the sorry piece of crap.

Richardson, on the other hand... He'd do anything to disrupt any aspect of the Eastern Empire Night Court. And he wouldn't hesitate to lie about James, if he thought that would advance his cause.

Even as I stoked my anger against Richardson, a niggling part of my brain said James *had* to be involved. There was no other way for a skanky, murderous, outcast vampire to get past Security Level Orange without triggering an alarm.

Mind reeling, I crouched low, keeping my offensive options open as I demanded, "How do I know you aren't lying?"

For answer, he hawked and spat on the floor, as if he were clearing a nasty taste from his mouth. I knew how he felt. My own throat was raw where his fingers had wrapped around my neck.

He ran a filthy hand through hair that could have used a shampoo or five and a month of leave-in conditioner. I took more pleasure than was strictly appropriate when he winced at the movement, but my glee was checked as he wiped his palm on the front of his black denim jeans. At least, I hoped they were black. The thought of stiff bloodstains turned my stomach.

Finally, he said, "Morton said you'd ask that. I'm supposed to say, 'The House of Usher is behind your couch and *The House of the Seven Gables* is next to your nightstand.'"

I'd written my undergraduate thesis on the theme of loneliness in American Gothic literature. I still kept my dog-eared copies of Poe in my living room. Hawthorne held place of pride in my bedroom.

And no vampire—even Maurice Richardson—could have discovered that information on his own. James was the only vampire I'd ever invited to cross my threshold.

I tightened my grip on the dagger, glancing again at the flickering computer screen. "Why did James send you?"

"To give you a warning."

I twisted my neck inside my collar, trying to ease the afterburn from my attacker's bony fingers. "Before or after you choked me to death?"

"I didn't know it was you on those stairs," he squealed.

"But you recognize me now?"

He whined, the animal sound rising from deep inside his body. "Morton said I was supposed to find you upstairs after I finished here. He said you were the only sphinx working in the courthouse."

The dagger was slippery in my sweaty palm. I considered

switching it to my left hand, but I didn't trust my enemy not to charge. "Go on, then," I said, trying to keep my voice level. "What were you supposed to say?"

"Morton says to get out of town. Now. While you still can."

The pure malevolence in the vampire's voice lifted the small hairs at the nape of my neck. I forced myself to scoff. "Tell James I'm not going anywhere," I said. "I've got an indictment hanging over my head."

"He said you'd say that too." He hawked up another loogie, then made another swipe at his filthy hair.

My fingers tightened on the dagger. "Then how are you supposed to respond?"

"Morton says no court case is worth your life."

"You tell him—"

He was faster than I'd imagined he could be. I'd been ready for him to jump me, for him to pin me to the ground and finish the strangling he'd started. I'd never considered that he'd simply knock me to the floor, spring over my body, and race up the stairs.

I dropped my dagger and grabbed at the leg of his jeans. He twisted to get away. I might have held him, even then, but I was startled by a metallic thunk, as something hit the crown of my head.

Blinking away stars, I loosened my fingers, reflexively clutching at my aching head. The vampire tore away, sprinting for the stairs.

"Wait!" I shouted, scrambling for the steps. But the door at the top of the stairwell clanged shut before I set foot on the first riser.

I circled back to see what he'd used to conk me. A flask glinted on the floor, its stainless steel sides scratched and dented. I clutched it and sprinted up the stairs, but the corridor was empty. My only link to James was gone.

Still clutching the flask, I raced to my office. Even as I ran, I realized I couldn't tell Angelique that I'd caught an invader in the Old Library. She'd mobilize all the forces at her disposal, doing everything in her considerable power to catch the vampire.

And she'd make sure he led her to James.

Even now, after months of silence, after nearly being strangled in my own workplace, after hearing that James had somehow—impossibly—thrown in his lot with Richardson, I couldn't set him up for Angelique's revenge.

The night court's actual Director of Security would certainly be treated as an extreme flight risk. He might *accidentally* be left in silver handcuffs. He might mistakenly be tied down in a room with full exposure to morning sun. He might just happen to encounter a broken chair leg, a shattered banister, an oak stake that would penetrate his heart.

Instead of storming Angelique's office, I stumbled over to my desk. Using two fingers, I gingerly opened the steel flask my attacker had thrown at me. A quick whiff of cinnamon told me everything I needed to know about its contents.

Lethe. The potion vampires used to make humans—and most other imperials—forget encounters with the supernatural.

Lethe wouldn't work on me. My sphinx blood saw to that. But Richardson's drone had been armed against any *other* imperial discovering his presence. A quick shot of Lethe and a direct command could make anyone forget they'd seen a vampire.

I had to call Chris. I had to tell him everything that had happened. I had to enlist his help to track the enemy vampire, to follow whatever trail existed back to James, back to Richardson, before the court or the EBI got involved.

Hurtling through my office door, I set the *I'll Be Back* clock swaying. I scrambled for my keyboard at the same time that I fumbled for my phone, ready to send an emergency email while I called.

My computer monitor glowed a bright, toxic green.

Crap. We'd upgraded the court's computers about a year ago. In the intervening time, I'd become spoiled. I hadn't needed to deal with a single frozen monitor, unlike the nightly blue screens of death that had been the norm when I started my job.

Muttering under my breath, I typed in Control-Alt-Delete, the time-honored three-fingered salute designed to clear a frozen screen.

Nothing.

I tapped on the Escape key, half a dozen urgent pecks.

Nothing.

Swearing, I reached to the back of the monitor to reboot the entire computer. Before I could flip the switch, though, the green screen shimmered. As I stared, a shape rose out of the disturbance. It twisted and rippled, the shocking scarlet of fresh blood.

I blinked, and the distortion resolved into a skull-and-crossbones.

I threw myself back in my chair, instinctively leaping as far from the screen as possible in the tight confines of my desk alcove. As I gaped, words began to stream from the bottom of my screen to the top, jagged blood-red letters that disappeared into the shocking green background like the first reel of a demented *Star Wars* sequel.

"Pay Up or Else!" said the scroll. "Your computer has been locked! We have access to all Eastern Empire files. Transfer one million dollars to our Bitcoin wallet: ZzZ9y4fRgvf5Rx4Hupb-E5JjQqXx. A timer will start once you read this message. You have 48 hours before all Eastern Empire records are destroyed."

8

M y fingers flew toward my mouse without my giving them conscious permission. A couple of quick clicks, and I'd turned off the computer.

Nausea twisted my belly. This had to be someone's idea of a joke. I forced myself to take three deep breaths. All I had to do was turn my computer on. It would cycle through its long boot-up process and then a shiny image of blindfolded justice—the emblem of the District of Columbia court—would appear.

There. Everything was fine. My computer wasn't possessed. The ransom demand had only been a prank. Everything was working exactly as it should. The computer displayed the appropriate mundane screensaver.

I flicked through the keystrokes to bring up my Eastern Empire files.

"Your computer has been locked!"

The same message appeared as before. Now, though, a countdown clock ticked across the bottom of my screen. Scarlet numbers peeled away as I wasted precious seconds.

Why would anyone target *me?* I was a harmless court clerk. I didn't wield any sort of power. I had no ability to change anyone's life in anything approaching a meaningful way.

Anyone. Even as I thought the word, I knew I was lying to myself. The computers hadn't been sabotaged by just *anyone.* They'd been hacked by Maurice Richardson.

Even as I turned my computer off again, I remembered the soft whirr of the terminal in the Old Library. The vampire I'd surprised down there must have used that machine to hack into our system.

That's why James had given him access to the courthouse.

Acid rose in the back of my throat as I turned my computer back on. This time, instead of logging in as me, I tried a dummy account, a fake username and password that I'd created over a year ago, when I was first updating the computer system.

The dummy account was locked too.

And if the dummy account was affected, that implied that every other account on the system had been sabotaged. And if every other account had been sabotaged—

"Sarah!"

I'd recognize Angelique Wilson's yowl anywhere. I pushed my chair back and scrambled through the *Staff Only* door.

"Sarah!" Angelique screeched again, barely cutting off her summons as I barreled around the corner into her office.

Automatically, I checked the almanac in my mind.

What? Most people don't have the phases of the moon committed to memory? Well, most people don't work for a slave-driver, cat-shifter boss. Most people don't have to worry about the one night a month when their boss might literally eviscerate them for the slightest mistake in filing.

We were one day past the full moon. I was safe. For now. Except, of course, for the little matter of the crimson letters dripping down the computer screen that Angelique turned toward me.

"What the Fox Terrier is this?" she demanded. Even now, with the computer system shut down around us, Angelique persisted with her idiotic dog-breed curses.

"I don't know," I said. "The same thing just showed up on my computer."

Angelique's eyes narrowed. Her crimson-painted fingernails reflected the letters on her screen as she typed in some frantic command. I wasn't sure how she managed to attack the keyboard with nails that extended half an inch, each one filed to a needle-sharp point.

"I don't have time for your Borzoi," she muttered as she worked.

"I've already tried turning my computer off and turning it back on," I said, wincing as she toggled her own power button from on to off to on again without a second's delay. The surge of electricity couldn't possibly help anything. But from the inexorable countdown clock that filled her screen, it didn't seem to cause more harm.

As Angelique's canine profanity scorched her office walls, I schooled my face to stillness. In the past six months, I'd become inured to my boss's tantrums.

I looked around the office as Angelique continued to explain that she was rather frustrated with her computer, and she truly wished it would function a mite more efficiently, especially because she had been in the middle of drafting a highly detailed and engaging memo about the Office of Security's annual budget. Or something to that effect.

A glass glinted on the corner of her desk. I recognized the tumbler immediately, one of a pair that should have been locked away in the credenza on the far side of the room. Now that my attention was snagged, I caught a faint breath of cinnamon on the air, almost drowned by the stench of the vampire I'd wrestled downstairs, the reek that still permeated my clothes.

Lethe.

Someone had dosed Angelique Wilson. And my money was on the vampire from downstairs, of course.

But what the hell had he been doing inside Angelique's office? He must have raced here directly from the Old Library.

While I'd been fighting the ransom demand, methodically cycling my computer on and off, waiting for the interminable booting routine to complete—twice—he'd done something to my boss.

But what?

Before I could begin to divine an answer, the telephone rang on Angelique's desk. It was an internal line; we could both see Judge Finch's extension displayed on the console. For a moment, I thought Angelique would let the call go to voice mail, but at the beginning of the fourth ring, she grabbed the handset. "Wilson," she snarled.

I could just make out a fast-paced question.

"Yes, Your Honor."

More garbled words.

"No, Your Honor."

Another response, this one shorter and more sharp.

"Right away, Your Honor."

Angelique cradled the phone, already glaring at me. "Judge Finch wants to see me in her chambers," she said. "But don't think we're finished here. Not by a Labrador long-shot. I know what you're up to, and you're not going to get away with it."

"What *I'm* up to?"

"Everyone knows your Gordon Setter history with Morton."

"J—James! What does James have to do with this?" Even as I protested, I felt my bruised neck flush crimson. James wasn't anything to me, not anymore. Chris was my boyfriend. Chris, who'd just declared he loved me, just six hours earlier.

Angelique's green eyes narrowed to daggers. "You think I'm an idiot, but I know exactly what's going on here. Your James Morton is the only imperial I know with access to lock down our entire computer system. He might be roaming the Empire right now, not feeling like coming into the office, but he sure as hell won't let me or anyone else take his job."

I gaped. I honestly couldn't imagine James conspiring to target the Acting Director. If he'd wanted to return to this office, he'd march through the door and claim it. But Angelique certainly wasn't interested in hearing *that* protest, not as she tugged on her suit jacket and prepared to face Judge Finch.

"You've got two days, Sarah. Unlock these files and turn in James Morton. Because if I don't have access to my computer before the ransom demand expires, you're going to be held accountable."

She held up one long index finger, tipped with its needle claw. "First, you'll be Foxhound fired."

Another finger, another claw. "Then, you'll be Affenpinscher arrested. Again."

A third finger, a third claw, rotated so that all three daggers pointed directly at my heart. "And then, you'll be put in German Shepherd jail, where I'll make it my personal mission to see you rot until you die."

Before I could respond, she shot her cuffs and strode to the door. She paused on the threshold, turning back to glare at me. "Make no Mastiff-loving mistake. You're going down for this."

"Going down?" I couldn't help it. I laughed. It was either that or melt into a puddle of terror, overwhelmed by how quickly my life could go from normal to insane. "What do you think this is? A cheap remake of *The Untouchables?*"

She snarled. "You can be touched, Sarah Anderson. You can be torn, limb from limb. And by the time I'm through with you, there's not an imperial this side of the Mississippi who'll do anything more than spit on your bleeding corpse."

Well, *that* got interesting in a hurry. And what a surprise— when Angelique was threatening bodily mayhem, she dropped her need to swear. She spun on her stiletto heels and headed to Judge Finch's office before I could stammer a response.

James and I aren't working together…
I have no idea how to unlock the files…
You can't send me back to that cell…

All those arguments, and a dozen more, were useless. The

only way I could save myself was to find James. Find Richardson.

That, or come up with a million dollars to release our ransomed files.

Right.

My meager bank account barely reached five hard-won figures. Four, after I made my rent payment each month.

The sphinxes might have enough cash on hand to appease Richardson, but I couldn't imagine convincing the Pride to sign the check—even if I *were* still a member of the Den. I shook my head, unable to imagine how *that* request would go.

Out of the corner of my eye, the overhead light glinted on the crystal tumbler that still sat on Angelique's desk. I stepped close enough to make out the ring of Lethe at the bottom of the glass.

What had Richardson's drone wanted from Angelique? What had he needed here, that he couldn't accomplish using the computer down in the Old Library? And what sort of sneak-thief invader left evidence of his tampering in full view?

Angelique had been distracted by the ransom notice. She'd been intent on targeting me. But I was certain she'd notice the tumbler as soon as she returned. As Acting Director of Security, she had to be familiar with Lethe. She'd understand that she'd been dosed, even if she didn't have any more answers than I did.

And that would pretty much seal James's arrest warrant, even without my testimony that the vampire in the basement had said James had granted him entrance to the building.

I should let Angelique bring him in. I should have faith in the court's machinery as they got to the bottom of this unprecedented attack.

But I didn't have faith. Not in the wake of Judge DuBois's death.

Not when I *knew* James was innocent. He had to be innocent.

Even if he'd given my attacker access to the Old Library. Even if every scrap of evidence shouted that James had allied himself with Maurice Richardson.

He wasn't innocent. But even with that knowledge, I couldn't imagine turning him in. Not until I'd made one last effort to find him myself. My earlier vision of silver bonds and oaken stakes still held. I had to give James a chance to survive.

That meant I had to deal with the tumbler. I could hide it in my desk. I could even try to carry it home. But given my boss's current unreasoning rage, she might very well search my workspace. She might even go through my bags before she let me out the door.

The safest thing to do was to return the glass to its proper place inside the credenza. But that meant working the discreet keypad set into the cabinet's front panel.

I caught my breath, listening for any hint that Angelique was about to return.

Silence—at least until my pounding heart made it impossible for me to discern approaching danger. I pulled my sleeve over my hand to avoid leaving fingerprints, and I picked up the tumbler. Setting the glass on top of the credenza, I kept my fingers covered as I typed 1234 into the keypad.

Nothing.

I tried 0001.

Nothing.

James Morton was a disorganized vampire. He couldn't alphabetize a filing cabinet to save his life. He had no qualms about leaving waist-high stacks of pressboard files in the safety of his own office.

But in whatever passed for his heart, he was the court's Director of Security. And he'd never use the two most common combinations in the entire world.

I contemplated typing 5358, the street address of his sanctum. But that would have created a security risk James would never countenance.

1911, then. The street address of *my* apartment.

The gears shifted inside the lock, and the door released, just enough for me to pull it open. A cut-crystal decanter sat inside, neatly stoppered next to a single matching tumbler. A faint circle indicated the resting place for a second tumbler.

I exhaled a breath I hadn't known I was holding. Until that moment, I'd somehow believed this was all a terrible mistake. I'd clutched the lie—that Richardson's vampire had been gaslighting me, that James wasn't involved with the break-in, the Lethe, the imperial files held ransom.

Maybe I should follow the instruction that foot soldier had delivered. Maybe I *should* get the hell out of Dodge. Flee DC. Abandon the only home I'd ever known.

But I had no way of knowing if I'd be jumping from the all-too-hot frying pan into a lethal fire. Until I understood the powers arrayed against me, I had no way of being certain how to reach safety.

I could wait for Angelique to return. I could show her the Lethe and explain that she'd been drugged. We could work together to discover what Richardson had wanted in her office. *What James had wanted.*

But I could still hear her snarled threat: "You're going down for this." I'd already been indicted for a series of crimes against the Empire. I'd forfeited my insignia just to walk free. I had nothing left to give as a token of my good will. Especially not when my own people, the sphinxes, had turned against me.

I set the glass precisely in the center of its dust-ringed circle. I closed the credenza door. I spun the dial and scrambled the lock. And then I headed back to my desk, to my computer and the terrifying countdown clock on its poisonous green screen.

I couldn't log out, not with the ransom demand holding my screen captive. Instead, I reached behind the terminal and killed the power button one more time.

Grabbing my purse, I headed out of the courthouse, cutting my shift short. Better to ask forgiveness than permission.

I had less than forty-eight hours to meet Angelique's ultimatum. If I failed, I'd be asking for a metal file hidden in a cake, so I could break out of my future jail cell.

And I couldn't think of a single imperial who would dare to bring me one.

9

O f course, I went to Chris.

Even awakened from the deepest of sleeps, he was the only person I knew who would look at my bruised throat and understand that I wanted revenge, not comfort. I told him everything, finishing with: "I need to find James."

It felt strange to talk about the man whose bed I'd shared before Chris's. Still, I forced myself to say, "I need to understand what's going on, because he would *never* join forces with Maurice Richardson."

"He's been gone for ten months," Chris said, his voice impossibly gentle.

"But he's still—"

"He watched you execute the man he respected most in the entire world."

Execute. Chris didn't hesitate as he said the word, but I knew he'd chosen it over "kill."

Chris went on just as carefully. "DuBois was like a father to him."

"I *know* that—"

"A father's death must be avenged."

There. That was the explanation my own brain had been

avoiding, every single minute since my attacker first muttered James's name. James Morton would only unite with his greatest enemy—Richardson—to get revenge against an even more malicious force.

Me.

"He wouldn't do that." My voice cracked.

I'd drunk James's blood. I *knew* him—somehow, some way, in the deepest parts of my brain, the ones that functioned without words.

But if that were true, wouldn't we have been drawn together over the past ten months? Even if we were only destined to have one final conversation, the words that finally, irrevocably pulled us apart... Wouldn't I still be bound to James?

"Chris..." I said, but I didn't know how to finish that sentence.

His eyes looked like caramel in the lamplight. "Tell me what you want."

Words. I needed words. Not this crazy tangle of emotions, not my constant stressing and spinning and wondering. I steadied myself with a deep breath, and my fists closed on the blanket, still rumpled from Chris's sleep. "I want you to help me find him."

Chris nodded. "I will," he said. But then his voice sharpened. "On one condition."

Energy crackled off those three words. Even if I'd been blind, if I couldn't read the lines that creased beside his mouth, I would have known we'd crossed a new barrier. Chris was about to change everything—between him and me, between *James* and me.

"What?" I asked, the single word loaded with trepidation.

"When we find him, you'll make him *commit*."

I heard the emphasis on the word. I understood it was important. But I had no clue what Chris intended. "What does that mean?" I whispered.

"You know the Ancient Commission."

Of course I did. Sekhmet had charged all sphinxes with the Ancient Commission, binding us to her service millennia ago. The goddess's youngest children, her vampires, couldn't manage the chaos of their predatory lives in a world ruled by humans.

So we sphinxes, Sekhmet's oldest children, protected our younger siblings. The Ancient Commission bound us to our mother, to the goddess. We protected vampires because Sekhmet commanded us to do so.

And we did it—*they* did it, the sphinxes in the Den—by confining vampires to tiny cinderblock cells, by feeding them strict rations, by binding them to specific sphinx masters.

Not all of them. Some vampires, like James, had lived proud lives free of direct sphinx control. But weaker vampires, ones that were Turned and abandoned by their creators, ones that wandered, starving and alone, on the fringes of imperial society…

Chris nodded at my wordless sound of frustration. "The Ancient Commission breaks vampires," he said. "We make them dependent on sphinxes for food, for safety, for the satisfaction of every natural urge. For centuries, that's been the only way to keep them safe."

I'd seen the results of that so-called safety. One of those battered and broken vampires had instigated the entire Judge DuBois debacle.

Chris went on. "The Ancient Commission only works if we find vampires quickly, within a week—at most—of their Turning. We need something else, for vampires who've long-since Turned. We need a new tool. A new bond."

I shook my head. Vampires already resented sphinxes enough. The scarcely masked enmity between James and Chris had taught me that much.

Chris went on, as if I'd spoken my objection aloud. "The New Commission will give vampires options. We'll teach them about the importance of a sanctum, and why they should keep its location secret from everyone." He reached for his nightstand

and pulled open the drawer. Inside was a pad of lined paper and three capped pens, nail clippers, and a bottle of aspirin.

At the back of the drawer was a pamphlet. "Have you seen this?" Chris asked, passing me the brochure.

Welcome the Night. Easily legible letters were picked out against a dark night sky. The paper was slick beneath my fingers. The document consisted of a dozen pages, each answering a basic question for new vampires. "How often do I need to feed?" said one. "Do I really need to sleep in the earth of my forefathers?" asked another.

"Where did this come from?" I asked Chris.

"Empire General. The new medical director at the hospital started a program a few months ago. A lot of newly Turned vampires end up on their ward, recovering from the shock of transition. This is supposed to make things easier."

I glanced at Chris's handwriting on the back of the brochure, cocking my head to better read his words. "How does it fit with your…New Commission?"

"Twelve pages isn't enough. Three paragraphs about setting up a sanctum?" He snorted dismissively. "But Empire General can get them started with that. And we'll take on long-term support. We won't just tell them they feed from Sources; we'll show them how to track down an actual living donor. We won't stop at noting they're immune from most human diseases; we'll get them on a schedule for self-care. Haircuts, nail trimming, regular appointments with a dentist who understands fangs."

"We'll be their personal assistants."

"If that's what they need. The thing is, we'll be helping them. They'll be better able to keep out of sight from mundane authorities."

"For how long?"

"Until we determine they can function on their own. We'll have a clearance program—they'll have to show they know how to hide a sanctum, how to locate a Source, what to do if they can't feed safely for an extended period of time. We'll issue a license, a certification that they're allowed to be free. They'll be re-certified every year."

I pictured a phalanx of sphinxes, stopping vampires on the street under a baleful moon. *Papers, please.*

"You'll treat them like second-class citizens."

"We'll treat them like an endangered species."

I shook my head. The vampires I'd met were proud. Powerful. They'd never submit to Chris's plan.

Chris sighed and reached toward the nightstand again, retrieving his cell phone from its charger. His fingers flew over the smooth glass surface, tapping out a password.

Staring at the screen with enough intensity that I knew he was avoiding my gaze, Chris threaded his way through email until he got to a recorded video. After a moment's hesitation, he clicked on the white triangle to make it play and turned it to face me.

At first, I couldn't make out what I was seeing. The images were dark; the clip had clearly been made at night. The camera moved closer, taking a moment to change its focus.

A mound of rags sagged against a stained and dented Dumpster. A slick of oil—or something darker—oozed across broken pavement. A rat glared up at the camera, not threatened enough to give up the bone beneath his yellowed incisors.

As I squinted, trying to reduce the image to meaningful shapes, a form appeared at the edge of the camera's field—a man who nodded to whoever held the camera. He held a club the length of a policeman's nightstick. But unlike any nightstick I'd ever seen, this one gleamed a sickly white.

I didn't realize it was silver, until the man prodded the tangle of rags.

The rat took flight as a body exploded from the pile, all arms and legs and ragged, uncombed hair. Only then did I realize the video came with sound. My ears were filled with an agonized screech, the wail of feedback through overtaxed speakers.

But I wasn't hearing feedback. I was hearing the cry of a creature in fear for her life.

The cameraman grunted as his colleague bashed the vampire's arm with his silver nightstick. The crack of bone was loud enough to be captured on video. The recording, though, didn't pick up the sizzle, the sound that would have matched the blisters that rose immediately on the vampire's skin.

She was thrashing now, desperate. She tried to lunge past her attacker, but he forced her against the filthy wall. She bared her fangs, hissing in defiance, or maybe only in pain.

That made the cameraman laugh, a gloating sound that coated the back of my throat with bile. "You've got a live one," he shouted at his buddy. "Go on," he said. "Pin her before she gets away."

Egged on, the attacker slammed his club across the vampire's throat. She bellowed at the blow, renewing her efforts to escape, but the man merely shifted his weight, using the leverage of one forearm and the silver rod. His other hand fumbled at the zipper of his pants.

Chris did something to the phone, and the screen went black.

Agriotis.

My head hummed with sweet blood-thirst. I hovered on the edge of my shift, one breath away from transforming into my true imperial form. My talons lurked beneath my flesh; I could feel the jagged edge of the teeth that longed to express from my jaw.

I wanted to kill those men. I *needed* to destroy them.

"Breathe," Chris said.

I didn't want to breathe. I wanted to step off the cliff of oblivion and descend into mindless, animal satisfaction.

"Breathe," Chris repeated, keeping his voice soft because he was only a handspan away.

Sweet, sweet vengeance. I craved it, for myself and for the

tortured vampire and for every other creature that had ever been tormented by a bully with a club.

"Sarah," Chris whispered.

My name pulled me back. My name and the distant inkling that I'd sworn never to yield to *agriotis* again. Chris had rescued me from madness in the past. He'd restored me to my human form; he'd fed me and grounded me.

I breathed.

And when I was able to form words, I whispered with deadly precision, "Who the hell were they?"

"We think they're salamanders. The video was found on the FireWeb."

"And the vampire?"

"A gargoyle found her before the sun rose. He brought her to Empire General. She's still on the Vampire Ward. Her physical wounds healed quickly enough, but…"

Her wounds went well beyond the physical.

Chris went on. "And there isn't anywhere to send her. She didn't have a sanctum before the attack. And she's in no condition to create one now."

"But she's a vampire!"

He nodded. "From what she told the doctors, she was Turned about five years ago. She dropped out of high school before that. She was addicted to heroin and couldn't hold down a job."

I shook my head. I didn't want to hear more.

"But she's a vampire," I repeated, because I couldn't think of anything else to say.

Chris leaned forward. "You've known James. And Judge DuBois. Judge Finch now, and a handful of lawyers. But most vampires don't live like they do. Most vampires don't have the advantage of education and money. Some don't even have Lethe to hide from the mundane world."

I stared at the darkened phone, feeling my fingers grow numb in the aftermath of near-transition. Chris gave me time, letting me fumble for an answer. He could afford to. He knew I couldn't come up with a meaningful response.

Finally he said, "That's why the New Commission is so important. I want to harness Sekhmet's power in service to vampires everywhere."

"You want to bind them!"

"I want to serve them. Protect them. All of them." His gaze met mine and held it, steady and unwavering. "I want every vampire to find the sort of bond James found with you. You made him better. Stronger. More successful. Safer."

"Until I drove him mad!"

"You didn't do that. The people who Impressed DuBois did that."

He waited, but I only shook my head. He was asking too much. I didn't have the right to make a decision that would bind every vampire in the Eastern Empire. I shouldn't be allowed to choose their future.

"Think about it, Sarah. James hired you for the court. *He* reached out to *you*. He gave you your insignia. He granted you your powers. He did that because he knew he needed you. He might not have had the words. He might not have had the knowledge. But he wanted this. He *needed* this."

I looked around the bedroom, at the neatly folded comforter resting across the foot of the bed, at the smooth pillow where I'd lain my head too many nights to count. I stared at the windows, at the blackout shades, at the sheers and curtains.

Everything about Chris's house spoke of order, of logic. He managed his life as a sphinx; he was in control.

I flashed on James's abandoned sanctum, the musty sheets and the tangled linen closet, the dry toilet and the bare kitchen shelves. Even in its abandonment, though, the sanctum was luxurious, with its dark kitchen cabinets and its fashionably distressed wood floors.

Chris was asking me to make a decision for the vampires who couldn't afford fine houses, who weren't guaranteed a safe and secure sanctum like James's. I had to speak for the dispossessed.

And then he added honey to his request. "If you do this, we can go to the Pride. We can show how well we work together, everything we've accomplished. Ptah or Sheut—none of that will matter. They'll let you back in the Den."

A longing rose inside me, hot and heavy, like slow lava flowing to the sea. I wanted to belong. I'd wanted to belong since I was a child, since I'd first realized I never fit in—to school, to work, to life in general.

I didn't trust that desire. Not with the searing images of Chris's torture video still playing out behind my eyelids when I blinked. Not with my throat still throbbing from Richardson's goon, with my thoughts scraped raw at the thought of James purposely *allowing* that creature into the courthouse.

Chris cared for me. I knew that. By his own admission, he *loved* me. But his prescription for my safety and health and well-being was inextricably linked to his own goals as Sun Lion of the Eastern Empire.

I needed guidance from someone who wasn't directly invested in the outcome. I needed advice from someone who understood all the old history, all the new challenges, who was aware of Eastern Empire politics and the Den and the Pride, but who stood outside all those worldly institutions.

I squared my shoulders and looked Chris in the eye. "I need to know what's right and what's wrong. That's more important than you or me or James. More important than the Den or the Pride or even the Empire." I swallowed hard, refusing to acknowledge the simmering burn of my bruised throat. "I want to speak with Sekhmet."

10

F or just a moment, Chris looked surprised. He'd expected me to listen to his argument and accept his point of view. That's what sphinxes did when the Sun Lion spoke, even when he didn't back up his argument with audio-visual aids.

But I wasn't exactly a sphinx. And I definitely wasn't the sort of woman to take a man's word just because he said so.

Besides, I'd always had a special relationship with Sekhmet. I'd seen her the first time I slipped into a magical trance. I'd watched her fondle the lion cubs that were her children, my siblings—sphinxes and vampires alike.

Chris had told me that first encounter was shocking. He hadn't bothered to say that my next visit—in Sekhmet's private gardens—was impossible. And I'd never managed to explain to him exactly what I'd seen the last time I visited our mother—the bloodthirsty goddess leading her troops into battle, taking no prisoners in the terrible fight for supremacy in the ancient world.

Now, he quickly smothered his surprise. "Do you want to work here? Or would you be more comfortable in the library?"

"This is good enough."

I lay down on top of the blanket and accepted a throw

pillow to tuck behind my head. I was suddenly reminded of my rank clothes, of the lingering stench from the vampire I'd fought in the Old Library. There was nothing to be done about that now, though. Seeking guidance from Sekhmet was more important than clean clothes. I shifted to a more comfortable position, and tried to clear my mind.

Seated on the edge of the bed, Chris gave me an encouraging smile. I could tell he was trying to make this easy for me, giving me control over the situation and letting me go as fast—or as slow—as I wanted.

My fingers closed around my bare wrist, mimicking the hematite bracelet that remained in the court's custody. In the past, I'd used it as a focus to block out the mundane world, filtering away all the things that truly didn't matter.

When I touched bare skin, my attention automatically shifted to my ring finger. Of course, my coral band was gone as well.

Even as I shoved down my burgeoning case of nerves, Chris passed me his wristwatch, his own insignia. The band was warm from his flesh, hematite and coral the identical temperature.

It wasn't the same as my own insignia. It wasn't even close. But the compassion behind the offering, the simple, straightforward understanding of my need, made my breath come uneven.

"Whenever you're ready," Chris said softly.

I blinked hard and settled the watchband over my wrist. It was large, and heavy too, and I adjusted it three times, trying to find a more comfortable position.

"You're safe, Sarah," Chris said.

I hadn't thought I was in danger. Not consciously, at least. But Chris's quiet reassurance soothed something I hadn't even realized was ruffled inside my mind. I closed my eyes and breathed in on a count of seven.

My diaphragm stretched. My lungs expanded. My chin rose, and I turned my face toward the window, with its impeccable curtains. I concentrated on the folds of the sheers. Even with my eyes closed, I knew they were perfectly placed, their soft curves framing the shades with precision.

"*Skepsi,*" I said, murmuring the ancient word that initiated the meditation of my people.

I imagined the glow from the reading lamp filling my head, flowing past my eyes, my nose, my mouth. It filled my throat, hot and pure and perfect. It melted away the roughness in my larynx, all the remnant pain that Richardson's soldier had left after our battle in the Old Library.

"*Phoni,*" I said, offering up my voice in service to Sekhmet.

The golden light overflowed into the hollow of my chest. It expanded between my ribs, illuminating them like the arches of a medieval cathedral. It flowed over and through me, soaking into the core of my heart and flooding all four chambers, hotter than blood.

"*Pathos,*" I said, offering up all the passion of my body, my mind, my being. I was swept along by a fiery tide. I traveled through time, through space, to the ancient core of my memory.

I reached Sekhmet.

The goddess held her lion form. I could see her ribs beneath her sleek flanks, rising and falling with every breath she took. She lowered her massive head to the grassy ground, twitching her ears as if bothered by a fly. Her whiskers moved as she whuffed out her breath, each puff resonating in a deep tone I could barely register with my ears.

As I watched, she raised one massive paw. Its heavy pads were curled inward, hiding her claws. Flowing like a tranquil river, she stretched her furred leg. Only then did I realize that she was blocking the escape of a naked toddler boy.

The youngster, though, would have nothing of containment. Instead, he shoved his head under his mother's paw, wriggling forward with clear intent to reach the sandy plain beyond the lush grass circle. In his chubby hand, he carried a doll shaped out of soft cotton rags.

The toy was ragged, as if it were well-loved. The head was

coming unraveled, and the arms were shapeless lumps. This was a long-established plaything, no recently created treasure.

Sekhmet's whuffing sharpened, but the boy didn't care. He tumbled down the slight incline, barely managing to stretch his legs as he came to a stop. His toy dropped from his hand, but he retrieved it immediately, plucking at it to make sure it was unharmed.

Only when he knew the doll was safe did he look up the hillock at his mother. When she issued an unmistakable command for him to return, he set his tiny jaw. His fingers tightened on the poppet, and he shouted, "No!"

Half a dozen toddlers appeared around Sekhmet, peering from behind her lashing tail, from between her braced forelegs. Identical obsidian eyes widened. Identical rosebud mouths puckered in awe. One little girl laughed, and then she shouted, "No!" as she clutched her own cotton doll. They all held them, all the children, and every toy was ragged with age.

The goddess had had enough. She climbed to all fours and surged down the hill. Reaching her disobedient son, she lowered her head, glaring directly into his startled eyes.

"N— No?" The child asked, defiance rapidly diluting to confusion.

Sekhmet opened her mouth wide, showing upper and lower rows of gleaming needle-sharp teeth. When her headstrong son clutched his toy and backed one step away, she roared.

The sound filled my ears. It resonated through my body. It found the marrow of my bones and shook until I thought I might drain away into the sand.

The pile of children atop the hill froze, their worn dolls falling from slack fingers. The brave explorer at the bottom of the slope dropped his own toy as he wet himself in terror.

Sekhmet lowered her head and caught her disobedient son by the scruff of his neck. She carried him as if he were in cub form, her mouth soft, her steps determined as she returned to her awed children. Reaching the top of the hill, she pinned the boy with one broad paw, ignoring his piteous whimper as she licked him, head to toe. The child's trembling gave way to contented mews, at least until he realized he'd lost his toy.

I picked it up.

I cradled the cotton form against my body, supporting its limp neck as if it were a true human child. It was warm in the sunlight, as soft as a sleeping babe. My fingers automatically moved over its loose cloth folds, soothing and straightening. Without planning to speak, I found myself whispering words of comfort, shapeless syllables about peace and quiet and safety.

When I looked up, the scene before me had transformed. Sekhmet was no longer a lion. Now, she was a woman, tall and terrible in a linen gown that fell in perfect pleats from her shoulders. Her straight black hair was twisted into braids. Her eyes were lined with kohl.

"Protect them," she said, but her lips never moved. She placed the words directly inside my head.

I couldn't look away. I couldn't search for the children behind her. I couldn't gaze at the doll cradled in my arms. All I could do was shape my own silent words, a question that moved from my mind to the goddess's. "The children?" I asked. "Or their toys?"

"There are no toys."

And because she was a goddess, she spoke the truth. The instant her words bloomed inside my skull, the doll disappeared from my arms. There was no poppet; there was no toy. There was only an ache, a longing, an emptiness that could never be filled.

I gasped at the pain of loss, staggering forward to beg Sekhmet for... something. For comfort. For a toy of my own. A child of my own.

But the goddess only turned away. And now, in the way of dreams, she no longer stood on a hill. She was no longer surrounded by her children or their playthings.

Instead, she stood, *we* stood, in the mouth of a cave. With the shadows behind her, she gazed at me. Her eyes were bright. Her mouth curved into a smile. She set a single finger against her lips, urging me to silence, as if we were playing a game.

She stepped into the darkness. I heard her laughter. And I heard a rumble, long and low, like a mountain coming to rest after a temblor. Mother Sekhmet whispered, "My love..."

She was with him. She was with Sheut. She could have summoned him from the shadows, brought him into the light, but instead she kept him secret. She forbade me to meet my sire.

I waited, because the goddess had not dismissed me. And after an hour or a day or a lifetime, I peered into the cavern, into a darkness deeper than night.

No. There was light *somewhere* in that cave. There was a flicker, like a distant aurora in a midnight sky. Like fish scales at the bottom of a pond. Like a rainbow splayed against velvet.

Still I waited, wondering what form my father took in the darkness of that cave. And all the time that Sekhmet was with Sheut, I nurtured a flame of resentment, a tiny crimson curl deep inside my heart.

She could have let me meet my father.

But she was a goddess. And she did whatever she wanted to do. And so I sat beside the cavern's mouth and tried not to feed the anger beneath my breastbone.

After forever, a lioness emerged from the shadows.

She moved like a dream, silent and lithe. She breathed upon me, and I shuddered—a long, slow ripple that cascaded from the crown of my head to the arches of my feet. Her tongue scraped my arm, and I exhaled my breath into two words: "Mother Sekhmet."

"Daughter," she said.

Those two syllables filled me with wonder. My soul grew light as a feather. My body melted into sunlight.

I might not know my father, but my goddess accepted me. I belonged.

Through the magic of my bliss, I heard Sekhmet speak again. "Find the Seal," she said. "And save the children."

"Find what?" I barely summoned the will to set my words in the midst of her majestic presence.

"The Seal."

"I— I don't understand."

She nudged me with her head, pressing her furred brow against my wrist. I looked down to where I'd worn my hematite bracelet, to where I should have seen Chris's watch.

Instead of Chris's insignia, though, I saw an imprint on my flesh. The shape was simple, like a child's drawing—an oval bisected on the long axis by a single line.

The lioness whuffed again, the same sound she'd used to command her wayward son. "The Lost Soul has it. Find my Seal and keep all my children safe."

As she said the words—Lost Soul—I sensed a being hovering beyond the goddess, a shadow that was ancient and dark and impenetrable. I could feel its savage hunger inside my mind. I could sense its yearning, its lust for power and control. But when I turned my head to stare at it directly, I found nothing.

"Please," I said to Sekhmet. "I don't understand! Who is the Lost Soul? What is the Seal?"

But she had disappeared. Sekhmet and the cavern and the magic of ancient Egypt—all of it drifted into nothingness.

I was sitting in Chris's bedroom. The reading lamp glowed in the darkness, its light barely reaching the edge of the bed.

"Sarah," Chris said, and I realized he knelt beside me, holding my hands where they rested across my belly, still curved to protect a toy that wasn't a toy, a child that wasn't a child. His fingers shifted, and he started to chafe my wrists. "Sarah," he said again, and I finally remembered how to speak.

"I saw her," I said. "Sekhmet and…" But I couldn't say *Sheut*. I couldn't name my father. I couldn't share the iridescence, the dark magic of the man I'd barely glimpsed. That was too personal, far too private.

"And…" Chris prompted.

I shook my head, trying to focus. "Her children," I said.

"Vampires? Or sphinxes?"

I bit my lip. It was impossible to reduce my vision to words. "Both," I said. "Neither."

I fought to sit up, but Chris spread his hand across my chest, urging me to lean back, to regroup, to gather my strength before I attempted so great a feat.

I concentrated on words, "They were children," I said. "Toddlers. But they were lions, too. They had toys, broken-down dolls." My voice grew stronger. "Sekhmet's children had toys. And the goddess told me to protect them."

"Them?" I knew Chris was asking the same question I'd asked the goddess.

I shook my head. "The children. The toys. It didn't matter to Sekhmet." And as I said the words, it all made sense. "Sekhmet wants us to protect her children and their possessions, the things they've made, the things they've Turned. Even if the Turned are old and ragged." I swallowed hard as the import of my vision spread through me. "Sekhmet accepts the New Commission."

Chris sank onto the floor, as if my words had melted the marrow of his bones. His head was bowed, and I wondered if he was actually praying.

His weakness somehow gave me strength. I sat up against the headboard.

"There's something else, though."

"Something else?" Chris was immediately on alert.

"She told me to find the Seal."

"What's that?" Chris asked, immediately perplexed.

I stared at his watch, picturing the symbol that had graced my wrist. "I don't know. She said it belonged to the Lost Soul. She said if we found it, we could keep all her children safe."

More confusion spread on Chris's face, but he didn't ask me to repeat myself. I thought about the impression I'd glimpsed beyond Sekhmet, the ravenous craving of power. I'd only encountered one creature who'd permeated my mind with that level of desire.

"Richardson," I whispered. "Maurice Richardson is the Lost Soul. He has Sekhmet's Seal, and we need to reclaim it."

Chris nodded, and I could see he was bursting with questions. He settled on, "Is the Seal a ring? To seal letters?"

I shook my head, staring at my wrist, trying to puzzle out the simple shape that had glowed there. "I don't think so. I don't know."

I felt as frustrated as Chris looked. Folding my fingers around my substitute insignia, I returned to my initial purpose in reaching out to Mother Sekhmet. "But first things first. The goddess supports your New Commission. And I will too. But you have to give me something in exchange."

Chris was too wise a warrior to agree to a demand without knowing the specifics. He waited, while I found the will to meet his gaze.

"I have to be the sphinx assigned to James," I finally said. I didn't bother to voice my own doubts, my own fears—I might not even *be* a sphinx. I just knew that if Chris was going to continue with his New Commission, if he was going to bind every vampire in the Eastern Empire, I had to be the one linked to James.

Chris's first reaction was to say no. I could read it in every line of his face, in the possessive way he set his jaw.

"It might not be safe," he said, reaching for an argument that went beyond the two of us, beyond the tangle of our relationship. I still hadn't told him I loved him. I still wasn't sure I could say the words.

"Nothing's safe," I said.

"He was Turned years ago," Chris said. It was almost painful to watch him back-pedal, to see him tease apart the program he wanted so badly to launch. "I don't know that we'll have anything to teach him, anything for him to learn."

"You said it yourself," I reminded him. "Vampires will be recertified every year. Every single one of them will need an advocate."

Chris's lips pressed into a stubborn line. I leaned forward and set my palm against his chest. I could feel the cotton of his T-shirt, the one he'd been sleeping in when I'd rung his doorbell. I could feel the tension in his muscles as he mustered every argument he could imagine to fight me on this. I could feel his rigid determination, the animalistic jealousy that he only kept tamed because he knew I could leave him in a second.

I waited until he met my gaze, and then I said, "I'll be James's advocate. That's the only way, Chris. The only way I'll do this."

He knew I wasn't bluffing. He swallowed, buying himself one more second. And then he nodded. "I understand," he said.

I wondered if he did. I wondered if either of us had the faintest idea what we were taking on.

But we were bound to find out soon. Because I had less than forty-eight hours to break the lock on the court's ransomed files. And James Morton was the person who held the key.

11

The sun was stealing into the bedroom by the time Chris agreed to my ultimatum. The rosy light should have made me tired; I was accustomed to sleeping away the day like a vampire. But when I closed my eyes, I could only see the red countdown clock scrolling away on my computer screen.

What did we have left? Forty-odd hours?

I couldn't sleep. Not yet.

But I didn't need Chris watching over me, anxious that I'd back-pedal and reject his New Commission. I insisted that he change into his running clothes, that he lace up his shoes and head out for his usual morning three miles. His daily run kept him sane, giving him the energy he needed to control the most demanding of his sphinx compulsions. I handed him his wristwatch as I sent him out the front door.

And once he was gone?

I ate. I ate a lot.

I raided Chris's kitchen, toasting three slices of the really good whole-grain bread he kept in the freezer. One got topped with thick slices of cheddar. Another provided a sturdy base for an open-face roast beef sandwich, the fresh deli slices rare the way I liked them. I transformed the third into dessert, slathering it with Nutella. I added an apple to my crowded plate and then I grabbed a banana for good measure.

What? Communing with the goddess was hungry business. Plus, I was blessed with the metabolism of a sphinx.

Or maybe—just maybe—I was trying to delay thinking about what I'd seen when I spoke with Mother Sekhmet.

Sure, there was the interaction with the little boy, my realization that I had to protect all Turned vampires. There was the chilling charge to find the Seal, whatever that was.

But there was more. More that I hadn't felt comfortable sharing with Chris.

And that alone gave me pause.

Chris had said he loved me. He'd taken that risk, before I'd even imagined I could say the same.

Moreover, he'd been one hundred percent supportive since I'd discovered my supernatural status. He'd taught me how to meditate. He'd made his library available to me, literally day and night. He'd answered my questions patiently, sometimes going over the same territory multiple times.

But I still wasn't comfortable telling him about the cavern in my dreams. I didn't want to discuss Sheut. I didn't want to talk about my father.

It wasn't the sex thing, the fact that Sekhmet and Sheut had clearly been engaging in…adult activities inside that jet-black cave. No child wanted to think about her parents doing the deed, but this was something more. Something deeper. Something at the core of *me* and who I was.

The Pride had banished me precisely because of what had happened inside that cave. I wasn't a sphinx, because my father was Sheut. That shadowy creature in the darkness—the source of that iridescent shimmer, that velvety unknown—was something *other*.

I couldn't share that with Chris. Hell, Sekhmet hadn't wanted to share it with *me*. She'd put a finger to her lips, insisting on my silence. She'd disappeared into the darkness instead of summoning her lover into the light.

Sekhmet was the bloody-jowled goddess of justice. She led her forces into battle without regard to arrows or lances or swords. She was bravery incarnate.

But she wasn't ready to introduce me to my birth father, and I resented her reluctance.

Birth father. Ha. Just like a modern melodrama. Phrased that way, my problems seemed so mundane.

Phrased that way, I knew someone who specialized in building the very bridge I needed, in making connections among reluctant, unwilling parents and their children.

I took out my phone before I could lose my nerve.

Of course Allison's number was in my favorites. I tapped it with a heavy finger.

Four rings.

Voice mail.

I wasn't ready to speak to her recording. I hadn't figured out what I wanted to say. I disconnected, before I could make everything worse.

Who was I kidding? Things couldn't *get* worse. I'd gone to her office and been given the heave-ho, as if I were a street hustler trying to con her out of a couple of bucks.

In the past ten months, I'd lost so much. My relationship with James. My community at the Den. If I didn't solve the mystery of the ransomed computer files, I'd lose my job.

I couldn't lose my best friend too. I couldn't give her up.

I touched Allison's number again. The phone rang three times. I took a breath, ready to leave a message, to say something, anything, to beg her to call me back, just this once.

And then she answered. "What do you want, Sarah?"

There were better openings. But I was beyond caring about degrees. Allison had answered my call. We were closer to communicating than we'd been in nearly a year.

"Hey," I said.

"It's 7:35 on a weekday morning," she said, her voice tight with annoyance, even through the speakerphone on her cell. "I'm driving Nora to day-care. I don't have time to talk."

My heart tightened at the mention of my goddaughter. When Allison had split from her no-good, two-timing hound of a husband, I'd thought that *I'd* be the one helping out with child-care. I'd pictured myself as the easy-going auntie, the one who scooped up a tantruming toddler and made her smile just by making a goofy face, the one who showed up with pizza, wine, and a juice box, just because.

I'd forfeited that.

"I need to see you," I said, hating how desperate I sounded. I didn't mind *needing* my best friend. That wasn't the problem. I didn't even mind letting her know just how *much* I needed her. But I despised having let things get to this point.

"I told you I'd call when I was ready to talk."

Allison's resolution still knocked the air from my lungs. But at the same time, a sliver of my heart was proud of her. When Steve first left, she wouldn't have advocated for herself so successfully. She wouldn't have said what she needed and stuck to her guns until she won.

"I know," I said. "And I respect that. But this isn't about us. It's not about our being friends. I need to talk to you professionally. About adoption."

She was silent for almost a full minute. I could hear Nora singing in the background, nonsense syllables that rose and fell like wind chimes. I caught my breath, not wanting to ruin my chances by saying something stupid.

"You cannot possibly be thinking of adopting a *child*," Allison finally said.

I'd say yes, if that meant we could talk face to face.

Before I could lie, though, Allison said, "Because your job kept you from spending time with the *friends* you had. You'd be insane to add a child to the mix."

"I'm not adopting," I hurried to say, even as her words stung like a fresh paper cut. "I just have some questions about how to approach things. About my…birth parents."

"You aren't adopted," Allison said.

"I didn't think I was." That was true. Sort of. Sekhmet and my birth mother and Sheut and my unknown birth father… They were all tangled inside my head. Before I could be overwhelmed by what was truth and what was metaphor, I rushed to fill the silence. "My mother never told the full story."

An ambulance went by in the distance, its siren rising and falling while Allison debated.

"I don't want Nora seeing you," she said at last. "She's had too many people come and go in her life."

That hurt. But the turn of the knife inside my chest was justified. Nora had been too young to remember me the last time I saw her. But at two and a half, she would feel the loss if I dropped out of her life a second time.

"We can meet anywhere," I said. "Any time. You name it."

"I leave for Denver this afternoon," Allison said. "I'm speaking at a conference."

This time it was my turn to wait. I didn't want to frighten her into changing her mind.

"Friday evening," she finally said. "Before you go to work. I'll be teleworking after my plane lands, and Steve will still have Nora. You can come by the house."

"Friday evening," I echoed, and I was astonished to feel my throat closing over the words. I whispered, "Thank you."

We both sat there for a minute, holding our phones. I didn't want to be the first one to hang up, and I hoped she felt the same way.

Then there was an outraged squawk demanding access to a dropped toy or a handful of Cheerios, or something equally pressing in a toddler's mind. "I have to go," Allison said, and she ended the call before I could say anything else.

I was pretty sure Allison's throat had been as tight as mine. Her words were high-pitched, as if she could barely squeeze them out. But maybe, just maybe, she'd managed to smile after she hung up the phone. Because I had—thrilled at the thought of finally getting back my best friend.

12

Having made progress with Allison for the first time in months, I felt energized, ready to start hacking through the heap of problems that had piled up in the past few days.

But I couldn't do everything at once. I couldn't figure out what the Seal was, at the same time that I searched for it, at the same time that I advanced Chris's New Commission, at the same time that I tracked down James, at the same time that I got to the heart of Richardson's holding the court files hostage, at the same time that I built a complete legal argument for my own pending criminal case. I was as likely to succeed at doing all of that simultaneously as I was to find a spare million dollars in my bank account.

So, it was time to set priorities. And my first priority had to be finding James. He represented my most likely chance of breaking the grip of Richardson's ransomware. And I had to find him before I could...mentor him in Chris's new program. Those were two excellent reasons to put a priority on tracking James down. At least, that's what I told myself, repeatedly.

Alas, finding James was far, far easier said than done.

And in the hours since I'd last slept, I'd researched my court case. I'd fought a vampire invader for my life. I'd watched the court files be locked down. I'd borne the brunt of my boss's fury. I'd discovered that my former whatever-the-hell-he-was-I-wasn't-even-sure-I-could-call-him-a-boyfriend seemed to be responsible for destroying every vestige of order in the imperial judicial system. I'd been taken to the very edge of *agriotis* by watching Chris's videotaped attack on a vampire. I'd communed with an ancient Egyptian goddess. I'd made my first progress in months on making up with my best friend.

No wonder I was exhausted.

Grounding was one thing, anchoring my physical body with food and drink. But sleep was the only option that could truly calm my jangled nerves, rejuvenating both my body and my mind.

I asked myself, "What would the Sun Lion do?"

Without waiting for Chris to return from his run, I headed upstairs. I took off my clothes, taking care to fold them neatly, even though every last scrap needed to be laundered, courtesy of my fight with Richardson's foot soldier. I pulled on the sleep shirt I kept in the bottom drawer of Chris's dresser, and I climbed into bed—the bed that Chris had made when he changed into running clothes before leaving the house.

The crisp sheets were a comfort as they settled over my body. The blanket's perfect drape felt like a feather-soft anchor. I shifted my head on my pillow, thinking that maybe I'd wait up for Chris to get home. Before I could imagine how we might entertain ourselves, I fell asleep.

I woke to the sound of the bells chiming at St. Agnes, the church across the street. A quick glance at the clock confirmed I'd been out for four hours. That certainly wasn't sufficient for me to recover fully from the previous night's demands, but it was enough for me to think clearly. For now. Especially after I showered and brushed my teeth.

Chris was waiting when I returned to the bedroom, one towel wrapped around my body, another holding my freshly shampooed hair off my neck. The grin on his face indicated he approved of my wardrobe choice.

"What?" I asked, a blush making my throat throb where Richardson's man had done his best to strangle me. I'd already done my best to ignore the angry purple bruises in the bathroom mirror.

"Come here," Chris said, inviting me to join him on the bed.

I wanted to. I always wanted whatever diversions Chris offered in the bedroom department. But at that precise moment, my desire was tamped down by the memory of my acid-green computer monitor, of the blood-red letters spelling out Richardson's ransom note.

"Can I get a raincheck?" I asked.

"Of course."

He almost hid his disappointment. And I almost gave in. But that would have meant pretending everything was normal. And Chris and I were both lousy actors.

I made short work of pulling my clothes from his closet. Freshly pressed black trousers, clipped neatly to a hanger. A white cotton shirt, cut with enough room for me to employ my hard-won fighting techniques if necessary. I plucked clean underwear from the dresser—a business-like bra and panties that reminded both of us that we had work to do.

When I was dressed, I folded my towel, creasing it in perfect thirds so I could return it to the rack in the bathroom. Only then did I meet Chris's inscrutable gaze. "Are we doing this thing?" I asked.

"Finding James?" One of us had to be brave enough to say things out loud.

I nodded.

"Where have you already looked?" he asked.

There. More bravery from Chris. Of course I'd looked for James in the past ten months. I'd tried every place I could think of—although that was a laughably short list. "He hasn't been back to his sanctum," I said.

Chris nodded. He knew that, of course. He'd met me there the day before.

"And no one's seen him at the courthouse."

Another nod.

"I've searched the *Imperial's* online records, and they don't mention any other address for him. I went through legal databases, too, Lexis and Westlaw. Nothing."

And that was it. I didn't have a clue where else to search for James Morton. As far as I knew, he didn't have any family, certainly no one who'd known him before he Turned, in 1872. He didn't have friends, at least not at the office. I'd never heard him mention a favorite restaurant or bar, a place to hang out and nurse a beer, to watch ball games on TV.

I couldn't imagine James Morton nursing a beer or watching ball games on TV.

But for the first time in ten months, I had a clue about where James was actually spending his time. I didn't want to believe it. If I closed my eyes, I could still feel the rogue vampire's hands around my throat. I could smell his foul sweat. I could hear him gasp out James's name in a last-ditch effort to keep me from breaking his arm.

"Richardson's house," I said. "We have to start there."

Chris nodded grimly. We'd been there before—two times, actually. Both visits had ended with dramatic fights against punishing odds. My stomach completed a queasy somersault as I thought about the cage in the basement of that house, the tarnished silver bars that had once seared James's flesh.

If anyone had asked me before today, I would have sworn he'd never go back to that hellhole.

But if anyone had asked me before today, I would have said that James Morton would never help sabotage the computers of the court he'd been hired to protect. He'd never send a vampire to choke me half to death. He'd never let his name be uttered in the same sentence as Maurice Richardson's.

"Foxhall Road," I said, as if there could be any doubt which house I meant.

Chris's dark blue Corolla was parked half a block down the street. He opened my door for me and waited until I was settled before closing it and walking around to take his seat behind the wheel.

The DC streets were filled with the usual weekday frenzy— double-parked delivery vans, scooters zipping in and out of traffic, pedestrians with death wishes crossing against every light.

Slowly, though, with apparent patience, Chris made his way across town. As he drove, I filled him in on the chaos at the courthouse, the locked down computers, my fight with Richardson's drone. I couldn't tell how much he'd already heard from other imperials.

Traffic cleared as we began the climb up Reservoir Road. Here, the lots were larger, and individual houses sprawled across well-maintained lawns. Most of the properties were protected with wrought-iron fences.

Of course Chris remembered where Maurice Richardson had lived. Neither of us would ever forget.

The iron gates to the property were open. No one was parked on the circular drive. Chris turned off the car's engine, but neither of us was in a hurry to get out. Instead, we studied the home before us.

The mansion was a classic colonial, perfect in its red-brick symmetry. Each double-hung window was framed by glossy black shutters. Three steps led up to the deep porch. Columns framed the space, their capitals crowned in graceful Ionic curves. A teak swing hung on the right, its wooden slats covered with a chintz cushion.

The house was abandoned.

I couldn't say how I knew. Sure, someone had cleaned out

the window boxes. The flower beds were covered in weed-deter-ring mulch. No newspapers yellowed on the front porch.

But anyone could hire a gardener. A housekeeper too.

The mansion didn't have a doorbell, but a gleaming brass knocker hung in the middle of the shiny black door. I raised and lowered it three times. When no one answered, I tried again, taking care to hit the strike plate as hard as I could.

Nothing.

Chris mustered the nerve to peer into the windows before I did. He cupped his hands around his eyes to keep out the glare of the spring sunshine behind us. He only took a moment to say, "The place is cleaned out."

I stepped up to his side and made my own inspection. My memories were perfectly clear. We should be looking into a library, a room lined with full bookcases.

Instead, we were spying on empty white shelves. The hard-wood floor sported a couple of gouges, the ordinary wear and tear of a hundred-year-old house. Not a stick of furniture was in sight.

I crossed the porch and checked another window. The parlor, I knew, complete with overstuffed furniture. Except this parlor was bare.

"He could be living upstairs," I said. A vampire's needs weren't very extensive.

In reply, Chris walked down the steps and past his car. He was halfway to the iron fence before he turned around. I came and joined him as he craned his neck to look up.

"Curtains," he said. I took his meaning immediately. Each window on the upper floor was framed with straight falls of white satin. No shades blocked daylight from the interior.

Any vampire living in those rooms would be fried to a crisp.

"The basement?" I suggested, but I couldn't keep my voice was shaking. I'd been imprisoned in that basement. I'd thought my life was going to end in that dank, dark space.

"I'll check it," Chris said.

I melted. Chris knew what it had cost me to come here in the first place. He was searching for James, a rival who'd saved my life with vampire blood, a man who'd claimed my heart before I even knew Chris existed, certainly before I knew that Chris and I shared a sphinx identity. But to save me, to protect me, Chris was willing to enter the hellhole of that basement alone.

"I'll come with you," I said.

Chris led the way to the back of the house, where we were less likely to fall prey to prying eyes. As I concentrated on taking deep, calming breaths, he selected a rock from a decorative border, hefting it experimentally in his right hand.

Approaching the back door, with its gingham-curtained window, he studied the frame. He pointed with his chin, indicating a sleek white rectangle attached to the glass. "The house is alarmed," he said.

"We can get in and out before the cops arrive." I sounded a lot more confident than I felt.

"Ready?" Chris asked.

I nodded, not sure I could fake certainty out loud one more time.

Shattering glass made a lot more noise than I expected. I was braced for a Klaxon to follow, but none blared.

"Silent alarm," Chris said. I wondered if that meant the cops would arrive sooner.

Before I could ask, Chris reached through the broken pane and turned the lock. "Careful," he said, leading the way over the shattered glass and into the kitchen.

Of course I knew to be careful. I'd broken into a house before. I'd broken into *Chris's* house before. But neither of us said anything to commemorate that stroke of awesomely bad decision-making.

Instead, we hurried toward the basement stairs. We'd already announced our presence by shattering a window. There was no premium in stealth.

Chris jerked the basement door open before I thought I was ready. He slammed on the lights, flooding the space below with a fluorescent glow. "On my count," he shouted, as if he were leading a mercenary force. "One! Two!" He trailed off and threw himself down the stairs while I was still wondering if anyone could possibly be foolish enough to believe we'd arrived with reinforcements.

I followed him down the stairs. Each step squeezed a little more air from my lungs. By the bottom, my ears were buzzing, and the roof of my mouth tingled.

The room was empty. No work tables. No tool benches. No hint of the stolen books that had brought me to Richardson's house the last time.

I caught a whiff of paint, the chemical tang of latex. The walls were unmarked white; the floor had been coated with battleship grey.

I forced myself to look across the room, to confront the silver cage in the corner. Its bars had been painted too; they were white now, as regular as the slats on a baby's crib.

The lights glared above everything. There was no place for a vampire to hide. No place for James.

A part of me was relieved. I still couldn't believe James had anything to do with Richardson. If I'd actually found him here, in this torture chamber of a basement… Something would have broken inside me. Something would have died.

"Let's get out of here," Chris said.

I nodded, but I couldn't make my feet move. I stared at the cage, at the now-harmless snow-white bars. If they'd been painted the first time I'd been here, James would never have been burned. He never would have drunk from me to heal himself.

"Sarah," Chris said, and now there was real urgency in his tone. His fingers tightened around mine, and I wondered when he'd taken my hand. "Let's go."

This time, my body obeyed his command. I climbed the

stairs without looking back. I stepped over the glass in the kitchen. When I cleared the door, I started running, sprinting to the Corolla as if a thousand enemy vampires were clamoring for my blood.

Chris didn't hold my car door. Instead, he skittered on the driveway gravel, almost losing his purchase as he ran to his side. As I pulled my door closed, he slammed the key home and threw the vehicle into gear. The wheels spun the first time he pounded the accelerator; he needed to stop, reverse a few inches, then try again.

Clearing the driveway, the tires bit hard into the asphalt of Foxhall Road. Chris gunned it until he reached the first stop sign; then, he squealed to a halt.

Before he could start into the intersection, we heard it—a siren rising and falling in front of us. Chris took his hands from the wheel, wiping them hard on the thighs of his pants.

It only took a moment for the police car to scream into sight. Its lights were flashing—red and white and a clear, piercing blue. Like good citizens, we waited for it to clear the intersection. I turned around to watch it spin into Richardson's driveway.

Chris looked left, then right, then left again. He let out a breath I hadn't realized he'd been holding. And then we headed toward safety, toward his home.

We hadn't found James Morton. But we hadn't been arrested for breaking and entering either. I was willing to embrace whatever victories I could find.

13

I went to work that night, because I didn't know what else to do. The mundane part of the evening was busy with last-minute filings, lawyers who were intent on making end-of-the-month deadlines even if they needed to work late to do so.

The imperial court was shuttered for the night. Announcements had been posted on various hidden networks—on Faebook and Wiccapedia and Snapbat.

Local newspapers had risen to the occasion as well. *The Imperial Inquirer* had dispatched a succubus reporter to glean as many facts as possible about the shutdown of the court's computers. She seemed disappointed to discover she'd have to deal with me to get information. I suspected she had better luck with the male imperials she interviewed.

I only gave her the basic facts: The court's computers were shut down, but our crack IT team was working on fixing the problem. We didn't have an ETA for the fix. No serious legal matters were in jeopardy. There was no reason for any imperial citizen to worry about life, liberty, or the pursuit of happiness.

In a minor stroke of good luck, the reporter's presence kept Angelique sequestered in her office. My boss wanted no part of the fourth estate. For all I knew, she spent the first half of the night filing her claws in preparation for ripping out the throat of whoever had brought us to a standstill.

Shortly after midnight, Angelique was summoned to Judge Finch's office. I gathered the judge wanted some reassurance that the Acting Director of Security was investigating the break-in appropriately.

I waited until the sound of Angelique's stilettos disappeared down the hallway, and then I dove into her office. Richardson's foot soldier—or someone working with him—had done *something* in there that warranted dosing Angelique with Lethe. If I could figure out what had happened, I might be able to backtrack to James.

I sat in the massive leather chair behind Angelique's desk, gently opening her unlocked drawers. The first was filled with a jumble of office supplies—pens, pads of paper, and a three-hole punch that rained little white circles over an assortment of clips, staplers, and other debris. My palms itched, but I resisted the temptation to straighten everything. My goal was to remain undetected.

The second drawer was devoted to official documentation—an orientation manual, human resources handbooks, and no fewer than ten different procedures manuals in various stages of completion. I riffled through them, taking care to leave the ragtag fringe of sticky notes in place along the edges.

The third drawer held personnel files. I couldn't resist finding my own—inexplicably placed in the middle of the alphabet, instead of under A, as my last name warranted. My fingers ached, but I didn't return the folder to its proper place.

I barely even peeked inside. I just glanced quickly enough to see that Angelique had not added anything to the official reviews James had left almost a year ago. I eased the drawer shut, taking extra care not to shift any of the contents.

Nothing in the desk was interesting enough to warrant a dose of Lethe—at least, nothing that remained. I couldn't rule out the possibility that the intruder had taken something valuable—blueprints of the underground court structure maybe, or diagrams of the alarm system... Maybe even something Richardson could use to blackmail Angelique...

Shoving aside that revolting idea, I looked for anything compelling on the surface of Angelique's desk. A jumbled stack of legal pads revealed some remarkably detailed doodles, including several graphic depictions of canine autopsies. But no listening devices had been planted beneath the leather blotter. The brass pen and ink set were similarly clean.

No miniature cameras had been affixed to the ceiling. The credenza was bare. The cushions on the couch appeared undisturbed. Two hangers hung innocently on the hook behind the door.

In short, my sleuthing proved useless. I could not find a single item out of the ordinary. I didn't spot a single surveillance tool, or anything else that had compromised the Acting Director of Security.

If I hadn't seen the Lethe-ringed glass myself, I wouldn't believe it had ever been left on Angelique's desk. But I *had* seen the glass. Angelique *had* been dosed. I just wasn't smart enough—or observant enough or *something* enough—to figure out why.

Returning to my desk thoroughly out of sorts, I tried to take solace in the roast beef and cheddar sandwich I'd brought for lunch. By the time I'd corralled the crumbs into my trashcan, I'd come up with another approach.

So far, I'd been thinking about the locked-down computers as a uniquely imperial problem. A vampire had locked our files, and so we were doing everything in our power to track down that vampire.

But the Eastern Empire Night Court wasn't the first entity to have its files attacked for ransom. It was time to do some research about hacking, ransomware, and Bitcoin.

Two hours later, I felt a lot smarter. And a lot more terrified.

Major US companies had been sabotaged in the past few

years. Entire municipalities had had files held hostage. In virtually every case, the victims had paid a ransom to regain access.

Sure, they'd hired computer experts after the fact. They'd removed vulnerable computer code and installed firewalls. They'd enlisted "white hat hackers"—guys who'd turned from their lives of crime to protect the innocent.

But first and foremost, everybody paid.

And with Bitcoin, those payments could never be traced. The words spun out before me—blockchain and cryptocurrency and digital assets. Half of what I read was hyperbole, and the other half was incomprehensible. Bottom line: Bitcoin transactions weren't monitored by any bank or government.

They were completely anonymous as well. No one could say who owned any specific Bitcoin account. If we somehow managed to pay our ransom, we couldn't go running to the Empire Bureau of Investigation and ask them to prosecute the owner of Bitcoin wallet ZzZ9y4fRgvf5Rx4HupbE5JjQqXx.

That last detail was a moot point, of course. The Night Court didn't have an extra million dollars lying around. Hell, the court hadn't issued raises to employees in the past five years. We were practically broke.

With my research complete, I was firmly convinced that nothing short of a miracle would free our files. I didn't bother making a report to Angelique. Instead, I headed out of the courthouse at the precise instant the clock ticked over to 5:00 am.

The thought of retreating to my basement apartment was depressing. Instead, I walked back to Chris's place. The early-morning air was cool, and the sidewalks were still mostly empty. Traffic was light enough that I could jaywalk across most of the intersections.

I hoped that physical movement would unlock something inside my mind. I'd remember some detail I hadn't consciously noticed when I fought the vampire intruder. I'd recall something James had let slip in the months we worked together.

It seemed like years since I'd thought of us as a couple. Intellectually, I knew we'd been together for months. He'd frequented my apartment, with its painted-over windows that protected him from dangerous sunlight. We'd taken long midnight walks on my nights off. Once, we'd gone to the National Arboretum, viewing the trees by moonlight.

But now, my memories of those nights seemed like half-remembered dreams. I knew James and I had talked—a lot. He'd lost his family, the wife and son who'd died over a century ago. I'd lost my mother when I was in college, long before I'd heard of Sekhmet and the shadowy Sheut. James and I had bonded through our loneliness, our differentness, our sense of never belonging.

But now my morning perambulation did nothing to shake loose useful memories. I didn't suddenly recall the address of a sanctum Chris and I could explore. I didn't come up with a favorite haunt. James remained lost to me.

I was more than a little frustrated as I climbed the steps to Chris's front door. *The Banner* was missing from his doorstep. He was already awake.

In fact, I realized after I let myself in with my key that he was already out on his run. Empty library, empty kitchen, empty office and bedroom.

I thought about waiting up, but I was suddenly overwhelmed with exhaustion. Maybe I was still recovering from my fight with Richardson's minion and my short sleep the day before. Maybe I was tired of living on a hyperactive edge, waiting for Angelique to fire me. Maybe I was depressed, because I knew that the following night, I'd lose the only job I'd ever loved.

Whatever the reason, I crawled into Chris's bed. I pulled the perfectly centered coverlet up to my chin. I shoved the pillow into a more comfortable mound.

Lying there, I kept hearing Richardson's foot soldier hissing his warning: *"Morton says to get out of town. Now. While you still can."*

James had avoided me for ten months. Why would he care about getting me out of town before some shadowy, unknown disaster?

Was he trying to protect me? Or was he trying to keep me from tracking him down before he... What? Before he took down the court? The entire empire?

Or maybe he actually intended to implicate me. If I fled and more bad things happened, it would be child's play to cast me as the ultimate bad guy.

I'd already been thrown out of the Den. Maybe James was trying to get me banished from the entire empire. How deep was his need to avenge Judge DuBois's death?

I had no way of knowing. But that didn't keep me from spinning out scenario after disastrous scenario, each one more convoluted, more dangerous, more deadly than the last. And not one contained a solution to the Bitcoin ransom clock that was scrolling down with every passing second.

14

I woke to the sound of fingers rasping against cloth.

Automatically, I surveyed my surroundings. Late afternoon sun shone through the windows. A car alarm shrilled a block or two away. The bed beneath me was soft, as irresistible as a tractor beam.

And those fingers... That cloth... I knew without opening my eyes that Chris had worked the buttons on his shirt, that he'd just slipped his arms out of the sleeves. I wasn't surprised by the breath of cool air as he raised the edge of the comforter. I fully expected his weight on the mattress behind me.

"Mmmm," I murmured as he slipped an arm around my waist. He responded by curling around me, big spoon to my little spoon. "What time is it?" I asked, not wanting to break the spell by checking the clock's angry red numbers.

He nuzzled my neck. "2:30," he whispered, just before he found the soft spot behind my ear.

I stiffened. "You shouldn't have let me sleep so long."

"You needed it," he said, pulling me closer.

The tingling along my spine worked wonders, making up for all sorts of lost sleep. I rolled to face him, letting the motion twine my legs between his. "We're almost out of time," I said. "The computer files—"

"I have someone else for us to talk to," he interrupted. "But he won't be home till six."

"Six?" I asked, even as hope flared high in my chest. I couldn't imagine who Chris had found, what new route he'd discovered. But his fingers were doing distracting things, feathering across the small of my back. I shivered and said, "Then it's awfully early for a wake-up call."

"So sue me," he muttered against my lips.

Litigation was the last thing on my mind.

And when I woke a second time, almost two hours later, Chris was propped up on one elbow, studying my face.

"What?" I asked, swiping at my hair to make sure it wasn't doing anything bizarre.

"I love you."

I love you too. That's what I was supposed to say. I knew that.

And I did love him, in all sorts of uncomplicated ways. I loved the guy who stopped by the courthouse in the middle of my shift, just because I'd forgotten to bring my lunch. I loved the guy who understood why coffee had to be stirred seven times, who didn't get exasperated when I rearranged the silverware drawer so all the forks were in perfect alignment, who understood that each and every book had to be in its alphabetized place, spine set flush against the front of the shelf. I loved the guy who held me when I woke trembling, tangled in nightmares about Judge DuBois.

But that wasn't what Chris meant.

Or rather, Chris meant all of that and a whole lot more. And this wasn't the right time to discuss that *more*... Not when I'd been kicked out of the Den. Not when I was searching for Sheut, for my key to a past that I could barely begin to understand. Not when Mother Sekhmet had charged me with finding the Seal, whatever the hell that was. Not when Chris was pushing for his New Commission for every vampire in the Empire, including James.

And not when the Eastern Empire Night Court files were going to be destroyed forever, in less than eight hours.

I barely caught the flicker of disappointment across Chris's face when I didn't respond. I let him sit up and clear his throat, as if he hadn't been waiting for anything at all.

"Let's get going," he said.

Six o'clock. That's when our mysterious contact would be home.

I grabbed a quick shower and twisted my damp hair into a messy bun. I threw on clothes that were appropriate for the office. Chris and I both grabbed slices of toast, standing as we ate in the kitchen.

"You'll need a coat," he said.

I gave him a curious glance, but I grabbed a light jacket as we headed out the front door. Of course, he was right. The temperature had dropped precipitously from the morning. The wind had picked up as well. I felt as if I was leaning into a storm as we headed into the night.

No car for us this time. We walked down the sidewalk, matching our long strides. And as we walked, I considered our destination. Clearly, we weren't heading out to the suburbs; we would have taken the Corolla for that. We probably weren't hitting a major tourist site, or we would have taken the subway.

We passed century-old townhouses and modern office buildings. We came within half a mile of the White House as we skirted the eastern edge of George Washington University.

At the far end of campus, smaller townhouses began their march to the Kennedy Center. These were modest two-story structures, each faced with clapboard or painted brick. Tiny front yards were mostly covered with flagstones, with the occasional brave herb garden sheltered in terra cotta pots.

The sidewalks here were rough, the brick paths long since broken by the eruption of tree roots. After turning my ankle on one slippery corner, I kept my eyes down, the better to keep from sprawling flat.

That was why I pulled up short when Chris stopped in front of the next building. He bent slightly to open the catch on the knee-high gate—more of a decoration than a deterrent. I let him lead the way to the front door.

Chris rang the bell. There was a pause, and then the door opened on a chain. A man looked out at us, half his body sheltered behind the glossy green-painted panels.

The guy could have made good money as an extra on a movie set. He was white, with an average frame and a medium complexion. He had unremarkable brown hair and muddy eyes. Nothing about him leaped out in any way. No one would look twice if they saw him passing on the street.

His face was impassive as he waited for us to speak.

Chris asked in a conversational tone, "Have you had a chance to see the moon tonight?"

The man shifted his weight, hiding more of his body behind the door before he answered carefully. "I expected a lot of cloud cover."

Chris completed the exchange: "The sky is clear. You shouldn't miss the view."

The man obviously wasn't put at ease by the formula. Instead, he cast a probing look at me. I considered informing him that the eagle had landed or Elvis had left the building. Instead, Chris said, "I'll vouch for her."

After a long minute of silent debate, the man closed the door, but only for long enough to slip the security chain from its track. As he gestured for us to enter, I belatedly realized the chain was silver.

I didn't see the stake until I'd stepped into the foyer.

The man held it tightly in the hand that had been hidden behind the door, his knuckles white against the oak. He wasn't taking any chances against vampire invaders.

Chris stopped just over the threshold, extending his hands in ostentatious proof that he wasn't armed. Of course, a sphinx didn't need weapons to defeat a human.

The man jutted his chin toward a casual living room. I led the way, taking in the Crate & Barrel couch, the television on the wall above the fireplace, a couple of scattered books and the *Banner's* sports section left open on the coffee table.

None of us sat. Instead, the man planted his feet just inside the doorway. He tapped the stake against his left palm, as if he were counting out the rhythm of a song only he could hear. He took his time, studying first Chris, then me. Finally, he said, "You're sphinxes."

Bingo. Or, in my case, close enough for Empire work.

Chris nodded and extended his hand, introducing both of us. "Tyler Hawkes," the man replied, but he didn't shake hands. At least he lowered the stake to his side.

"We're looking for James Morton," Chris said.

If I hadn't been watching Tyler so closely, I would have missed the moment he thought about lying. But at the last instant, something made him settle on the truth. He said, "I haven't seen him in six months."

Chris frowned. "What was your usual Muster?"

"First and third Wednesday of the month."

Usual Muster... Recognizing Chris and me as sphinxes... The oaken stake and silver chain...

"You're James's Source," I said.

Tyler turned flat eyes on me. "I was."

I stared at him more closely now. In the past two and a half years I'd learned a lot about vampires. I knew how to fight them. I knew how to heal them. I knew how to drink their blood to cure my own mortal wounds.

But despite all that information, I'd perpetuated some myths in my own mind. Blame it on Hollywood, but I'd always assumed James's drinking blood had a sexual twist. I'd never imagined he'd feed from another man. Not that there was anything wrong with that.

When I'd thought about feeding—and it had come to mind more often than I cared to admit—I'd usually pictured James in a well-appointed hotel room. He kept champagne on ice for his so-called victims. He started the evening with oysters on the half shell and ended with thousand-count Egyptian cotton sheets. He brought along gifts for his women—boned corsets or sheer thigh-high stockings or, once in my overheated imagination, a studded leather collar.

Sometimes, I pictured him prowling through a brothel. He chose his Source from a chorus line of waiting pros. He ordered her to bathe before he took her to bed, and he drank her blood without looking her in the eye.

As a sphinx, or whatever the hell I actually was, I should have known better. I'd been taught about vampires' needs. Blood meals were no more about sex for vampires than K-rations were seductive for soldiers on the march.

And yet... I'd felt *something* when James fed from me. I'd shuddered when his fang sliced into my jugular. I'd almost fainted at the delicious pull as he sucked blood from the wound. He'd made me feel safe and protected. Cherished.

But Richardson certainly hadn't done the same. He'd ripped through my flesh like a scythe downing reeds. I'd been stunned by the pain, paralyzed.

Feeding was different for every vampire. But I knew one basic rule applied, at least for vampires on the right side of the law: Sources were like campgrounds. Vampires were supposed to leave them better than they found them.

I wondered if *Tyler* found sexual satisfaction serving James. Or maybe he'd reaped other benefits—tuition at the nearby university, or tickets for the close-by Kennedy Center...

Whatever the arrangement, Chris had clearly been aware of the relationship long before we'd arrived on the doorstep. "Six months," he said, tinging his words with disbelief. "And you haven't taken on another vamp?"

Once again, Tyler considered lying to us. Once again, he

chose to tell the truth. But his fingers tightened around his oak stake. "James said it wouldn't be safe. He said not to trust any other vampire, not to welcome anyone across the threshold. He said they'd take me for a blood herd."

A blood herd. A group of captive Sources. Richardson had been convicted of running them at least twice in the past. Convicted, but always let go, because of technical mistakes, procedural irregularities...

Once again, Chris displayed his ostentatiously empty hands. He kept his voice low and his tone casual. "Is James seeing another Source?"

"You'll have to ask him." Tyler's tone was instantly flat. I suspected a Source didn't last long if he couldn't keep his vampire's confidences.

"I want to," Chris said, his voice purposely unruffled. "But I have to find him first."

"I can't help you."

"Can't?" Chris asked, as if he were reading a crossword puzzle clue out loud. "Or won't?"

Tyler settled a little more solidly on his heels. "You knew enough to find me. So you probably know I've Sourced James for thirteen years. In all that time, he's never done anything to hurt me. The least I can do is return the favor."

I had to answer that. "We don't want to hurt him. We're trying to help him."

Tyler gave me a tolerant smile, but the expression didn't move past his lips to the rest of his face. "If I see him, I'll tell him you stopped by."

"Please," I said. "We need to talk to him tonight."

"Then I hope you have another option." He pointed toward the front door with the stake. "Good evening," he said.

Our interview was clearly done.

Chris must have reached the same conclusion. He followed without another word.

Neither of us tried to shake Tyler's hand. Before the door

closed, though, I tried one more time. "If you have any way of reaching him, please tell him…"

What? I needed his help? I wanted to apologize for executing his mentor? I was willing to beg for anything, any scrap of information he could share that would end my legal prosecution, that would let me keep my job?

"Good evening," Tyler said again, and this time his tone of dismissal was final.

An hour ago, I hadn't known James had a Source in the West End. Now, I felt like I was leaving something valuable behind as Chris and I walked away from Tyler's home. On the one hand, I was thrilled that James had kept his Source safe from Richardson's blood herds. James had had enough presence of mind to worry about his human ally. He hadn't been completely destroyed by the events on the steps of the Jeffersonian Memorial.

But on the other hand, James's caution only made me more concerned. If he wasn't feeding from Tyler, where *was* he getting his meals? Was he actually using Richardson's blood herds? Was he risking discovery by stalking random humans?

I rubbed my arms, trying to chase away a chill that had nothing to do with the weather. My voice was miserable as I asked Chris, "Now what do we do?"

"Now," he said. "You go to work."

"And the ransomed files?"

Chris took his time answering. We passed another three houses. "You'd better hope whoever has them is bluffing. Because the way I see it, we're fresh out of moves."

15

I shuffled up the sidewalk in front of the courthouse, automatically taking my phone out of my pocket in preparation for passing through the metal detector. I reached for my absent hematite bracelet as well. Failing to find it, I automatically swiped at my missing coral ring.

With the court's security ratcheted up to Orange, the magnetometers were set on stun. I half expected them to alert to the metal eyelets on my walking shoes.

"Look what the cat drug in!" Earl exclaimed as I passed through the machine.

I tried for a wan smile, the best I could manage under the circumstances. Before I could retrieve my phone, Earl passed me a padded manila envelope. A scuffed label was slapped on the front of the package, bearing my name and the court's address.

"What's this?" I asked.

"A kid dropped it off, about ten minutes ago."

I looked over my shoulder, at the plaza in front of the courthouse. Full night had fallen as I made my way from Tyler's townhouse.

"A courier?" I asked, studying the envelope with suspicion. I wasn't expecting any special deliveries.

Earl shrugged. "He rode up to the door on one of those scooters. Took off down Pennsylvania, after he left this."

I turned the envelope over. The back was smudged, and the sticky seal had been imperfectly applied. There was no indication where it had come from.

Earl was a human security guard. Built like a linebacker, he had the patience of a boulder. Night after night, he and his colleague Bubba kept watch at the courthouse's front door, utterly unaware of the courthouse's subterranean dimensions.

But they still followed the edicts of the court's Director Of Security, whether they understood supernatural threats or not. Earl nodded toward the envelope. "I put it through the scanner. No ticking time bomb there." He laughed at his own joke, one I might have found funnier if I hadn't been worried about the ransom bomb ticking away in my office.

"I swabbed it, too," he said. He pointed a blunt finger toward the sniffer, the machine that analyzed squares of activated cotton to determine whether any given item had been in contact with explosives. "You're good to go."

"Thanks," I said, conscious as always about giving away too many imperial secrets.

Holding the envelope by one corner, I made my way to the clerk's office. There, I found a handwritten sign on the door: *Clerk's office temporarily closed.* A scrawled URL directed people to the mundane night court's website.

Steeling myself, I headed into the battlefield of my office.

I was granted one small mercy: My boss wasn't standing in my desk alcove. But she—or some other imperial—had logged in to my computer.

The garish green screen hurt my eyes. The ransom demand screamed its long string of nonsense letters and numbers, the Bitcoin account where I was supposed to send funds.

The countdown clock raced beneath the demand, a constantly decreasing flow of numbers. The "days" field was zeroed out. As I watched, the "hours" field slipped from four to three. The numbers continued to spin away as I crossed the room.

As always, one of the day clerks had moved things around on my desk. I twitched the stapler back to its proper place. I turned the pen holder to the correct angle. I shifted the computer keyboard, lining it up properly with the edge of the desk.

Only then did I slip my finger beneath the sealed flap on the padded envelope. Sure, Earl said it was safe. But he didn't know the full range of threats that could destroy the Eastern Empire.

I tilted the envelope, and a cell phone slipped into my palm.

Keeping in mind Earl's assurances that the package wasn't laced with explosives, I caught my breath as I pressed the phone's power button. The screen sprang to life with a photograph of a hastily scrawled note: *Open Me.*

I recognized the urgent slant of the words, the quickly dashed links between the individual letters. I would know James Morton's handwriting anywhere.

My heart squeezed hard enough to hurt. I reached behind myself blindly, fumbling until I found the arm of my desk chair. I sank into it and pulled the phone close.

I stared at the virtual number pad, at the four blank spaces waiting for numbers. I'd taken this test before. I'd broken James's code, when I'd forced my way into the credenza.

1911, I typed. The address of my apartment.

The screen wavered and cleared.

A single icon sat in the middle of an empty black screen. I could make out the outline of an old fashioned wallet, the kind with a snap-tab to keep it closed in a man's pocket. A stylized letter B blazed from the center of the icon.

I tapped the wallet.

A new screen phased into focus. The same stylized B decorated the upper left corner. Below the letter, a legend read, "Your Bitcoin address." A long series of letters and numbers ran on for three lines. Beneath the address were the letters BTC and a number: 144.75969889. Beneath that, in letters almost too faint for me to read, a notice said, "Worth about $1,000,000."

I stared at the phone, waiting for the screen to fade away. Surely, it would shift to the same noxious green as my computer screen. It would start to scroll with its own crimson letters, another mocking countdown.

But the message remained: Solid. Placid. Reliable.

An arrow blazed at the bottom of the screen, next to the words, "Transfer Bitcoin now." My finger shook as I touched the emblem.

A new screen opened. "Enter Bitcoin address," it said at the top of the page. A convenient virtual keypad opened.

It couldn't be this easy. I couldn't simply stop the ransomware by transferring funds from a random account.

It wasn't a random account, though. James had written the note on the first screen. He'd programmed the passcode, four digits that only I would guess.

He was giving me the funds to save the court's files.

I glanced at my computer screen. The numbers seemed to flow away faster now, draining into the ether.

The index finger of my left hand trembled as I set it beneath the first letter on my computer screen: Z. One by one, I edged beneath the scrambled letters, typing each into the new phone with my shaking right hand.

ZzZ9y4fRgvf5Rx4HupbE5JjQqXx.

Ignoring the hurtling clock, I read the sequence twice, to be certain I'd made no mistakes. I shifted my grip on the phone. I hovered over the button that said, "Transfer Now."

I tapped it.

The screen shifted. A notification popped up telling me I'd transferred 144.75969889, and asking me to please be patient while the blockchain was verified.

Please be patient. I wanted to throw the phone against the far wall. I'd read enough about Bitcoin to know that the currency consumed massive amounts of computing power. The blockchain was an impenetrable tangle of electronic encryption.

How long would it take for a computer to sort out that information? Could the operation be done in three and half hours?

I couldn't leave my desk. I couldn't stop staring at the cascade of numbers in the countdown. I couldn't stop thinking about everything I'd done as the clerk of court—the files I'd created, the records I'd organized.

Everything I'd done for the night court would be destroyed if the Bitcoin transaction didn't process in time. But there was nothing else I could do, no one I could talk to, nothing I could say. I could only offer up a silent prayer to Sekhmet that I'd used James's gift in time.

The *Staff Only* door opened behind me. I wasted a moment thinking James himself might be there, coming in from his office as if nothing had ever changed. My greeting caught in my throat, though, as Angelique pounced.

"Where the Rat Terrier have you been? Do you have a Springer Spaniel's idea how crazy things have been here? The Saint Bernard judge is about to lose her Otterhound mind over that thing."

I ignored her ridiculous obscenities. Instead, I stared at the computer she waved to, at the tumbling clock inured to her talons.

"Sarah!" Angelique said, snapping my attention back to her face. "I take it you've done absolutely nothing to respond to this disaster?"

No swearing. She was serious now. She was about to fire me.

I could tell her what I'd done. I could tell her I'd gone to Richardson's house, trying to find James. I could tell her I'd spoken to James's Source, Tyler. I could explain how none of it had worked, how I hadn't come close to landing a hook in Richardson's ransomware.

I could tell her that James had given me the means to save us all.

I looked back at the screen. Less than three hours left.

Angelique cleared her throat. "If that's the case, then you leave me no option but to—"

The countdown stopped. The flow of crimson was staunched, the clock frozen at 2:58:12. The numbers glared against the acid-green screen.

"What the everlasting Pointer—" Angelique said.

Before she could complete her sentence, my computer screen flickered. The green and red disappeared, replaced by a boring field of black. In the center, rotating as if it had been in motion since the creation of the universe, was the Night Court logo, a scroll of parchment pierced by an ornately carved sword.

My hands moved as if they belonged to someone else. I automatically cocked my wrists over the keyboard, holding them at an ergonomically sound angle. I typed in my username. Tabbed to the next field. Entered my password.

I didn't waste time gloating as the normal court desktop filled the screen. Instead, I turned to Angelique. "I'm sorry. Did you want me to pull up a file?"

"In my office," Angelique said. "Now."

I thought about telling her I couldn't leave my desk unattended, not during normal court hours. But I'd already pushed my luck, cutting off her tirade. And even *I* would admit that my question had been insubordinate. My ransoming the court records and saving the day at nearly the last possible minute could only carry me so far.

I took my time, though, getting to my feet. I was careful not to let her see me tuck James's Bitcoin phone into my pocket.

Angelique slammed her office door closed behind me, hard enough that I jumped at the noise. As I watched warily, she stalked to her desk, taking her time to plant her hands on the blotter.

Apparently she and I had read the same books about how to make an impact in the midst of an awkward power dynamic. By looming over the desk, she added the furniture's mass to her own. She seemed more imposing, more capable of carrying out a threat.

Or maybe I only thought that because I could see the razor-sharp tips of her fingernails.

"What the hell just happened out there?" she demanded. *Hell.* Not *Harrier* or something-hound, or something-even-stupider-terrier. My job was on the line. Possibly, even, my life.

"I don't know." Until I said those words, I wasn't certain I was going to keep James's Bitcoin phone secret.

Angelique was an apex predator. Her shifter hearing had evolved to detect the heartbeat of her prey, to calculate the precise moment that adrenaline sent a creature into full escape-mode overdrive. Her eyes were designed to sense the slightest hint of motion—the tiniest gathering of muscles prior to a leap toward freedom. She could literally smell fear.

But sphinxes tracked prey as well.

I focused my energy by taking a trio of deep breaths, using each to siphon off more of my jagged fear. Angelique was my boss, not my judge or jury. She most definitely was not my executioner. At least not that night.

"What stopped the countdown?" she demanded.

I looked directly into her eyes. "I don't know," I repeated.

At the same time, I told myself I was only speaking the truth. I *didn't* know what had happened. I didn't know why James had sent me the phone. I didn't know why he'd decided to spare me, spare the *court*, from almost certain doom.

"Did you find James Morton?"

"No," I said. That was the truth as well. I hadn't found James. If anything, he'd found me.

"What about Maurice Richardson?"

"No." This was getting easier and easier. She didn't even know the questions she should ask. She didn't have a clue what was happening in the middle of her own courthouse.

"You've been indicted as a murderer and a security risk, Sarah. You had *something* to do with that computer hack. I don't accept for one Basenji second that the ransom demand was spontaneously withdrawn. Give me one good reason I shouldn't fire your Malamute ass," Angelique said.

"I'll give you three," I said, before I could remember my vow to stay on her good side. "One: I'm innocent until I've been proven guilty in an imperial court. Two: You don't have a shred of evidence that I had anything to do with the ransom threat— either making it or keeping it from destroying our files. Three: I'm the best damn clerk this court has ever seen."

She opened her mouth. Closed it. Took a moment to study her fingernails, where they glinted scarlet against her desk.

"I don't trust you, Sarah Anderson."

The feeling is absolutely mutual. But I wasn't suicidal. I only thought those words; I didn't say them out loud.

She narrowed her eyes, as if she could read my mind. "I'm formally placing you on probation."

I started to protest, but I managed to bite back my words.

"That's right," she said, her voice shifting to a frozen register. "One more violation, no matter how small, and your employment will immediately be terminated. Do I make myself perfectly clear?"

I glared, not about to give her the submission she craved.

But I knew she was serious—she hadn't mentioned a dog in her last threat. And bottom line, she held all the cards. If I was fired, I immediately became a flight risk—insignia held by the court or not. Judge Finch would lock me up for months, maybe even years, before my trial was complete.

"I want to hear a verbal response, Sarah. Do you understand the terms of your probation?"

"Yes," I said, as sullen as any teenager.

Angelique turned her head to an angle, as if she'd missed my answer. "What's that?" she asked.

"Yes, ma'am," I said, nearly gagging on the syllables.

"Excellent," she said. "Now get your Chow Chow ass out of my office and get back to your Weimaraner work."

I had no choice. Biting my tongue and clenching my fists, I returned to my desk. I took a stack of papers from my inbox and started to file them, one after another.

The computer system worked flawlessly. And after I completed each document, I slipped my hand into my pocket, reassuring myself that the Bitcoin phone was still there.

However tenuous, the device was the only link I had to James. I just had to figure out how to reach him.

16

I'd assumed the locked-down files would put my preliminary hearing on hold, maybe even buy me a week or two of living in denial.

I was very sadly mistaken.

I was fiddling with my inbox, discarding dozens of spam messages that had arrived in the past forty-eight hours. My to-do list was longer than a qilin's mane, and I hadn't even begun to check the electronic stack of new cases to be filed.

Chris strolled into my office a few minutes before midnight. I'd shot him a quick message the instant I sat down to my freed computer, giving him a heads-up that the files had been released. Brushing my fingers against James's phone, I'd decided to give Chris all the details later. In person.

But here he was. And for just a moment, I thought he'd come to keep me company at lunch, and I started to explain that I didn't have time for a break—not with the gigantic backlog from two days of lock-down and Angelique on the warpath.

But after the past forty-eight hours of intensive sleuthing, Chris should have been sound asleep in his oh-so-comfortable bed.

And he wasn't carrying any delectable treats, so he hadn't come to feed me.

And he was wearing a suit.

I gawked. I'd never seen Chris in a suit before.

The charcoal plaid was so subtle it almost looked plain grey in the office light. The jacket was expertly tailored; its lean lines complemented Chris's runner's physique. His white dress shirt was impeccably ironed, and his black tie was dotted with tiny images of a blazing sun—a subtle reinforcement of his title: Sun Lion of the Eastern Empire.

"Ready?" he asked.

I stopped just short of asking him what I was supposed to be ready for. Of course, time, tide, and Judge Finch waited for no computer disaster. It was time for my preliminary hearing.

I wished I'd worn one of my own suits when I reported for work that evening. At least I could carry a legal pad into the courtroom, as if I hadn't been completely taken by surprise by the criminal case that was going to determine the rest of my life. I gripped the strap on my purse as if it were a lifeline.

Swallowing hard, I was surprised to find my throat as dry as Sekhmet's desert. Instead of trying to speak, I resorted to a single curt nod. Chris held the office door for me, waiting with apparent patience as I set the *I'll Be Back* clock.

This was probably the exact type of activity that would jeopardize my probation in Angelique's eyes. I didn't have a choice, though. If I failed to appear before Judge Finch, I'd be thrown back into the subterranean jail. And I was *certain* imprisonment would be cause for termination.

The courtroom was crowded as Chris and I filed past the benches in the gallery. A low hum of excitement increased in pitch, and I could feel the gaze of scores of imperials as we took our places at the defendant's table.

Judge Finch had already downed her blood cordial, transforming into her vampire self. Her fangs looked particularly sharp as she gestured to her bailiff, Eleanor Owens. The robust griffin wore carnelian jewelry for the evening, a heavy necklace and matching bracelets that sparkled against her uniform. Her eyeshadow echoed the crystals, glittering blood-red as she planted herself before the bench.

"Oyez! Oyez! Oyez!" she intoned. "All persons having business before the Honorable, the Night Court of the Eastern Empire, are admonished to draw near and give their attention, for the Court is now sitting. May Sekhmet watch over all proceedings here and render justice unto all."

A business-like sphinx sat at the prosecutor's table. I'd never seen him before. He wasn't a member of the Den. But I recognized a kindred spirit when I saw his six legal pads, each lined up precisely in front of his briefcase, complete with uncapped felt-tip pens standing ready—two black, two blue, a red, and a green. Extensive notes covered the top sheet of paper.

A dryad sat in the last chair at the prosecutor's table. I realized she was the young lawyer who had managed my arraignment, the creature who had nervously twined her fingers in her hair for the better part of that appearance. Now, she hid behind a fortress of legal books—a copy of the criminal code, a matching volume of the court's rules, half a dozen reference volumes on criminal procedure, and a hefty Italian-English dictionary.

Undaunted by the pair, Chris shot the locks on his briefcase. I couldn't help but note that he only had one pad and only one capped pen. There wasn't a word scribbled on his paper.

"Antonio Russo for the Empire," the prosecutor stated, a lilting accent spicing his words. "Sphinx resident in the European Confederacy."

So. That was how the court had resolved the requirement that I be prosecuted by an imperial of my own race. They'd brought someone in from across the ocean. That was an elaborate expense for a sphinx like me. Or not-a-sphinx. Whatever.

I glanced at Chris. His face was perfectly smooth. He didn't seem surprised by Signor Russo.

Of course he wasn't surprised. Even at this preliminary stage of my case, Chris must have exchanged filings with the opposition. I wondered what else he'd accomplished while we'd both been running all over the District, trying to track down James and release the ransomed files.

My heart expanded inside my chest, Chris's matter-of-fact attitude warming me like a physical flame. He'd protected me when I didn't even realize I needed protection. Once again, he'd put my welfare before his own.

That was a more touching display of love than any utterance of words. Surprised to find tears filling my eyes, I blinked hard. I was newly determined not to disappoint him.

For now, Chris stood a little straighter and directed his response to Judge Finch. "Christopher Gardner for the defense," he said. "Sun Lion of the Eastern Empire."

If the judge was impressed with his title, she gave no sign. Instead, she shuffled a stack of papers on her desk and glared at the ranks of benches behind us.

"Before we begin," she said, "I'd like to say a few words to the observers in the gallery."

I heard an anticipatory shuffle behind me. I wanted to turn around, to see who was gaping at the proceedings. But Chris shifted his weight, bringing his arm close to mine. I glanced down at his hand and caught his index finger pointing toward Judge Finch. *Pay attention*, he was saying. *Ignore everyone—and every-thing—else.*

I closed my fingers around my hematite bracelet, the better to concentrate. Of course, that bracelet was gone. I tried to disguise my motion by fiddling with the cuff on my blouse.

Judge Finch continued. "I've already cleared the press from this courtroom, when it became apparent that *some* reporters couldn't observe the rule against audio and video recordings. I will not hesitate to bar any other imperial from this room for any disturbance whatsoever."

As if to underscore the judge's fiat, Eleanor shifted her

weight, settling the boulders of her hands on her hips. The expectant buzz behind me ceased immediately. If I'd been the recipient of her glare, I might have crumbled to dust.

And then the hearing began.

The details were boring. Russo called witnesses, carefully guiding them through a tick-tock of the events on the night of June 25. Chris applied his journalist's skill at shorthand, taking complex notes while Russo presented his case. With the judge's permission, Chris asked a handful of questions in cross-examination. Russo declined to re-direct.

The preliminary hearing was supposed to work to the advantage of both sides. Chris and I could learn how the Empire was building its case. Russo could see the outline of my defense. All of us could gauge the advantage—or disadvantage —of my plea-bargaining to lesser charges.

As the night wore on, Russo's Old World accent lulled the court, blurring the line between respect and skepticism. With every round of question and answer, I felt less able to defend my actions on that summer night ten months earlier.

The blood and the horror and the shimmering power of *agriotis* seemed like half-remembered nightmares. I couldn't explain—even to myself—what I'd been thinking and how and why I'd acted as I had. Over and over again, I brushed my fingers against my missing insignia, hoping to calm my seething thoughts, trying to gain some perspective.

Chris did his best to shelter me. He presented some procedural challenges, obscure Empire rules that caught Russo by surprise and sent the dryad scurrying to her legal tomes. He kept a running tally of facts we'd been unable to counter, and he started a list of expert witnesses we should start to gather.

There was no jury, not at this preliminary stage. Judge Finch certainly wasn't betraying a hint of emotion. But as the clock ticked closer and closer to dawn, I had to believe that she was inclined to decide against me. Against the sphinx who'd killed a vampire judge.

Finally, she gaveled the hearing to a close. She noted that she'd take all of the arguments under advisement, and she'd issue a written decision on several procedural matters that had been presented. The narrow-eyed glare she cast toward me made it abundantly clear she was not dismissing my case for lack of cause.

"All rise!" Eleanor barked, and a weary courtroom of observers stumbled to its collective feet. The instant Judge Finch cleared the bench, the gallery exploded with speculation.

Chris wasted no time escorting me through the crowd, actually raising his briefcase to block my view of the spectators. Indignation sharpened the tone of discussion, and a few people called out to Antonio Russo, asking him to clarify some of the points he'd made.

Muttering under his breath, Chris caught my elbow with commanding fingertips, speed-walking me to the courthouse door.

Bubba looked up as we approached. "Ms. Anderson," he said. "Looks like folks are getting an early start out there."

His words didn't make sense. It was the end of a long night. Nothing "early" about it.

But I was wrong. I was naively, incredibly wrong.

The press had gotten an early start, mobbing the courthouse plaza before dawn.

To Bubba's human eyes, they would have looked like a scrum of eager spectators—humans hoping to snag a seat in an important trial heard by one of the day-court judges. To my imperial eyes, though, they looked like a cadre of imperial journalists.

Three different reporters—a naiad, an ifrit, and a witch—all representing *The Imperial Inquisitor*. A vampire for *The Nightly Moon*. *The Centaur Sentinel*. *The Paranormal Post*. *The Sylph Standard* and *The Elemental Gazette*. *The Shifter Dispatch-Tribune*.

That wasn't even considering the online media. Smartphones took the place of bulky video equipment. Screens were held above heads, dull eyes that came to blinding life as Chris and I reached the top of the courthouse steps.

"Sarah!" one of the reporters shouted, and the others immediately took up the cry.

"Ms. Anderson!"

"Mr. Gardner, over here!"

"Come on, Sarah! Look this way!"

They bayed like a pack of wolves scenting fresh blood. When I froze, the most daring sprinted up the stairs. Phones were shoved in my face, microphones jammed so close to my lips that I had to take a step back.

"Hey, Chris! What did you think of Mr. Russo?"

"What's it like to walk free, Sarah?"

"How did it feel to stake a vampire?"

That last question caught all of us by surprise. We were standing on the steps of the District of Columbia Superior Court. Mundanes making their early way to work were already staring at the crowd. No one had cast a protective circle around us. No one had taken any precautions to preserve the Empire's secrecy.

"No comment," Chris said, taking my hand and leading me down the stairs.

That should have been the end of it. The reporters should have dispersed, building their stories on whatever documents had been filed in the case, whatever orders Judge Finch saw fit to issue.

But Chris's fingers on mine ignited new passion in the mob.

"Hey Sarah! Is it true you two got married last night?"

"Chris! Is that why you weren't taking calls on Monday?

"Should we start a pool for baby names?"

"Come on, Chris, give her a kiss. Just a quickie!"

The questions rolled on, louder and more boisterous. The cameras were back, brilliant white flashes blinding me as I tried to find the steps beneath my feet. The shouting, the jostling, the utter, uncontrolled chaos… It felt like the worst of a pitched battle.

My heart shifted into overdrive. My vision sharpened, as if someone had snatched away a veil. I caught my breath, and my throat was drenched with scent—blood and sweat and the individual reek of each of my enemies.

"No!" Chris said. The syllable carried all the urgency of the Sun Lion, all the power a sphinx could summon. He kept his voice low, though, pitched only for my ears. All that intensity, all that command, targeted directly at the *agriotis* that threatened to demolish the reporters.

"Get out of here," he whispered, pitching the words for my *agriotis*-enhanced ears. As I struggled to master my shift, to keep my murderous demon from breaking loose, he insisted, "Go home."

And then he left.

I knew what he was doing. He was drawing half the pack to himself. He waved down a cab and purposely gave the driver his address, saying the words loudly enough that a dozen of the journalists flagged their own taxis and scrambled in pursuit.

I didn't have time for an Uber. I barely snagged my own cab, yanking open the red-and-grey door and tumbling into the back seat with the closest reporters on my heels.

In his urgency, Chris had been too loud. "Go home," he'd said, breaking through the spell of my *agriotis*. I heard the pack baying as my cab pulled away.

"1911!" someone called, raising a phone screen in victory.

"Corcoran Street!" shouted another.

"Go!" I shouted to my cabbie. "Just drive!"

He drove.

Of course, the swarm followed me. I lost half of them at a Starbucks over by the White House after I threw money at my driver and fled into the caffeine-starved crowd milling in front of the counter. I wasted no time fighting my way to the back of the shop, to the exit that opened onto a quiet side street.

Another cab. Four more reporters gone.

A scramble down the elevator at the Foggy Bottom Metro station, slapping my card onto the fare gate.

I ran onto a train and watched the door slam in the face of a determined warder and a sylph. I traveled three stations, searching the crowd for other imperials.

No one.

I changed trains three times, just to be sure. Changed subway lines too, ending up on the Red. As morning commuters came and went, I slouched in a seat in the middle of the car, studying the crowd until we arrived at Woodley Park and the National Zoo.

The doors opened. I waited. Passengers boarded. I waited. Bells rang, announcing the conclusion of the stop.

Using my elbows and fingernails, I shoved with all my weight, pushing my way to the exit just before the door slammed closed. The train rushed by me, picking up speed as it fled to the next station.

For one blessed moment, I stood on the empty platform.

I was alone.

I was safe.

My fingers jangled with excess adrenaline as I climbed the escalator out of the station. My legs ached, teetering on the edge of cramping from the control I'd exerted to keep from completing my *agriotis* shift. My arms trembled from exhaustion.

Food. I needed food. I'd skipped lunch the night before, heading into my forgotten hearing.

I stumbled into another Starbucks. I couldn't drink coffee, not now, not when I needed to sleep off my nightmare flight. But I could get a breakfast sandwich.

I gulped down the treat, chasing it with a bottle of water. As I was swallowing the last bite, I ordered two more sandwiches and another water.

Finally, fortified with egg and cheese and blessed, salty bacon, I headed into the warren of roads that cut through Rock

Creek Park, on my way to James's sanctum. I forced myself to wait at trailheads, making sure no one was following me. I followed two false paths before I let myself take the actual one I needed.

At the top of the hill, I knew I should head for the alley and the privacy of the townhouse's garage. I didn't want the neighbors to see me. I didn't want anyone to ask questions.

But I was too tired to hide any longer. My feet kept catching on the sidewalk, as if the toes of my shoes were too heavy to lift. It took two tries to find my keyring in my purse, and three to fit the key into the lock.

I turned the knob, letting my weight push the door open. I barely remembered how to extract the key, how to close the door, how to slide the chain and turn the top deadbolt, the middle one, the bottom.

I wasn't going to make it up the stairs in James's sanctum. I might not even make it to the couch. I dropped my purse on the foyer floor and tried to summon the strength to move to the living room.

And for the second time in a week, fingers closed around my throat in a deadly, strangling grip.

17

J ames.

I knew the scent of him, the ghost of pine and snow.

I knew the feel of his hands—even around my throat—the memory of a hundred training sessions in the Old Library.

I knew the weight of his body as he pressed me against the door, as he levered his knee between my legs, as his hips pinned mine.

Against my will, I whimpered as his thumbs pressed against the bruises left by Richardson's soldier. I was too tired to fight. I was too exhausted to summon everything I'd learned in the sub-basement of the courthouse, falling over and over and over again on blue mats spread across the hardwood floor.

There were no mats here. I might break a bone on the foyer's marble floor. And even if I succeeded in taking James to the ground, I had no faith that I could apply my other vampire-fighting lessons. Not now. Not when I was already spent.

"James," I whispered, barely forcing his name past his fingers around my throat.

He snarled, and I heard a soft *pop* as he expressed his fangs. Before I could consciously realize that he'd been holding himself back, that he'd caught me without even using his most dangerous weapon, he shifted his grip.

One hand grabbed both my wrists, locking them in an iron vise as he stretched my arms over my head. With his other, he caught my chin, forcing my jaw back with the V between his thumb and index finger.

I'd sought him for months. I'd practiced what I'd say when I found him. I'd rehearsed apologizing, begging for forgiveness, arguing my case, telling him I'd do it all over again if that's what it took to free Judge DuBois.

But he didn't give me a chance.

He slashed my jugular, slamming an icicle into my throat.

Pain rocketed through me. I twisted my arms, fighting to break free from his grip. At the same time, I jackknifed my body, driving my knee into his groin.

He anticipated me easily, turning his body to deflect my feeble blow. He tightened the pressure on my wrists until my hands went numb.

Another slash against my throat, this one not as deep because I was fighting now. I thrashed my head, determined to keep him from filling his mouth with my blood.

I knew James was capable of softening his bite. He could roll his tongue over my veins, soothing away the sting of his fangs and raising my own delicious shivers of anticipation. He could worship my throat, leaving me limp and spent and trembling before he even started to slake his own needs.

But he hadn't bothered with any of that. He was attacking me like a predator pulling down a meal on the open veldt.

"This is for Robert," he growled, forcing my chin up to give him better access to my throat.

Robert. Judge DuBois. James wanted revenge as surely as if I'd killed for sport.

I reached for *agriotis*, for my birthright as a sphinx or whatever I was, but I was too tired, too far gone to complete the transition. Merely trying made my wounded throat sting as if I'd been submerged in a vat of salt-water.

My strength was gone. All I had was my capacity to think, my ability to string words together—at least until James ripped my throat out.

"I miss him too!" I gasped.

"You barely knew him," James snarled.

"I knew the way he ran the court." I answered quickly, before he could close for the kill. "I knew the way he kept order in the Empire. He was fair. He understood justice."

Somehow, impossibly, James was listening. It was as if he craved some benediction, some confirmation that Robert DuBois had been a worthy man, a great man, a man who should still live.

I continued, because I couldn't think of anything else to do. "He didn't deserve what happened. He never should have been Impressed. But by the time we found him, by the time you and I got to the Jefferson Memorial, the only thing he wanted was freedom."

James stiffened above me, his muscles as taut as bowstrings. He'd been there. He knew. But he didn't want to remember.

"He begged me, James. He pleaded for me to release him. He knew it would hurt you, hurt me, hurt the entire Empire, but it was better than submitting to anyone else. I didn't have a choice. I had to honor the man. I had to give him one last gift."

I was panting, desperate. I had to convince James. I had to make him understand. "I did my best to save him," I whispered. "I swear by Mother Sekhmet."

James shoved himself off me.

Wiping at his mouth with the back of his hand, he staggered back a step. He howled, a wordless sound of unadulterated grief. He was close enough that I could feel the heat of his flesh, his body grown warm from the blood he'd swallowed, *my* blood.

"Sarah," he finally said, and he reached shaking fingers toward my throat.

I batted his arm away, ducking past him to the center of the entry hall. "Don't touch me!"

He pulled back, but he demanded, "What the hell are you doing here?"

I couldn't explain it all—the hearing, the scrum at the courthouse steps, the paparazzi who'd chased me through the city. Even if I'd had the strength, he would have pounced on my last words, on the possibility that I'd delivered strangers to his sanctum.

Instead, I heaved a deep breath, trying to ignore James's flinch as I exhaled, long and steady and slow. "I needed some place safe to stay," I finally said.

"You think I'm safe?" No sane person could make that mistake, not with James's fangs glinting wetly in the dim light of the corridor. Not with his fingers flexing, as if he were even now fighting to keep from pinning me to the door.

"I didn't know you'd come back," I said. With a conscious effort, I kept my hands open at my waist, my fingers splayed. I tried not to look like a threat…or prey.

I couldn't keep my heart from pounding, though. And my breath still came in short, sharp pants that I tried to disguise through stiff lips.

"You stink," he said. Ignoring my outraged squawk, he reached into the pocket of his trousers and came up with an immaculate white handkerchief. "Clean yourself up." He shoved the cloth toward me.

I ignored the offering. The last thing I wanted was to move closer to him. Not when I could still feel a slow trickle of blood down my throat.

"Take it," James said, waving the handkerchief like a white flag. "It's bad enough you're dripping fresh blood. But you reek like a steakhouse on top of that…"

He'd warned me not to eat meat, the very first day he'd trained me in the Old Library. He'd told me my diet made me smell like prey, and I'd become an inspired vegetarian overnight.

Now, I swallowed acid at the back of my throat. I wished I hadn't eaten those breakfast sandwiches. At least I could have ordered them without bacon.

The breakfast sandwiches, and the roast beef I'd had the day before. Pork loin and chicken before that. With James out of sight, I'd readily embraced my carnivorous side.

"Sorry," I said, but I didn't bother trying to sound sincere. I did, though, take his handkerchief.

I folded the clean square into quarters, and then in half again before I pressed it against my throat, hard. It hurt, but not as much as the open wound had stung. I increased the pressure steadily, ignoring the rising ache in my veins.

As I worked, James sagged against the wall. There weren't any windows in the foyer, and the ones in the adjoining living room had been covered with steel. The only light came from the empty dining room, from the soft yellow glow of the chandelier.

I didn't need a window to know it was broad daylight outside. The sun had risen as I fled the paparazzi horde. James should have been asleep two, three, maybe even four hours ago.

His eyes were dilated, as wide as a lemur's. My blood wasn't enough to fight the compulsion of his vampire body to sleep, not when he had to be spending an enormous amount of energy just fighting his instinct to drain me dry.

Nevertheless, he struggled to stay upright. "Just as well you're here," he said. The words were a little slurred, as if he'd had one too many glasses of wine.

I lifted my makeshift bandage gingerly. My neck still stung, but a quick swipe of my fingers confirmed I'd staunched the flow of blood. "Why?" I asked, wary.

Instead of answering, he tried to stagger toward the door. His fingers closed around my wrist.

All his brutal strength had flown. He was no longer an apex predator defending his lair against an unknown enemy. Now, he was a drained warrior who could barely keep his balance.

Instead of pulling away, I let him lean against me. It was that, or watch him pitch to the floor.

"C'mon," he said, reaching blindly toward the doorknob.

"Come where?"

"Richardson," he slurred. "Have to see. Have t' unnerstan…"

There was no way in hell I was letting him take me to Maurice Richardson, even if he *could* navigate the city streets by day. "What the hell, James?"

I shifted his weight, and he slumped against the wall. As he sagged to the floor, legs akimbo, I knelt to retrieve my purse. It only took a moment to pull out the burner phone. It seemed like a century since Bubba had given it to me, not one long night and part of a nightmare day.

"What the hell is this?" I demanded, shoving the phone toward him.

He shook his head slowly, like a punch-drunk fighter trying to get back into the ring. "Richardson," he repeated, nearly losing the last syllable as his eyes closed.

"What about Richardson?" I insisted. "You gave him access to the court! Angelique was dosed with *your* Lethe!"

James murmured something, but I couldn't make out the words. Frustrated, I kicked at the sole of his shoe, brandishing the phone in front of his slack face. "You don't get to do this! You can't help Richardson one day and fight him the next! It doesn't make sense, James! I don't understand what's going on!"

I could have yelled for hours. I could have smashed the phone to pieces on the marble floor. I could have twined my fingers in James's tangled hair, pulling with all my might, but none of that would change a thing.

He was out cold. Like any vampire in the middle of the day, he was completely incapable of action. Maurice Richardson could be plotting a nuclear war against the Empire, and there was nothing James could say or do till sunset that evening.

Even in the midst of my frustration, I understood all that. I was a sphinx. Or I *had* been one. Whatever.

In all the ways that mattered, I was *James's* sphinx. He had chosen me for the clerk's job. He'd given me my insignia. I was bound more closely to him than if we'd been joined through the Ancient Commission, or Chris's untested, untried New Commission.

But my own strength was drained—not by sunlight or by Earth's turning on its axis. I was exhausted because I'd depleted my reserves, physical and mental, trying to manage whatever the hell James was doing.

I was too spent to drag him to the comfort of his own bed. It was all I could do to snag a blanket and spare pillow from the linen closet upstairs and stumble back to the foyer. My own eyelids drooped as I untied his laces, as I slipped off his shoes.

After only a moment's hesitation, I loosened his belt as well. There wasn't anything seductive about the action. I might have been undressing a mannequin, for all the thrill I felt.

I knew James's body. He'd meant something to me; we'd meant something to each other. But that was before that horrible June night. It was before Judge DuBois's death and James's disappearance, and Richardson's mistrial.

It was before everything went wrong.

I settled my palm against his shirt, imagining I could feel a heart beating inside his chest. His flesh had cooled now, the rush of my blood completely dispersed.

He was safe here, in the hallway of his sanctum, and he was as comfortable as I could make him. I climbed upstairs to his bed and fell asleep, alone.

18

J ames was gone when I awoke.

That should have been impossible. He should have been sun-drunk until dusk, too sleepy to rouse. Even if he clawed his way up to wakefulness, he shouldn't have been able to leave the safety of the house, not without head-to-toe garments shielding him from the sun, and I'd seen nothing like that in the near-empty sanctum.

On the other hand, he could make do with tinted windows on the vehicle he'd parked in the garage.

I found fresh drops of oil on the concrete floor. Whatever car he was driving needed a new gasket, sooner rather than later. But it had been sufficient to spirit him away without a morning confrontation.

Once I was certain I was alone in the house, I studied my bruised throat in the bathroom mirror. A pair of lurid scabs stood out against the rather ghastly green that remained from my throttling by Richardson's soldier. I probably should have been grateful James hadn't attacked me while I slept.

Nausea washed over me as I remembered the piercing pain of his bite. He'd been defending his sanctum, I told myself. He'd been maddened by the scent of meat on my breath. He'd been trying to avenge Judge DuBois.

In the end, at least, my words had penetrated his madness. He'd understood that I'd acted to *save* the judge, not to murder him. My confession had saved my life.

I couldn't spend the night waiting for James to return. I had to get to work. Angelique had made it perfectly clear that my job was on the line. She'd be overjoyed to catch me violating my probation.

But I had no delusions. The pack of reporters who'd chased me from the courthouse that morning would likely be gathered on the plaza, waiting for me to start my shift.

They could be banned from the actual clerk's office the same way Judge Finch had exiled them from the courtroom. I just needed some way to *get* to my office, past the ravenous hordes.

I just needed…

I made my way down the stairs to the empty kitchen. A car key glinted on its tiny hook beside the door to the garage—a sleek electronic fob bearing Toyota's oval logo.

I'd seen the Prius when I'd checked the garage for James's escape car, the one with the leaky oil pan. I hadn't consciously acknowledged it; its windows were clear above its sleek silver paint. It couldn't have spirited James away from the house, so it hadn't been important.

But it was my salvation now.

I glanced at the Florida license plate, with its jaunty legend: The Sunshine State. That must have been James's idea of a joke for a car owned by a vampire. The tag was current, and a parking pass for the courthouse garage hung from the rear-view mirror, a perk for the court's Director of Security.

As I slipped behind the wheel, I offered a quick prayer to Sekhmet that the engine would start. After all, no one had used the Prius for months.

Either Sekhmet was listening or Toyota's engineers were geniuses. In any case, the dashboard lights flickered through their start-up sequence, settling on a single green glowing word: Ready. In eerie silence, I backed out of the garage and headed for the courthouse.

In the end, it was easy to reach my desk. The city streets were relatively empty. The guard at the garage entrance waved me through with the quickest of glances at the hanging parking pass. I found a space close to the elevator, and I cleared security without the rabble outside ever suspecting I was in the building.

The message light on my desk phone was flashing. I picked up a pen as an electronic voice announced I had seven messages. The first was from Chris's cell.

Chris.

How had I forgotten to contact him? We'd left the courthouse together, surrounded by the scrum of reporters. I'd scrambled for a refuge, settling on the sanctum in Rock Creek Park. I'd fought with James.

Sure, I'd been slashed and bleeding. I'd been terrified and more than a little confused. I'd been exhausted.

But none of those were valid excuses for overlooking my boyfriend, the one man who'd had my back for months.

I listened to the other six messages. Each was from an increasingly worried Chris. I cut off the last recording and dialed his cell.

It was my turn to get voicemail. "I'm sorry," I said. "I'm safe." There was too much to tell him, too much to explain. I couldn't say it all, so I settled on, "I'm at the office. Call me."

I left the same message for him at home. My palms were sweating by the time I terminated that call, and I couldn't draw a full breath. Looking over my shoulder at the glass eye of the surveillance camera that kept the clerk's office safe, the one that fed a direct line to Angelique's desk, I placed a label on my malaise.

I felt guilty.

Guilty that I'd forgotten Chris. Guilty that I'd spent the

night—however platonically—with James. Guilty that I'd let our one known link to Maurice Richardson slip away.

I turned my back on the camera and forced myself to take a steadying breath. I couldn't change things now. There was no way to go back in time, to call Chris promptly, to wake before James disappeared like a wraith.

Sweet Sekhmet, how had my life fallen apart so quickly?

Sekhmet… The goddess had stopped James's attack. At least I'd called on her, just before I finally penetrated James's murderous haze. She watched over me, however flawed I was as her servant.

And I absolutely *was* flawed. Sekhmet had told me, days ago, to find her Seal before Richardson did. I'd ignored her request, letting it fall by the wayside as I grappled with other, more worldly concerns.

I owed the goddess. It was time to seek her Seal. And the best thing was, I could start with the tools right in front of me.

The Seal—whatever it was—was unlikely to have been the subject of litigation in Eastern Empire courts, but I shouldn't overlook possible easy solutions.

Most cases filed in the Eastern Empire Night Court were civil disputes between two supernatural parties, different races who couldn't resolve their disagreement in their local jurisdictions—Hecate's Court or the Dryad Circle or the Council of Giants, that sort of thing.

Other cases were criminal matters. As I'd seen in my own indictment, cases were brought by the Clans of the Eastern Empire against individual imperials.

But there was a third category of cases—actions against individual *items*. It sounded strange, but a case could actually be filed against an individual parcel of land.

Not long ago, there'd been a series of actions against an absentee vampire's multiple sanctums, when the missing occupant had ostentatiously failed to safeguard the properties from prying mundane eyes, putting the entire Empire at risk of discovery. A gnome's axe had been sued when it was left behind after cutting down a dryad's grove, with no elemental owner in sight.

Not many of those cases were filed in any given year. Their names were odd: *The Clans of the Eastern Empire v. A Cast-Iron Witch's Cauldron. The Clans of the Eastern Empire v. 1527 Massachusetts Ave.*

Maybe, just maybe, Sekhmet's Seal had been the subject of such a case.

I searched for the word *seal*. When I didn't find it, I tried some synonyms. I found thirty-one actions involving a *charm*, but not one of those items had been forged in ancient Egypt, at least not as far as I could tell from court filings.

There were fourteen *talismans*, but none of those was Egyptian either. I found four *amulets*, three *jujus*, and one each for *periapt*, *philter*, and *phylactery*.

Setting aside my thesaurus, my heart started pounding when I spotted the word *scarab* in a random court filing. I immediately pictured a faience beetle, a classic Egyptian symbol. But I was swamped with disappointment when I realized Scarab Realty had managed a string of sanctums some time in the 1920s.

In between all those searches, I actually completed some paid work. A mundane junior associate arrived from one of the largest law firms in town, and I walked him through filing his legal complaint—all before the stroke of midnight when the statute of limitations would have terminated his client's breach of contract claims.

My usual trio showed up—Davey and Eugene and Alicia—looking for their nightly bread and butter.

Angelique passed through the office half a dozen times, a record in all the months I'd worked for her. Happily, I was busy with human patrons each time she stalked past my desk. She didn't get a chance to hiss her disapproval over my very existence.

By midnight, I was certain the Seal hadn't been the subject

of any arcane litigation. That meant I'd have to seek further afield.

I had to research Maurice Richardson.

I shouldn't have been surprised. All roads in DC seemed to lead to the vampire kingpin. But knowing that my computer system had once been locked down by Richardson's lackey made me paranoid.

Had the ransom software installed a back door into my machine? Would Richardson be notified the instant I typed his name into a search engine? And if he was notified, would he dispatch his foot soldier to finish the strangling he'd begun in the Old Library? Maybe Richardson would send James this time, to drink his fill once and for all.

I winced as my fingertips scraped the new scabs on my neck. But I couldn't live the rest of my life in fear that Richardson and his troops might find me. Despite the major breach of the past week, the courthouse was still probably the safest place in the world for a sphinx. Or unknown imperial. Whatever. We had armed guards at the front door. We had the security of our secret warren below the mundane court.

I was better off researching Maurice Richardson from the court computer than from anywhere else in the Eastern Empire. My own cowardice was the only thing holding me back. It was time to find out what the Empire's greatest criminal mastermind had been doing since he'd last stood at the defense table in the courtroom down the hall.

Four hours later, I had a more complete picture than I'd hoped.

Fact: Last July, a mistrial had been declared in the Eastern Empire's case against Maurice Richardson, two weeks after Judge DuBois died.

Fact: Last August, a new case was initiated against Maurice Richardson, with half a dozen claims, including murder and impressment.

Fact: Last September, Maurice Richardson failed to appear

at a preliminary hearing in his new case, resulting in the issuance of a bench warrant for his arrest.

The trail ran cold after that. There was no reference to Richardson in any publication—imperial or mundane—after his September disappearance. He could be anywhere. He could be dead.

But he wasn't dead. James had tried to take me to him just that morning.

With Richardson impossible to track down, I returned my attention to the Seal. But mundane newspaper reporters would never realize the importance of one ancient item, not without the context that was engraved deeper and deeper inside my imperial mind.

I researched historic Egyptian treasure, in general. And I found the proverbial landmine.

Fact: In 1997, a record-setting lot of Egyptian artifacts had been auctioned at Sotheby's. The unknown purchaser had never come forward to place any item in a public collection or to otherwise provide any information about his identity.

Fact: Ditto, a 2002 record-shattering auction at Christie's, for another set of Egyptian artifacts.

Fact: Ditto, an auction four years ago at Wellingham's. Another set of Egyptian artifacts, another sky-high record. But someone at Wellingham's wasn't as well trained as his peers at the bigger auction houses. An employee speaking on condition of anonymity confirmed to the press that Lost Soul Enterprises had acquired the goods in question.

Fact: Prized Egyptian artifacts had been offered in each of the last four years, but they failed to meet their reserve.

There was no such thing as coincidence, not where vampire overlords were concerned. Sekhmet's Seal must have been in the Wellingham's lot. Lost Soul Enterprises—Richardson—had finally secured his goal.

All I needed to do was find a way to wrest the Seal from Richardson.

A headache pounded directly behind my eyes. Sighing, I reached behind my neck, trying to probe deeply enough at the base of my skull to banish the pounding pain. The heel of my palm, though, only pressed against my bruises, setting off a new wave of discomfort.

The phone rang on the corner of my desk. I answered before I could sink into an ocean of self-pity. "Clerk's office," I said, my eyes still closed.

"Sarah."

Chris. His voice shot through me like a bolt of lightning. I sat up straight at my desk. "Where are you?" I asked, and then I hurried on before I could question the defensiveness flooding my tone. "I tried to reach you—"

"I'm home now."

His voice was terse, but I thought I heard an emphasis on the first word. He was home—unlike me. I hadn't returned to his home—or my own—the night before, and he wanted to know why. Racking my brain for a safe response, a fair one, I asked, "Are the reporters there?"

"Not now. They must have found fresh meat."

Meat. The word made me think of James, of his visceral disgust as he shoved his handkerchief at me.

I wanted to ask another question, to know where Chris had been when I'd tried to reach him. But before I could do that, I had to apologize. Tell him I was sorry for ignoring him all day. Tell him where *I'd* been. Why I'd forgotten him.

But somehow, I wasn't ready to do that yet. Instead, I said, "I've been doing some research." Maybe Chris would think that was what had distracted me. Why I'd forgotten to call. "About the Seal," I elaborated. "I think Richardson's after it."

I told him everything I'd found, about the auctions and the mysterious buyer and Richardson missing his court date.

The more I talked, though, the more frightening Chris's silence became. I had to fill the gaps. I had to make my work seem even more time-consuming, even more complex than it had actually been.

I needed to justify an entire day of silence.

"All right," Chris said.

"All right?" I wanted him to be proud of me. I wanted him to be impressed.

"What do you want me to say, Sarah? It sounds like you're heading down the right path."

Chris sounded angry.

Chris never sounded angry. He was the Sun Lion. He was implacable.

"Fine," I said, knowing that my own rage wasn't justified. Before I could make more of a mess of the conversation, I said, "I have to go. Angelique needs a report before I sign out in the morning."

Of course Angelique didn't need a report. I was making a nasty habit of lying to my boyfriend.

Chris said something, and I said something else, and I don't know which of us was happier to end the phone call.

I stared at the phone after I'd cradled the handset. We hadn't fought. Hadn't even exchanged a cross word. But he hadn't asked me to come by after work. And I hadn't volunteered to appear on his doorstep.

A gulf was expanding between us, and I didn't know the first thing about how to build a bridge.

19

At the end of my shift, I headed home. That seemed the least complicated of all my options—seeking out the quiet privacy of my basement apartment instead of figuring out a path to peace with Chris or forging yet another elaborate, untraceable route to James's sanctum.

At least I didn't have to deal with Metro. I had a private car waiting for me downstairs. James's Prius started without a hint of hesitation, and it glided silently out of the garage.

Alas, my downscale home didn't come equipped with a private garage. My neighborhood wasn't made for car owners either. It took me fifteen minutes to find a parking space, and then I was a full three-block walk from my front door. Maybe I would have been better off taking the subway after all.

I stooped to collect a handful of advertising flyers from the bottom of the stairwell. They went straight into the recycling bin, but I owed it to myself to go through the stack of actual mail that had piled up in my mailbox. There might be something I wanted, tucked among the endless catalogs and credit card offers.

Fat chance. There wasn't a handwritten address or actual

stamp in sight. I shoved the door closed with my hip, automatically turning the dead bolt and flipping on the light switch.

I was half-way to the kitchen table when I heard the quicksilver voice: "Why bother with a security chain, if you aren't going to use it?"

Yelping in surprise, I dropped the mail, letting it scatter across the linoleum floor. Automatically, I surveyed the kitchen counter for a weapon—a knife, a pair of scissors, even a ball-point pen.

Of course my sphinx nature would never have left anything —weapon or otherwise—sitting out on the counter. My best hope was to grab a frying pan from the pot rack above the stove. If only I'd invested in some serious cast-iron, instead of a lightweight skillet barely capable of frying a couple of eggs...

Even as my fingers closed around the plasticized handle of my thoroughly inadequate bludgeon, my brain overruled my adrenaline, and I identified my intruder's voice. He was sitting on my couch, clear across the shadowed living room. He wasn't close enough to slash open the scabs atop my jugular.

"James," I said, measuring out his name with perfect neutrality as I turned to face him.

"Sarah," he answered, matching my tone precisely.

Once I released my frying pan, my fingers itched to pick up the scattered mail, but I wasn't going down on my knees in front of my unexpected vampire visitor. Instead, I channeled my anxiety into a demand: "What the hell are you doing here?"

"You stopped by my home yesterday," he said reasonably. "I thought I'd return the favor."

I couldn't imagine a more bogus explanation. But I *had* given him a key, over a year ago. Before that, I'd invited him to cross my threshold. Irony of ironies, I'd extended the welcome because we'd both feared Richardson might send minions to attack me.

The night before, when James had caught me entering his sanctum, I'd felt like an invader. I'd owed him an apology, or at least an explanation. I'd needed to justify my dispatching Judge DuBois.

But now we were on my turf. James was the one who needed to do the explaining. I almost succeeded in keeping my voice even as I asked, "Richardson ordered you over here?"

James's anger was immediate, unmistakable, and glacial. "Richardson doesn't order me to do anything."

But I'd seen his rage before. I didn't flinch. "So you're willingly working with him." When that statement didn't goad him into a reply, I said, "You acted on your own volition when you drugged Angelique Wilson."

"I didn't dr—"

"You or that miserable excuse for a vampire hacker. I don't see a lot of difference." I didn't bother squelching the reflex to cup my fingers around my bruised throat. "Tell me you didn't have anything to do with getting him into the courthouse."

James glared. "It's complicated."

"Try me," I shot back. "Over the last two years, I've gotten pretty good at *complicated*. Start with the phone you left for me at the courthouse. Where did you get a million bucks and a Bitcoin account?"

"The money was mine. I could use it any way I wanted."

"So you chose to do a little breaking and entering?"

I didn't realize how shrill my voice had become until he answered with a voice as dry as Sekhmet's desert. "Nothing was broken."

"What the hell are you doing here, James? What do you want from me?"

"I told you last night. I want to bring you to Richardson."

Last night, the thought of going to Maurice Richardson had terrified me. In fact, I was still frightened. I'd felt his cold fangs on my throat before. I knew he could kill me without a flash of guilt.

But now I knew that Richardson had been buying up lots of Egyptian treasure, searching for Sekhmet's Seal. And then, he'd stopped. I had to believe he'd found the goddess's token. And I'd do a hell of a lot to learn exactly what it was. Even if that meant taking a few risks.

Okay. A lot of risks.

But I wasn't inclined to make things easy for James. Not after he'd broken into my house and scared the living daylights out of me. "You told me a lot of things last night. You said you were going to rip my throat out because I executed Judge DuBois."

His jaw tightened. Another woman might not have seen it, might not have realized he was swallowing an emotion. But I'd spent almost a year with James, learning how to parse every one of his expressions. In our time together, he and I perfected the art of silence, carrying on entire conversations without exchanging a single word.

My belly swooped, traitorously reminding me of some of those *conversations.* I couldn't keep from glancing down the hall, toward the bed we'd shared as we'd refined our…unique style of communication. Blood rose in my cheeks, a blush hotter than any sphinx—or unknown imperial or whatever the hell I was—should have allowed.

Of course, James saw.

He was a predator, and I was flashing every sign of being prey. "I'm not going to rip your throat out," he said, as if that had anything to do with what I was thinking.

"Pro tip," I snapped. "If you want to talk to a woman, don't break into her apartment in the middle of the night. Try knocking on her door like a civilized person."

"Acknowledged," he said, with all the compassion of a computer.

"And you might let her wounds heal before you jump her again."

"Strictly speaking, no one jumped anyone," he pointed out, with a wry glance at my abandoned skillet. His amused tone sparked another rebellious swoop beneath my waistline. My mind was doing its best to play the cold, calculating imperial. My body clearly had a completely different agenda.

"And," James continued. "It's not exactly the middle of the night."

He was right. It was nearly daybreak.

But he was wrong about everything else. I didn't know what he was doing with Richardson. I didn't understand why he'd enabled the attack at the courthouse. I really couldn't say why he'd saved us with his burner phone.

I shouldn't be standing in my living room talking to him. I *certainly* shouldn't be curling my fingers against the trembling in my belly, shouldn't be thinking about my bed down the hallway, about all the times James and I had...

I should be at Chris's house that very minute.

But Chris had explicitly refused my company for the day.

And James was shooting his cuff. He was working the pearl buttons on his sleeve with a precision that would be the envy of any sphinx. He was holding my gaze, a gaze I hadn't realized he'd snagged, as he extended his wrist toward me.

"Say the word, Sarah, and you can drink." His lips pulled back, and I realized he was waiting for me to answer before he expressed his fangs.

One sip of his vampire blood, and my wounds would be healed. The scabs he'd inflicted on me when he attacked the night before. The bruises from Richardson's man. Hell, one good gulp of vampire blood, and my tired arches would feel like they were ready to slip into dancing shoes.

"Sarah..." James said, and I heard an entire conversation in my name.

He was apologizing for wounding me the night before. He was justifying his presence in my home now. He was asking me to trust him, one more time.

I stared into his blue eyes. If he'd wanted me dead, he could have waited just inside the door. He could have slashed my throat before I'd realized he was anywhere in the vicinity. He could have drained me dry before I had a chance to fight.

I collapsed onto the couch, pretending my legs were trembling because I was tired after a long day of work. I slipped off my shoes and pulled my knees to my chin, wrapping my arms around the backs of my thighs to press my skirt close, preserving some vague semblance of modesty.

"I don't want to drink," I said.

He nodded and lowered his arm, finally breaking the stare that had bound us. He paid too much attention to his sleeve as he fastened his buttons.

I let my head loll back, ignoring the fact that the motion stretched my neck, spreading a veritable buffet before a bloodthirsty monster. Not that James was particularly bloodthirsty. Not that he was a monster.

Staring at my ceiling, I said, "I'm sorry." I blinked, and I could see the marble plaza in front of the Jefferson Memorial. I could see Judge DuBois's withered husk in the moment before James carried away the corpse.

"I'm sorry," I said again. "I wish none of it had ever happened—Judge DuBois and Elena and the sphinxes. I wish I'd never trusted them. That I'd never tried to be one of them. I wish we could go back to the way everything was before, when you were the Director of Security and I was the Clerk of Court, and all we had to worry about was whether a handful of mundanes might try to have a motion heard after midnight."

"I don't," James said.

I sat up straighter, looking at him over my knees. "You don't what?"

"I don't want to go back that far. I don't want to give up what we had, you and me. Before DuBois... Before the end."

This time, he was the one who looked down the hallway.

I shook my head. "You left. Even before the judge... You... I... Chris..." That's what I had to tell him. That was the truth I had to speak. "Chris and I—"

"I don't want to hear about you and Gardner."

"But we were—We are—"

"I don't want to hear about you and Gardner."

The second time, I heard more than his words. I heard his tone. I bit off one last try at explaining. I wasn't sure what I was trying to say, myself. I'd never succeed in putting my thoughts into words.

I waved my hand, dismissing my half-fledged sentence.

"Thank you," James said, as if my cowardice was a gift.

Coming from any human, those would have been throw-away words. But vampires didn't say thank you. They didn't like the implied sense of obligation.

James was offering a true connection. He was giving me a chance at achieving a deeper bond. I did him the honor of not shoving aside that gift. "You're welcome," I said.

"Come on," he said, extending his hand. "Let's go before it's full daylight."

"It's practically full daylight now. You're not going anywhere."

"My car has tinted windows."

"I figured that out already. Tinted windows aren't enough."

"I'm parked right out front."

Of course he was. The fire hydrant at the curb had never meant anything to him. He'd perfected a vampire's lack of respect for rules and obligations, for order.

"You want me to see Richardson, right?" I tried to pretend the thought didn't spark panic somewhere deep in my lungs. "But he has to be asleep by now. He's not going to risk third degree burns, just to meet with me."

Frustration twitched across James's lips, but he didn't argue. He couldn't. I was right.

Besides, the sun was beginning to exercise its relentless pull over James. His throat tightened with a close-mouthed yawn. His pupils were dilating again, the same reaction to daylight I'd seen inside his sanctum.

"Okay, then. We'll sleep." His words started to slur. "And we'll go tonight. Wake me an hour before sunset."

I shook my head. "No."

"Sarah—"

"No!" I repeated, more sharply than I'd intended.

I'd lied to Chris, by omission at least. I wasn't going to lie to James as well. But I wasn't going to let him make my decisions, either.

"No," I said a third time, in a carefully modulated voice. "I promised Allison I'd see her tonight."

"Allison!" Even in his sun-drugged state, James's disdain was transparent.

"She's my best friend," I said defiantly. "And I've ignored her for too long. I'm seeing Allison tonight."

"After that—"

"After that, I'm going to work. Trying to clean up the mess you caused. You and Richardson, and that asshat who jumped me in the Old Library. You can take me…wherever you're going to take me, tomorrow night." It would be Saturday. At least my job wouldn't hang in the balance. Only my life.

James wouldn't endanger my life. He'd had ample opportunity to kill me, if that was what he wanted. I had to believe that. Otherwise, I had to regret everything, every second of our entire relationship.

Nevertheless, the thought of seeing Richardson face-to-face made my all-too-sphinx-like blood run cold.

"Sarah…" James said, but he never finished the sentence.

This time, I didn't have to summon the strength to carry him up a flight of stairs. My bedroom was just down the hall. I could easily have maneuvered him that far, could have settled him on the comfortable mattress, slipped a down pillow under his head, spread a warm duvet over his body.

But that would be one more mistake I'd have to confess to Chris. One more secret I'd have to share. And I had a feeling it would be difficult enough to make him understand all my other choices, the ones that had led me to this juncture.

For the second night in a row, I brought James a pillow. A pillow and a blanket, despite the fact that his vampire body didn't have a clear sense of warmth or cold. Once again, I removed his shoes, loosened his belt, and resisted the urge to do more.

I didn't have the right to do more. Not any longer. That part of our lives was over. Abandoned. Lost.

Tonight, I'd see Allison. And after that, I'd go to work. I'd call Chris, and I'd make things right.

And then, only then, would I master my fear and let James take me to Richardson.

20

I didn't sleep well.

Maybe that was because my vampire former lover was conked out on my couch. Maybe it was because my sphinx current lover was making it very clear he didn't want to see me. Maybe it was because I was plotting what to say to the woman who'd been my best friend for years, in a final, last-ditch gamble to regain the camaraderie that had come so easily before I found out I was a sphinx. An unknown, unknowable imperial. Whatever.

If those weren't reasons enough to toss and turn, I could always lapse into hopeless musing on my deteriorating relationship with my boss, my mystifying bond to the ancient Egyptian goddess I called mother, and my so-far-fruitless search for the vampire kingpin who was tracking down an ancient treasure that I'd been tasked to find.

And I could toss in the mystery of my father—and my apparently unique supernatural nature—just for good measure.

Viewed that way, it was sort of a miracle I slept at all.

By mid-afternoon, I gave up punching my pillow into submission. After confirming that James was still sun-comatose on the living room couch, I headed into the bathroom for a bracing shower, purposely turning the hot water to icy cold three times in quick succession, all in an effort to clear my foggy brain.

I took time to dry my hair, using a round brush and an indecent amount of expensive hair care product to make my waves lie flat. I chose a jet-black pencil skirt that always made me feel competent. I took my time with make-up, holding my mouth in a perfect O as I applied a double coat of mascara to my lashes.

Allison had told me to come over "Friday evening" before I went to work. I didn't want to get there early and disrupt her telework routine.

I recognized the twisted voice of my internal lies. I was delaying because I was nervous. Because I was afraid Allison would throw me out of her house before I had a chance to knock down the wall I'd built between us. Because I wasn't sure we'd still be friends if she sent me away one more time.

Standing in the living room, I looked down on James's deadly still body. Lost in whatever passed for vampire dreams, he hadn't stirred during the day. The blanket was exactly as I'd left it, spread across his chest, draping down to the floor.

My fingers twitched as I considered straightening its already immaculate corners. I thought about lining up his shoes, which were in perfect order beneath the coffee table. I debated setting out a coffee mug, a cereal bowl, a shiny stainless steel spoon, or at least an array of clean towels.

James didn't eat breakfast. I knew that, from all the nights we'd slept together. He didn't eat breakfast, he didn't toss and turn in his sleep, and he knew full well where to find the linen closet if he needed a washcloth.

Enough. It was time to head to Allison's home. To what might be our last-ever conversation.

Sucking in a sharp breath against that realization, I grabbed my favorite denim jacket and stepped out the front door, taking care to turn the lock behind me. I fast-walked to James's Prius, three blocks away. Once settled in the driver's seat, I resisted the urge to fiddle with the radio, delaying until I could find the perfect station. Finally, irrevocably, I maneuvered into traffic.

Only as I stood on Allison's front porch did I realize I should have brought something—flowers or candy or even a greeting card. A box of miniature Cake Walk cupcakes would have been the perfect ice-breaker. We could have put off real conversation for an hour or more, playing Cupcake Tarot, drawing squares of paper and selecting corresponding treats to represent our past, our future, and our present.

Too late now.

I knocked.

Allison opened the door, wearing yoga pants and an over-size sweatshirt that hung to her knees. Her hair was twisted into a messy bun, with an uncapped Bic pen holding it into place. "Sarah," she said, her voice perfectly level.

"Hey," I said. Not *Thanks so much for letting me come over.* Not *I've really been looking forward to talking to you.* Not *Can I tell you I'm sorry a million times over, in a way that finally makes sense so we can be done with all of this, and we can go back to being friends?*

At least she stepped back and let me come inside. I followed her into the family room, a cheerful space scattered with toddler toys. A ream of paper was spread over the couch, but Allison quickly shoved her work into a single messy pile. My fingers twitched, wanting to tap the pages into order. I didn't dare follow through on the compulsion.

Allison gestured toward the recliner where her ex-husband used to sit. She waited until I perched on the edge before she said, "So. You think you were adopted."

Okay. She wasn't offering me coffee or tea or anything resembling a snack. But at least she'd started the conversation.

I cleared my throat. "I think... Maybe... Yeah." With a gift for rhetoric like that, it was hard to believe I'd dropped out of law school.

Allison's eyes narrowed. "You never mentioned anything before. Did you find something in your mother's stuff?"

Allison knew full well my mother had died seven years ago. I wasn't likely to have discovered new documentary evidence recently. I said, "Not exactly."

"Then she said something to you before she died?"

The question was reasonable enough, but I heard the challenge behind it. I squirmed. "Not really."

Allison frowned. "I'm not following you here."

There was a reason for that. I wasn't exactly making sense.

The truth was, I'd asked to speak to Allison about adoption because I wanted an excuse—any excuse—to talk to the woman who used to be my best friend.

But I *was* trying to figure out my feelings about Sekhmet and Sheut, about being different from every other imperial I'd ever met. That was sort of like being adopted, wasn't it?

I tried again. "I never knew my father."

"That doesn't mean you were adopted, though," Allison pointed out quite reasonably. "I've seen the photograph on your nightstand."

Of course she had, in the days when she used to visit my apartment, before I'd painted over the windows with sage-green paint. Nestled inside a heart-shaped brass frame, there was a photo of my mother holding me, her wrist encircled with the white plastic of a hospital band. I was only a few hours old, swaddled in a pink blanket with a matching fleece hat pushed back just far enough to show the tiny strawberry birthmark at my hairline.

When I didn't answer quickly enough, Allison said, "You knew your mother. You *loved* your mother. And she loved you too."

There was no way to say I was asking about my other mother—my spiritual mother, the root of a family tree I could never share with any mundane friend. I was asking about Sekhmet. And Sheut.

Wiping my palms against my thighs, I admitted, "I'm not saying this right. I guess what I'm really thinking about is *parentage*, not adoption. I've never known who my father is. And for the first time in my life, I'm thinking about what it would mean if one man was. Or a different man."

"Do you have specific candidates in mind?" Allison asked.

I shrugged.

"Did your mother ever talk about these guys?"

My flesh-and-blood mother had always refused to discuss my father, no matter how many times I'd begged. But Sekhmet? She'd shown me an image of Sheut, disappearing into the shadows.

I couldn't explain any of this to Allison. She'd never understand. I could barely understand it myself. Sekhmet and Sheut were more than just my spiritual parents. Their ancient physical beings had determined my current corporeal self. They'd made me a sphinx, an unknown imperial, whatever. Something close enough that I'd fooled James and Chris and the Den for the past two years.

Once again, Allison was waiting. Once again, I had to find something to say, something that wasn't a complete lie. "She gave me hints," I said. "I saw a…a photograph. I just thought you'd understand. With your job, and everything…"

She said, "I *do* understand. I understand you want answers. I understand how hard it must be with your mother gone, so you can't ever ask her. But none of this has anything to do with *adoption*."

I couldn't tell Allison about the crazy, shaky line that went from Sekhmet to my mother to me. The one that went from Sheut to my mother to me.

Instead, I gave up and asked Allison how work was going. And it turned out, that was the conversation we should have been having all along.

I listened to her answer, about a new push for bipartisan legislation about accessing adoption records in foreign countries. I saw how excited she was to be having an impact, to be making a difference in the lives of children and adults throughout the world.

Suddenly, it felt good to sit there. It felt good to be talking, despite the fact that dozens of topics still felt too dangerous, too raw for us to share.

"Listen to me," Allison finally said. "I sound like a little old woman whose only companion is a cat. I could go on like this for hours."

"I like it," I said, smiling. "I like knowing what's going on in your life."

"But…" Allison said, accurately reading my tone.

"But, I have to get to the office." I stood reluctantly, collecting my purse and keys.

She walked me to the front door. We stood there for a moment, suddenly awkward again. I wanted to hug her, but I didn't know if I should.

"Thank you," I said instead.

"I don't think I helped very much."

"No," I said, protesting her doubt. "You did. A lot."

I stepped outside, into gray twilight. For just a moment, I wondered if James was stirring yet, if he was awake and alone in my apartment.

"Thanks for coming by," Allison said. "For listening."

"We'll do this again soon?" I asked.

She bit her lip, but she nodded. I did hug her then, an awkward, half-body clutch. Before either of us had to figure out anything else to say, I hurried to James's car. I was afraid to look back as I drove away.

21

For once, I made it through an entire shift at the courthouse without a disaster, either imperial or mundane. In fact, my shift was so boring, I almost fell asleep at my desk. Only my constant fear of Angelique policing my work kept me sitting upright, typing away, trudging through the interminable backlog of cases that had been misfiled in the decades before James hired me.

At the end of my shift, I faced a dilemma. James's Prius was parked in the courthouse garage. On the one hand, I could drive it back to his house—taking due care to keep from being followed—and return it to his garage. On the other hand, I could go to my own home, searching once again for parking on the street, and entering my basement apartment ready—hoping?—to find James waiting there. On the third hand (what? Most people—humans or imperials—don't have a third hand? Work with me here...), I could drive the car over to Chris's house.

The third hand won. Not because it was any easier to find parking in his neighborhood—it wasn't. But because I could still hear the scarcely bridled anger in Chris's voice the last time we'd spoken. I could still hear the tortured silences as he digested everything I'd told him, all the details of my research about the auctions at Sotheby's and Christie's and Wellingham's.

I'd done my best to scrape a path toward normalcy with Allison. It was time I devoted at least the same level of energy to doing the same with Chris, the man—the sphinx—who loved me.

As I waited for Chris to answer the doorbell, I barely resisted the urge to run away. It would have been simpler to use my key to enter the house. But I was uncertain of my welcome, and I declined to take that risk.

At least he answered the door quickly, fast enough that I suspected he'd watched me walk up the sidewalk. Clearing the threshold, I moved forward automatically, anticipating our usual kiss of greeting. Chris apparently had the same idea; he leaned forward too.

We both stopped short, though, of actually touching lips. It could have been an accident, a casual miscalculation born of haste and coincidence. There was a split second where I could have laughed and thrown myself into his arms with enough force that there'd be no doubt of my intentions. We could have kissed for real, with the passion we'd shared countless times over the past ten months.

But I missed that chance. And then there was nothing left to do but curl my arms around my belly, my fingers clutching tighter than necessary as I took a deep breath.

"Hungry?" he asked, leading the way back to the kitchen. The question was easy enough. We'd long since grown accustomed to sharing a morning meal—his breakfast and my dinner. "I just finished cooking the bacon. It'll only take a minute to fry up some eggs."

I glanced at the plate on the counter, next to the hot skillet on the stove. Eight crisp pieces of bacon glistened on a bed of white paper towels.

He'd cooked enough for both of us. He'd known I was

coming over, even if I hadn't been sure until I exited the parking garage.

Or maybe he hadn't known. Maybe he'd just hoped and was willing to throw away a few strips of bacon if he'd calculated incorrectly.

I slipped off my jacket, clutching the fabric just to give my hands something to do. Chris's motivation didn't really matter now. The important thing was that I couldn't eat the bacon. I couldn't eat any meat, not when James was taking me to Richardson in less than twelve hours. I didn't even trust a couple of over-easy eggs, unless Chris scrubbed the frying pan first.

My stomach growled, reminding me I'd been skimping on regular meals of late. I forced myself to smile as I said, "I'll just have an apple."

Chris's face tightened. "So James really is back."

I froze. Part of my brain shouted that I should say something, *anything*. Chris was a sphinx. He was the Sun Lion, for Sekhmet's sake. He'd devoted his entire life to protecting vampires. He could hardly fault me for doing my best to protect James.

But I could hear the lie behind those words before I even spoke them. Chris wasn't faulting me for protecting James. He was faulting me for failing to tell him I was protecting James.

The distinction was far from semantics.

My silence stretched out for long enough that Chris had a chance to cross his own arms. He schooled his face to impassivity, and I watched him take a deep breath, hold it for a count of five, then exhale slowly and evenly, exactly the way I'd been taught.

His voice sounded almost conversational when he asked, "Did you sleep with him?"

"No!" My answering shout echoed off the sleek stainless steel of the refrigerator.

Chris waited.

"He's back, yes. He was waiting for me inside my apartment last night."

Where I wouldn't have been, if you'd let me come over here. I thought it. But I didn't say it out loud.

His eyes went to the scabs on my throat.

"It's not James's fault," I said. "I startled him. He bit before he realized it was me."

Chris's eyes narrowed, and I realized I'd elided over the truth. I hadn't clarified that James had attacked me in *his* home, the night *before* he'd come to mine.

Like a guilty teen trying to justify a curfew violation, I stammered on. With each phrase, my words got faster, my voice rising in pitch. "He offered to heal me, to let me drink from him. He tried to make things right. That's why he was there in the first place. He wants to help."

"He wouldn't need to help, if he kept his fangs where they belong."

"You're the one who told me to see him!" Before Chris could deny my words, I scrambled for a clarification he might accept. "You want your New Commission. I was just bringing James into the fold."

"Is that what you're calling it these days?"

I'd never heard Chris's voice drip with sarcasm. For a moment, I thought I'd slap him, but that would be simple melodrama. Instead, I turned to leave.

"Wait!" Chris called, before I made it halfway to the front door.

Sekhmet help me, I stopped. Maybe it was the honest fear I heard beneath Chris's shout. Maybe it was the sudden realization that if I walked out of the townhouse, I was never coming back. Maybe it was the niggling feeling that always struck when I was in Chris's presence, the balance, the harmony, the *rightness* of being with another sphinx, even in the midst of this gut-churning fight.

"Sarah…" Chris said, loading my name with an encyclopedia of pleading. Of apology. Of longing.

I turned slowly. "I told you I didn't sleep with him. I'd never lie to you."

Tension spun out between us like a strand of spider silk. I willed him to hear the honesty beneath my words. I waited for him to accept the truth.

He swallowed hard. And then he sighed, opening fists I hadn't even realized he'd clutched tight.

"I'm sorry," he said. "That wasn't fair," he said. "And I apologize."

It took me a moment, but I found the right response. "Apology accepted."

I almost believed myself.

He waited, and I knew he was giving me a chance to follow through on my inclination, to leave, even though he'd capitulated. I weighed my options. But despite it all, the angry words and the queasy specter of jealousy, I didn't want to walk out that door.

"I've been doing some research," he finally said. "Following up on your leads."

"My leads," I repeated. He relaxed a little, recognizing a truce when he heard one.

"About those auctions. I talked to a few people, called in some debts from my days at *The Banner.* I found out who's behind Lost Soul Enterprises."

"Who?" I asked, even though I already knew he was going to say *Maurice Richardson.*

"Mohammed Apep."

"Not Richardson?" I was shocked.

"Not Richardson," Chris confirmed.

That didn't make sense. When Sekhmet had told me about the Seal, I'd sensed ruthless destruction, a bottomless appetite for power. I'd been certain I was seeing the vampire overlord who'd tyrannized the Empire for generations. "Apep..." I said in disbelief. "Why do I know that name?"

"He's a billionaire recluse who hasn't been seen in public for twenty years."

I made the connection. "The one who makes all those donations?"

"One and the same."

Facts came flooding back to me. Mohammed Apep had made his money in finance, running a hedge fund or a private equity fund or one of those things. A secular Muslim, he'd been born somewhere in the Middle East. His parents had moved to the United States when he was two or three years old. His father had worked as a cobbler; his mother was a seamstress. He'd worked his way through public school, got a scholarship to Harvard, and had become one of the ten wealthiest men in the country before retiring abruptly, almost thirty years ago.

In interview after interview, Apep stated that he could only have achieved his success in a country as generous as the United States. He'd vowed to return the favor, underwriting countless projects in and around DC. He'd financed a replacement roof for the Botanical Garden, stepping in when the federal budget fell short. He'd paid for the restoration of the Ulysses S Grant statue at the foot of the Capitol. He'd overseen the replacement of the dome at the National Gallery of Art, the carousel on the National Mall, and the National Archives display cases for the Constitution and the Declaration of Independence. He'd endowed a chair at American University, a professorship focusing on the history of civilization.

And despite all of those good deeds, no one had seen his face since his retirement. There were countless stories from reporters who'd tried to track him down—Apep was living in Dubai, in Singapore, at an ashram outside of Bangalore. Wherever he was, the checks kept coming—the checks and the special projects to save his adoptive country.

I stared at Chris. "Apep bought the Seal from Wellingham's?"

"According to an old article in *Vanity Fair*, he's been a collector for decades. Revisiting the culture of his people. The Metropolitan offered to build a new gallery for his collection, next to the Temple of Dendur. The Chicago Institute of Art proposed an entire new wing. But the Smithsonian thinks they have the inside track."

"Why?" My mind was still reeling. Mohammed Apep was Lost Soul Enterprises. But Maurice Richardson could still be Mohammed Apep. It wouldn't be the first time the vampire kingpin had masqueraded as a mundane in a position of power.

"Apep gave the Smithsonian the first Egyptian artifact he ever acquired. A faience charm. The Amulet in the Form of Two Deities."

A shiver rippled down my spine. "Which deities?" I asked, too quickly.

Chris met my eyes. "According to online records, Sekhmet is one."

"And the other?"

"Is listed as unknown. 'In the form of a man.' But the head is broken off."

Sheut. I had no way of knowing. No reason to be sure. But even as my mind seized the thought, I knew I was right.

I wanted to see the amulet. I *needed* to see it. If I could touch it, extend my imperial powers into it, I could finally make my yearned-for progress on my search for my father.

I thought back to my childhood visits to the National Mall, to countless school field trips in all the museums. Would I have recognized the significance of an Egyptian charm when I was only a kid? Would Sekhmet have called to me before I had any idea of my true nature?

"Maybe I saw it when I was a kid?"

Chris shook his head. "It's not on display."

I was filled with immediate outrage. How could something

as valuable as a Sekhmet amulet not be on display? Of course, the average mundane curator had no clue how important Sekhmet was to an entire race of secret imperials. Two hidden races—sphinxes *and* vampires. And whatever the hell I was too.

Chris's answer overrode my huff of displeasure. "The Smithsonian owns millions of items, but it only has room to display a fraction of that. Apep's gift only mandated that it be kept available for anthropologists to study, not that it be kept permanently on display."

I sighed. "I'd give anything to see that amulet."

"Anything?" Chris said, with a glint in his eye. "What are you doing tonight?"

It was Saturday. For once I wasn't working. But I'd promised James I'd go with him to Richardson.

I wasn't about to tell Chris I'd made that commitment. Our truce was still too fragile. Instead, I gave him a leery look. "What *am* I doing?"

"How about breaking into the National Museum of Natural History?"

22

I stared at Chris in shock. *I* was the one who was supposed to be impulsive, to act first and think later. He was supposed to be the voice of law and order.

But here he was, without a hint of hesitation, proposing that we break into a federal building.

"You've got to be kidding," I said. At the same time, my hands actually ached at the thought of holding the amulet. I could picture the faience, bright blue glass with darker cobalt-colored creases. Cool to the touch, it would warm to my body heat almost immediately.

My longing for the amulet was like a physical pang. But I retained just enough logic to ask, "Why would you even consider doing that?"

"The Seal," he said.

I glanced at my wrist, at the band of flesh where Sekhmet had displayed a bisected oval. Skeptical, I asked, "The amulet is the Seal?"

He shook his head. "I don't think so. If it was, he wouldn't have bought those recent lots at auction. Or he might have, but he wouldn't have *stopped* after the Wellingham sale."

"They why break into the museum?"

"Apep must have held the amulet. With any luck at all, he left enough of his essence on the charm. We'll be able to follow him, like bloodhounds on an astral trail. We'll use the amulet to track the Seal."

I didn't need much convincing. The thought of holding Sekhmet's amulet made my breath come fast.

"Okay," I said.

"Okay?"

"I'll do it. I'll break into the National Museum of Natural History." Less than two weeks earlier, I'd been locked up in an Eastern Empire cell, and I'd hated every second of my imprisonment. What the hell was I doing, signing up for a possible stay in DC's municipal jail? If we got caught this time, Chris couldn't simply call himself my lawyer and get me off the hook.

But when I closed my eyes, I could imagine the faintly rough surface of the faience amulet, feel its ancient power beneath my fingertips. Shoving aside the thought of living behind bars, I asked, "What do you need me to do?"

"For now? Get some sleep." I started to protest, but Chris overrode me. "You'll need to be at your most alert. Go upstairs. I'm going to pick up a few things."

There was no reason to protest. Not when I was already fighting not to yawn. If anyone could organize an assault on a government building, Chris could.

I headed upstairs and changed into one of the sleep shirts I kept in the bottom drawer of Chris's dresser. I slipped into my side of the bed, curling up with my head on my pillow. I managed to keep myself from reaching behind me, stretching to feel the absent warmth of Chris's body.

When I slept, I dreamed of Sekhmet and lions and a cave. But every time I looked at my wrist, it was bare.

23

E ight hours later, I stood behind a family of four, waiting my turn to pass through a metal detector to gain access to the National Museum of Natural History. It took a conscious effort not to scratch my temple, where a fine woven mesh anchored a stringy-haired black wig that made my entire scalp sweat. I had to remind myself not to scratch my prosthetic nose either. Instead, I tried to content myself by pushing my heavy-framed black eyeglasses higher on the bridge of that rather impressive nose. At the same time, I ground my false teeth together, trying to adjust to the new bite that shoved my lower jaw forward enough to ache.

I felt as if a spotlight was focused on my forehead, directing every security guard in the museum to pay special attention to my intentionally slouched shoulders. I tried to mimic Chris who stood behind me, chomping on a wad of pink bubble gum, utterly nonchalant as he flipped through screen after screen on his phone.

When we finally cleared the checkpoint, I shuffled into the museum's central atrium. A massive elephant stood above me, head lifted toward a gigantic dome. The hall of mammals stood to my left. Dinosaurs roamed to my right. I waited for Chris to take the lead, and we headed toward a wide stone staircase on the far side of the chamber.

Tourists were heading upstairs, most of them chattering about the Hope Diamond and other bejeweled treasures. Chris, though, shuffled *down* the steps, taking his time as we made our way to the basement.

The hallways beneath the main floor were utilitarian. Banged up white walls channeled us toward a first aid station, lost and found, and the maintenance department.

If I hadn't been watching Chris with the eagle eyes of... well... the eagle displayed in the Birds of the World exhibit on the first floor, I would have missed his hand gliding into the front right pocket of his ragged jeans. I followed suit, reaching for my own plastic identity card.

I slipped the blue-and-gold lanyard around my neck, casually making sure my stark-eyed photograph faced my chest. A couple of hours earlier, Chris had fashioned the cards in the privacy of his home office. The multi-rayed sun matched the real ID he'd commandeered from Shannon Masterson, the housemate of a boyfriend of a sister of the sphinx who taught second grade in the Den.

Shannon worked as an entomologist in the live butterfly exhibit on the second floor. I could only imagine the story Chris had concocted to, um, borrow her credentials. Or maybe he hadn't lied to her face. Maybe he'd simply ordered his sphinx to somehow dose Shannon's Saturday brunch Bloody Mary.

I didn't want to know the details. I'd been sleeping, of course, living out my strangely time-shifted life. All I knew was that my ID card had still been warm when Chris pressed it into my palm. My fake name was printed in a font that resembled the one on Shannon's card. The holographic shimmer of the real ID was only simulated with colored printing on my jury-rigged duplicate.

With any luck, no one would get close enough to detect the difference.

Chris slouched with affected disinterest, but nothing could change the watchful dart of his eyes as we passed multiple doorways. He was counting in his head, keeping track of the order, measuring the path he'd mapped earlier that day.

One right turn, into another dingy corridor. A left. Another right.

We stood in a locker room. Small metal cabinets lined the walls, pressed metal slats looking like disapproving mouths. Chris and I didn't have anything to lock away, though. We hurried past the lockers to the large supply closet at the far end of the hall.

We'd timed our arrival well. The daytime shift of janitors was still out working. The night shift hadn't arrived yet. Afternoon breaks were finished.

Chris wasted no time donning a bright blue service apron. He passed one to me, and I slipped it over my head, almost catching the collar on my wig. I quickly pocketed the shop rags he passed me, along with a spray bottle of sanitizer.

I'd read somewhere that anyone could get past any door, if they only held a clipboard and looked official. Well, no one questioned a janitor with an over-size yellow trashcan on wheels.

Not even when the janitor in question took the wrong hallway and ended up at a dead end in front of the museum's lost and found office. Chris muttered as we backtracked through the corridors.

He shouldn't have gotten lost. He'd explored this entire floor earlier in the day, pretending to be an unlucky tourist tracking down his lost cell phone, hoping against hope that a good Samaritan had turned in the device.

But the hallways were tangled—and nondescript—enough that Chris lost his way a second time. We ended up at an elevator bank that only went to the museum's first and second floor. Ultimately, we were forced to work the basement like a labyrinth, consistently taking left turns in the tangle of hallways until we found the service elevators that went all the way up to four.

In the privacy of that elevator, I longed to review our strategy. But I knew that privacy was merely an illusion. The elevators were equipped with security cameras, unblinking eyes that recorded my every breath for posterity. I pretended to find a hangnail fascinating, worrying at my cuticles until the heavy doors opened onto the fourth floor.

The museum's public space presented one view to visitors—broad granite and glass hallways filled with the treasure of a nation. The maintenance areas in the basement presented another view—utilitarian anonymity for day-to-day functioning of the institution.

The fourth floor displayed yet another side of the museum. The hall was filled with rank after rank of compact shelving. Each ceiling-high unit was labeled with an arcane combination of letters and numbers, the labels centered above the heavy ship's wheel that let users maneuver shelves along well-worn metal tracks.

My order-seeking mind immediately grappled for meaning in the coded letters and numbers. I needed more information, though. I had to know what items were filed on the shelves behind the neat labels. Casting a quick glance up and down the hall to make sure Chris and I were alone, I darted into an opening in the stacks.

Fumbling in a pocket of my work apron, I found a pair of blue nitrile gloves. Slipping them on to conceal my fingerprints, I studied the boxes on the shelves. Each was equipped with a handle, like a shallow dresser drawer. A label above each handle held an alphanumeric code, close kin to the one on the shelving unit.

Conscious of Chris waiting in the main corridor, I eased open a drawer. And I barely caught a strangled gasp of surprise against the back of my throat.

The drawer was filled with stag beetles, each insect the

length of my palm. They had arched legs and wicked antlers, and their cupped wings looked like iridescent shells in the dim light.

They weren't moving. I knew they weren't alive. But my wig started itching with renewed vigor, and I could feel sweat pool between my fake nose and my trembling upper lip.

All right, then. EN on the labels must mean Entomology. I shoved the drawer closed and grabbed hold of my yellow trash-can, moving quickly enough that Chris had to lengthen his stride to match mine.

EN was Entomology. HE was Herbarium—countless folders of dried plants, each with a legend showing who had collected the item, and where, and when.

The herbarium stretched on for what seemed like acres. When we finally reached a fork in the corridors, Chris suggested that he go to the left and I go to the right. We'd been lucky so far, not running into anyone else. We hoped that the real janito-rial staff didn't serve the fourth floor on Saturdays, but we had no way of knowing for sure.

We agreed to text each other, whoever found the ancient Egyptian relics first.

After the herbarium, I discovered an assortment of blown eggs, each nestled in fine cotton wool. There were hundreds of wolf skulls, every one accompanied by a map that indicated where the specimen had been collected. I found hundreds of trilobite fossils, each deceptively heavy in its cushioned box.

The range of artifacts was stunning. The number of exam-ples within each category was mind-numbing. My order-craving self longed to study each record, to determine the similarities and differences between the items.

But I wasn't roaming the museum as a continuing education student. I was searching for one specific item. And I didn't have a lot longer. Chris's entire plan hinged on our leaving the museum with the general population of visitors, by 5:30 at the latest.

Just as I was giving up faith, my phone buzzed in my pocket. I glanced down to see a cryptic notation from Chris: N27.

I was about to text back a question, when I realized he was giving me coordinates. Leaving my camouflaging trashcan behind for speed, I hurried to the twenty-seventh rank of shelves on the north side of the building.

Sure enough, Chris's yellow can sat in the corridor. I found him halfway down a row of shelves. AN said the labels. Anthropology?

"Did you find it?" I asked, my voice breathier than my quick trot across the floor could justify.

"Not yet," he said. "But I think I'm close. Everything in this row is made of glass."

I joined him, pulling out drawers at random. There were blown glass baubles, the type of thing that would hang on a chandelier. *Murano*, said the card inside the box. Date: 1748 CE.

Chris moved down the aisle, selecting another gliding drawer, this one nearly a foot deep. He was rewarded with a jute-wrapped bottle, a container that could have been the model for countless bottles of Chianti. *Firenze*, said the card. Date: c. 1432 CE. We were heading in the right direction.

I took three long steps, bending down to open yet another drawer. This one housed three tiny vials, each one nearly opaque with opalescence. *Roma*, proclaimed the card. Date: c. 300 BCE.

Another stride back into history. A drawer at waist level, chosen at random. A bright blue ibis, the size of my palm. *Luxor*, said the card. Date: c. 1100 BCE.

Chris opened the next drawer, the one below. I felt him catch his breath at the same time I did. A miniature mummified cat gleamed back at us, each turn of linen bandage picked out in fine blue-green glass. *Heliopolis*. C. 2500 BCE.

I barely waited for him to slide the drawer home before I leaped for the next one. A charm in the shape of Horus, the falcon-headed god. The next was Anubis, the jackal.

My fingers trembled in front of the lowest drawer. I could sense this was our goal. It contained the treasure we'd risked so much to find. The roof of my mouth buzzed, and my fingertips tingled, as if I were already in communion with Mother Sekhmet.

I offered up a silent prayer as my fingers wrapped around the handle. I glanced at Chris and read the eager anticipation on his face, crystal clear despite his own wig and fake teeth.

Holding my breath, I slid the drawer open.

It was empty.

24

"No!" Chris moaned, as we both stared at the white cotton batting.

But my body knew more than my mind. My fingers understood that the amulet couldn't be missing. The treasure couldn't be gone.

I opened the drawer above the empty one, double-checking one more time. Jackal-headed Anubis laughed at me.

I opened the drawer below to find an open-mouthed hippo.

My fingers burned. I couldn't be wrong. I grabbed the handle to the left of the empty drawer and yanked hard. A spray of iridescent fragments glinted from their cushioned bed, some long-shattered vessel.

The drawer on the right. In my vision, it glowed with the red of sunset. The red of blood. I caught my breath as I reached toward it. The drawer glided on silent casters.

The amulet glowed from its pure-white bed, ancient blue glass seeming to shine from within.

Sekhmet stood on the left. Her figure was carved with soft curves, the lines of her linen gown creased with a darker blue. Her head was shaped like a lioness, the ears brought out in indigo-rimmed relief. Her eyeteeth glinted above her mysteriously smiling lips.

The other figure was broken off at the neck. It was a man; that much was apparent from his short linen garment, from the solid legs that held him erect. But whether his head was shaped like a mortal man, or a desert creature, or some mythical, chimeric beast, I couldn't begin to guess.

I stripped off my nitrile glove, baring the fingers of my right hand. As I reached for the amulet, Chris's grip closed on my shoulder. But he must have felt something—my determination, or the wild electricity jangling through my body from the amulet itself. He dropped his hand and let me touch the charm.

As I had imagined, the faience glass was cool against my palm. As soon as my fingers wrapped around the object, though, it began to warm.

The taste of lemons sprayed across the back of my throat. The fingers of my left hand automatically moved to touch my hematite bracelet, to bolster my bond with Mother Sekhmet through my insignia.

But my bracelet was still in the custody of the Eastern Empire court. My finger ached, too, where my coral ring was missing. I clutched the amulet tighter.

I expected to feel Sekhmet's touch, her dynamic presence stealing over my brain. I didn't know if she would come to me in human form, or in her lion shape, or somewhere in between. I wasn't sure if I'd find her at home with her cubs, or striding through bloody battle. But wherever she appeared, however she was formed, she was my mother and I longed to greet her.

But Sekhmet didn't come to me.

Instead, I slipped through shadows. The hot desert sun was behind me. My body was chilled, as if I'd slipped behind a massive granite wall to escape a punishing summer heat.

I blinked hard, but my eyes couldn't parse the darkness. A tiny part of my mind warned that I should be frightened.

Anything could come out of the shadows. Anything could rise from the abyss.

I wasn't afraid, though. I was still. Calm. I was cradled in a moment of quiet, a minute-hour-day-life outside the chaos of the everyday world.

Standing in the darkness, isolated from anything I'd ever known before, I could not feel my arms. My hands were floating...somewhere, separate and apart from me, from sensation. My legs were numb.

But my feet were still anchored, steady against solid stone. And as I swayed gently in the darkness, something brushed my ankles.

My eyes were still useless in this foreign space, but I somehow sensed a Presence. Not with my eyes, not with my ears, not with my tongue or nose or fingers.

I *knew* the Presence in a way I'd never known anything else before. My heartbeat matched it. Slow and sinuous, my body melded to the thing that wrapped around my legs. It pulsed around me, in me, through me. It became me.

Or I became it.

Or I had always been it.

I didn't know. I couldn't say. I didn't have the words. But I *was* the serpent that twined around my human body, and it *was* me.

Come, it said, or it thought, or it vibrated the cells in my body to make me understand. I understood its longing, its hunger, its desire. It wanted my company. It wanted to share its whole existence with me.

I started to follow. I tasted a new world with the whorls of my fingerprints. I heard a symphony of new colors. I smelled a cascade of images, all the world that could be mine, all the power I could possess.

There was a wildness in the serpent, a glory and a wholeness and a separateness I'd never imagined before. I could transform.

I could be more than a woman, more than a sphinx, more than whatever imperial form I'd struggled to comprehend.

All I had to do was leave behind the world I knew.

All I had to do was tumble into the maelstrom, the chaos, the swirling destruction that could never be placed into order.

All I had to do was leave myself behind forever.

I wanted to go. I was terrified to go. I refused to go—not now, not without bidding farewell to everyone I knew, to Chris and to James and to Allison, too.

As I hesitated, a light grew in the distance. I could see it with my eyes, the way I'd seen a million lights before. It glowed red as sunset. Red as blood.

It grew closer, warmer, somehow more solid. And the part of me that wasn't me, the part of me that was the serpent recognized the life force of the other.

Now there was a distance. I wasn't part of the serpent any longer. I could feel it, with my flesh and with that strange other sense, the sense of *knowing* beyond my five normal senses. I knew it, but I was separate from it.

I felt it greet the other. I felt it take the light. Take the light and give the darkness and merge and split and join together again.

The light was Mother Sekhmet. I knew that now. I'd always known it.

And the serpent was Sheut. Sheut was primal and unknowing and unknowable. Sheut came from a time before words, a time before humanity, a time lost forever.

But Sekhmet's carmine glow spread over me. And Sheut's shadows flowed beneath me. And I was known. I was safe. I was loved.

25

C old.
       Absolute, unfathomable cold.

I shuddered, a massive trembling that quaked from the crown of my head to the curl of my toes. My teeth started to chatter so hard I thought my jaw would break.

I opened my eyes. When had I closed my eyes? I licked my lips. When had my throat gone dry? I tried to stand, to straighten my legs, to throw my shoulders back from their fetal curve.

"Sarah," Chris said, and the sound of my name pulled me back to the present. I knelt on a tile floor. Chris crouched beside me.

"Sarah," Chris said again. We were huddling in an aisle in the fourth-floor archives of the National Museum of Natural History. My hand was splayed across an empty field of cotton wool.

I stretched my fingers, making a wordless sound. Somehow, Chris understood me. He unfolded his own fingers, revealing Sekhmet and Sheut.

We'd found the amulet. And finding it, we'd failed.

Like naive children, Chris and I had thought we could

follow the amulet's power to the Seal. We'd treated it like a lark, a jaunt in the park.

But the amulet wasn't a trinket, to be treated like a flashlight in the night. We would never control it. The raw essence of Sekhmet and Sheut was powerful beyond anything we'd imagined. We would never bend it to our will.

By the same token, though, we couldn't return it to its cotton-lined bed. It was a living thing. It could never be imprisoned in the dusty archives of a museum.

I grabbed the amulet before Chris could return it to its drawer.

"We have to go, Sarah."

Clutching the charm, I tried to stand.

"No," he said. "You have to leave it."

I pulled away from his solicitous hand.

"It's not safe," he said. "We have to go out the main door, past all those guards."

I cradled the amulet close to my heart.

Chris swore, shooting a glance at his wristwatch. I caught a glimpse of his insignia, the hematite and coral worked into the band. He was the Sun Lion. He had the emblems of his power as sphinx. He was unbroken, and yet he didn't understand.

"Sarah—"

"No." I put all my meager strength into the word, enough power that shadows surged across the periphery of my vision. Those weren't Sheut shadows, though. They weren't mysterious or comforting. They were a sign that my body was too weak, that I was about to faint.

Chris's lips twisted into a frown, but he didn't try to argue any longer. Instead, he stood, stripping off his blue apron as he straightened his legs. He reached for my arm and hauled me upright, somehow holding me steady as he worked my apron over my head.

I held the amulet fast, which couldn't have made things easy. I didn't care.

"Come on," he said, hurrying me down the aisle to the main corridor. When I stumbled, he caught me with a rough grip on my biceps. I wasn't about to use my own hands to break my fall.

"Give that thing to me," he said.

"No!" That seemed to be the only word I knew.

"I'll give it back," he said. "We just have to get out of—"

"No," I repeated.

"Fine!" he snapped. "Put it in your pocket, though. You can't walk out of here holding it in plain view."

I shoved my hand in my pocket, but I wouldn't let go of the glass. Chris duck-walked me to the yellow trashcan he'd left by the entrance to the Anthropology archives. He tossed our aprons into the plastic-lined maw and planted my left hand on the rim. "Come on."

We pushed the can together. Chris moved us forward, while I shuffled like a patient in rehab. Each step, though, brought more strength to my spine. Every rank of shelves we passed cleared my head.

Bathrooms were located near the elevator. Chris pushed the trashcan into the men's room, shoving hard enough that the door swung closed behind it. He slipped an arm around my waist, taking most of my weight as he pounded the button to call the elevator.

As the doors closed behind us, I rubbed my thumb against the amulet in my pocket. I could feel the potential there, the vast stores of energy I had sampled mere minutes before.

Sekhmet.

Sheut.

We reached the main floor, and Chris half-led, half-carried me out of the elevator. An announcement was squawking overhead: The museum was closing in five minutes. We stumbled past the elephant, past the mammals, past the ancient dinosaurs.

A security guard stepped forward, his face creased with concern. "May I help you, sir?"

Chris shook his head. "No, thanks," he said. "She just needs some fresh air."

The guard looked doubtful, but he led us to the closest door, one marked *Entrance Only.* He pushed hard on the brass handle, helping us to pass outside.

Chris slipped one arm around my waist, guiding me down the interminable flight of steps. My feet dragged, my toes catching on the smooth planks of granite. It took forever to reach the sidewalk and even longer to gain a row of parked vehicles.

The breeze shifted, carrying the scent of cooking meat. We stood in front of a long line of food trucks, specializing in everything from tacos to Thai to mouth-watering kabobs.

Chris dragged us toward the closest truck, barking out an order for lamb on a skewer. I mewed a protest, and he scowled, but he quickly changed his order to falafel.

He handed over his money and collected the fried chickpeas, along with a monster-size Coca-Cola. We staggered to a bench, and he twisted the cap off the bottle, ordering me to take a drink. I started to shake my head, but my throat was suddenly raging with thirst. I downed a quarter of the bottle without coming up for air.

As I drank, Chris tore a ball of falafel in half. He blew on the steaming food to cool it, testing it against his lower lip like a father protecting his toddler. He passed it to me, and I barely took the time to chew before I swallowed.

Another bite, and I felt my body stabilize. A third, and I could sit up on my own. By the time I finished the falafel, and its pita wrap, and every bite of the accompanying lettuce and tomato, I was feeling close to human.

But I wasn't human. I'd never been human. Once and for all, the amulet hidden in my pocket had made that perfectly clear.

26

I f Chris ever decided to give up his Sun Lion gig, he could get a great job as a general caretaker. After he finished feeding me falafel, he called an Uber. He helped me into the back seat, holding his hand over my head to keep me from bumping against the doorframe.

I didn't realize we were heading to my place until the car pulled up in front of my apartment. "I thought—" I started to say.

"You'll sleep better in your own bed."

I wasn't sure about that. Chris's bed was pretty damn comfortable. But I was far too exhausted to argue.

Instead, I concentrated on maneuvering down the stairs, carefully placing one foot after the other. Chris hovered by my side, his fingers poised near my elbow as if he could pluck me to safety with the strength of his thumb and forefinger alone.

Chris used his own key to let us in. It wasn't until the door swung open that I had a premonition. Or maybe my common sense finally kicked in.

James stood just inside the front door, feet planted, eyes narrowed. "What the hell did you do to her?" he snarled as Chris crossed the threshold.

Chris stepped in front of me, as if I had something to fear from the vampire in my home. "Get back, Morton."

James expressed his fangs with an audible pop. Chris squared up, equally ready to take or throw a punch.

"Stop!" I shouted. "Both of you!" I closed my hand over the amulet in my pocket, praying to Sekhmet for the strength to stay on my feet.

"You," I said to James. "Stand down. Chris didn't do anything to me."

James gave an ostentatious sniff, as if he could smell magic on me. I straightened my spine, hoping to give him nothing more to comment on than fried chickpea batter and an extra helping of tzatziki.

Clearly, James remained unconvinced. I straightened my spine and said, "Chris was just seeing me home. I put too much energy into a working this evening. He grounded me. I'm fine."

"You aren't fine," Chris said. "You need to sleep." He turned a pointed glance on James. "So I'm sure you're leaving now."

Predictably, James bristled. "Sarah and I have an appointment."

"Crap," I said. I'd put James off so I could visit Allison, but I'd promised him we could meet on Saturday. I turned to Chris. "We're going to Richardson's tonight."

"Absolutely not," he said. "You're in no shape to walk across the room, much less drop in on the most heinous vampire in the city."

I actually felt my heels dig into the carpet. "Do *not* tell me what I can and cannot do."

"Sarah, be reasonable! You just—"

"I just committed a felony on federal property. I just bluffed my way past dozens of security guards, carrying contraband that could have me imprisoned for years. I just ate a perfectly restorative dinner, and I'm feeling fine."

I wasn't, not entirely. I was drawing on a tiny filament of

energy, a thread of electric anticipation that sizzled like a fuse inside my brain. At least this wasn't the trigger to forbidden *agriotis*. It was something new, something different. It must have been planted inside my skull when Sheut possessed my body.

I suspected I would crash hard after I'd exploited this pool. But I still had the capacity of diving deep for a few hours more.

Chris gave me a dirty look, and I realized he was embarrassed to have James hear about our exploits. But he said, "If you have to see Richardson, then I'll come too."

"No," James said, before I could begin to muster a response.

"I'm the Sun Lion—"

"I'm well aware of your title," James said, somehow giving the impression that he was plucking a speck of lint off his lapel, even though he didn't move an inch.

"Then you're well aware of the fact that the Den is responsible for vampires throughout the Eastern Empire. For *every* vampire. And even if you think you've somehow declared yourself exempt from oversight with your disappearing tricks and your abdication of responsibility as Director of Security for the Night Court, Maurice Richardson is still very much under our control."

"Vampires aren't *controlled* by sphinxes," James said stiffly. "At least those of us who aren't bound by your goddamn Ancient Commission."

"Speaking of which—" Chris began, but I cut him off before he could raise the specter of his New Commission.

"Excuse me!" I said sharply. "Do I have to remind you two that you're standing in *my* living room? I'm the one who makes the rules here."

Chris ignored my declaration. "No time like the present," he said pointedly—a not-too-subtle command to broach the subject of the New Commission.

"We don't *have* time," I snapped. "Not right now."

James looked conflicted. Obviously, he was winning the battle with Chris. I was agreeing to visit Richardson. But he had to be intrigued by the broad hints Chris was dropping. James had to question what the Den—or, at least, the Sun Lion—was planning for all vampire-kind.

I could stand up to the sparring Chris and James. I would manage the visit to Richardson. But I couldn't fathom telling James about the New Commission. Not that night. Maybe not ever.

I took a step toward Chris, determined to stop him in his tracks. At the last possible second, I softened my voice from the harsh command I'd tested in my head. "Go," I said.

"But—"

"James wouldn't take me there if it wasn't safe."

Chris wasn't buying it. "Until a week ago, James wanted your life in exchange for DuBois's."

Well, that put the truth out there, in rock-hard black and white.

Chris pressed his advantage. "Take a look in the mirror, Sarah. You'll have a scar forever from James's idea of safety."

I barely resisted the urge to raise my fingers to my throat. I already knew what I'd feel—a pair of scabs where James had bitten me. But he hadn't meant to hurt me. And he was my only link to Richardson.

My brain knew that Maurice Richardson hadn't bought the auction lots of Egyptian artifacts. Mohammed Apep had. Chris had told me that.

But my heart wasn't ready to give up on the notion that Richardson had Sekhmet's Seal. He was too embedded in every shadowy deal that took place in the Eastern Empire. Maybe he *was* the reclusive Apep. Maybe he'd spirited the Seal from Apep's collection.

Maybe I was absolutely, stone-cold wrong. But I wouldn't put anything past Maurice Richardson. And I couldn't hold back if there was a hint, a chance, even the vaguest suspicion that I could execute my goddess's order by following James to Richardson's camp.

I cupped Chris's jaw with my palm. The line of his flesh was different from the familiar feel embedded in my memory. He still wore the costume he'd donned for the museum's security cameras.

I still wore mine.

I pulled my hand away and stripped off my wig. "Go," I said again. "James will keep me safe."

He eyed the vampire, clearly doubting James's ability to protect me. "At least tell me where you're going."

"South East DC," James said promptly, as if an entire quadrant of the city was enough of an answer.

"Can I get an address?"

"No."

Chris didn't want to leave. He didn't want to trust James. But he was man enough, *sphinx* enough, to let me determine my own fate. After a long, silent moment, he nodded toward my pocket, toward the amulet hidden from the light of day. "Do you want me to take that?"

I shook my head. "I've got it."

He hesitated for a moment longer, but then he stalked out the door.

I was walking a tightrope. There were only so many times I could push Chris to his limits. Only so many times I could send him away, without regard for the emotions that flowed beneath his calm, orderly sphinx exterior.

But I had my limits too. I needed to keep my word. I'd promised James, and I couldn't go back on that now.

I waited until the door closed before I looked down at my wig. "Give me a minute, okay?" I said to James. He nodded as I ran my hand through my sweat-dampened hair.

Back in my bedroom, I peeled off the prosthetic nose. I reached into my mouth and snapped free the false teeth that had twisted my jaw. I folded the disguise into a tight bundle. I'd have to discard it outside the apartment, somewhere that wouldn't incriminate me if it were found.

Speaking of incrimination…

I pulled the amulet out of my pocket. What the hell was I going to do with it? I couldn't take it with me, not to Richardson's lair.

I pulled open the top drawer of my dresser. The sensation felt strangely familiar, and I realized that I'd opened and closed hundreds of drawers that afternoon, studying the museum's holdings.

In the end, I buried the amulet in a pair of socks, plain white anklets that I tucked into a corner of the drawer. My fingers tingled as I shut them away, and I wondered if I could harness the amulet's inherent power to give it added protection.

But even I knew it was too soon to call on my magic again. I couldn't risk another conversation with Sekhmet and Sheut. I couldn't chance going too far, too deep, and never finding my way home again.

Rubbing my hands against my ragged jeans, I headed to my bathroom. I ran my fingers through my hair, massaging my scalp from the nape of my neck to my forehead. I washed my face with freezing water and brushed my teeth, twice for good measure. I pulled my hair up into a high ponytail.

I considered changing clothes, but there was no need. No vampire would give a damn about my sartorial flair. Better that I keep wearing my comfortable clothes. Clothes I could move in, if the occasion required. Clothes I could fight in.

I raised my chin and opened my bedroom door. James sat on my couch, patient as a statue. I tried not to squirm as he surveyed my appearance.

"All right." I said. "Let's do this."

I turned the deadbolt as we left, pretending that would be enough to keep the amulet safe from discovery forever. Or at least until I was through confronting Maurice Richardson.

27

I expected James to lead me to his Mercedes, to the car that had always seemed to express his calm sophistication and his iron sense of control.

Instead, he took me to a broken-down Ford Fiesta. The car had probably been red at some point in its life, but now it was rust-colored. Or maybe it simply was all rust. It took three tries to start, and from the underfed-Doberman growl of its engine, a tune-up was long past due.

"Where in South East are we going?" I asked as James pulled into traffic.

He ignored me. Or maybe he couldn't hear me over the engine's roar.

In any case, it didn't take long for us to reach our destination. James drove past Nationals Stadium, the ballpark dark after an afternoon game. The nightlife at nearby bars and restaurants was bustling, though. Customers and music alike spilled out into the street.

We left the revelry behind and crossed the Anacostia River. On the far shore, we entered a different city—one that still called itself DC but played by a different set of rules. Irons bars covered the windows and doors of the narrow townhouses. At

least one home in every block was boarded up, graffiti splat-
tering the plywood.

James turned onto a narrow street. The shell of a car rusted
on the corner, all four tires stripped away. A fire hydrant leaked
into the road, leaving a wet streak that looked like blood. The
streetlamp in the middle of the block was dark, the globe
around its broken bulb shattered into jagged teeth.

The Fiesta looked perfectly at home when James maneuvered into a parking space. I winced as the tires crunched over a
glass bottle that had been hidden in the dark.

"Let's go," he said.

He led the way up the steps of a sagging rowhouse. Its tiny
patch of lawn had long since turned to dust. The front porch
was filled with a dilapidated couch and the stench of mildew.

I almost missed the vampire lurking in the shadows.

It was the foot soldier who'd attacked me at the courthouse.
He didn't seem aware of the fact that he'd lost his shirt. His ribs
stood out like fenceposts, the slats made starker by the loose skin
that dripped from his collarbones. His arms were wasted twigs,
ending in broad, flat fingers.

"Jimmy," he croaked to James, stirring himself to stand. I
felt like I needed a shower after he studied my body, starting and
ending with the scabs on my neck. "Got yerself a feeder?"

James didn't respond—not to the nickname, and not to the
crude word for a Source. Instead, he tapped a number into the
keypad that took the place of a lock on the door—the first sign
that the house we were entering was different from the others on
the block.

"C'mon, Chief," the vampire whined. "Give us a taste,
yeah?" He licked his chapped lips. "Just a sip. I'll be careful. No
sloppy seconds for Jimmy."

James might have been deaf, for all his reaction to the plea.
Something whined inside the door—or maybe that was the
other vampire, realizing he was going to be left high and dry.
The door creaked open.

James stepped in first. That lapse of courtesy set my nerves a-jangle. His action meant he worried more about what waited inside the house than he did the lackey on the front porch.

I swallowed hard and followed him. In my mind, I recited all the reasons James couldn't want to hurt me now.

He could have drunk his revenge months ago.

He could have drained me dry in the foyer of his house, just the other night.

He didn't have to send the Bitcoin phone; he could have left me—and the courthouse—to our fates.

He could have executed me in the privacy of my own home.

Nevertheless, my mind flashed on the wall of weapons in the Old Library far beneath Judge Finch's courtroom. I'd give a month's salary for any one of those blades. Hell, I'd easily drop my next paycheck for a single length of silver chain.

I'd sworn off *agriotis*. I'd promised I would never again access a sphinx's supreme speed, the lightning perception that could turn me into a murdering machine. But in that moment, on that porch, staring at James's tautly muscled back and bracing myself to enter Maurice Richardson's lair, I shoved my senses toward my only superpower.

I felt the edge, as if I were a blindfolded child pushing a toe past the drop-off of a curb. I knew it was there. I sensed the danger.

But I couldn't reach the other side. After a day of short sleep, after the tension of breaking into the museum, after my wild ride through the darkness with Sheut, I was exhausted. I didn't have the strength, the raw energy to convert my terror into rage. I couldn't use my *agriotis*, even if I hadn't made a vow. Even if I were willing to forfeit a little more of my soul.

I followed James into the room.

And I almost laughed when I saw the interior. The rowhouse was narrow, no more than fifteen feet across. Just inside the front door, stairs launched upstairs, disappearing in shadows. Richardson was nowhere in sight.

The ground floor consisted of three rooms. In better times, they'd probably been a parlor, a dining room, and a kitchen. Now, they were stripped of conventional furniture. Even the stove and refrigerator had been ripped out, pipes inexpertly capped at awkward angles.

Of course the kitchen was bare. Vampires didn't need kitchens.

But apparently vampires needed computers. Two dozen of them, balanced on uneven tables and plugged into grimy surge suppressors. In front of each screen sat a vampire, fingers poised over clacking keyboards.

Each man—and they were all male—was mesmerized by his screen. From across the room, I could make out swiftly flowing columns of numbers. A couple of screens sported horizontal rivers of data instead, ticker tapes reeling by.

Like fishermen plucking trout from a river, the vampires typed into their keyboards, slamming in letters and numbers, trying to beat some unseen clock. Every one of them was singularly focused, apparently oblivious to James or me or the world outside the rowhouse front door.

"What are they doing?" I finally asked, barely voicing the words.

James answered in his normal voice, which seemed like he was shouting. "Tracking Richardson's investments. Trading mutual funds. Stocks. Bonds. That one's following Bitcoin." He nodded toward a vampire in the middle of the devastated kitchen.

So that was the secret to the million-dollar account. "You got tips from him?"

James bit off his humorless laugh. "I got tips from all of them. I've skimmed more money in the past six months then I've earned in the rest of my life combined."

He wasn't boasting. He was simply stating a fact.

"And those guys?" I asked, taking in the entire boiler room operation. "Are they skimming too?"

"They're too busy searching for trends. Companies filing bankruptcy. Companies bringing innovations to market."

A tiny piece of a jigsaw puzzle slipped into place. "So the attack on the courthouse…"

"Part intelligence work," James said. "To find vulnerable companies in the mundane records, insider trading at its finest. But part rearguard action, too, to keep the imperial court from interfering here."

I stared at the mesmerized men. Not one had shifted in his chair—only their fingers moved, typing furiously. Their fingers and their eyes, studying the screens, scanning, scanning, scanning. "How long do they sit there?" I whispered.

Again, James replied at his usual volume. "From sunset to sunrise. Richardson used to keep them working an hour after dawn, but they made too many mistakes. The extra hour of trading resulted in lower income."

"What keeps them there?"

James looked at me as if I were insane. Or maybe just very naive. "They're Impressed."

I squeaked my surprise. "All of them?"

James's voice was grim. "Every last one."

I'd known Richardson had no qualms about Impressing vampires. He'd done it to James, decades ago. Technically, it wasn't even a crime. Vampires did it to other vampires, and if anyone took exception, they could fight it out amongst themselves. The Eastern Empire wouldn't enforce the situation.

"But the guy outside… Is he supposed to be in here?"

James scowled. "He flunked out."

"What does that mean?"

"Even Impressed, he couldn't make a decent trade. He lost more for Richardson in a month then all the other traders combined."

"Then why is he allowed to stick around?"

"He keeps the stock in line."

"Stocks?"

James shook his head. "Stock. Singular. Livestock." He gestured toward the stairs.

I had no idea what waited at the top of those steps. I was reasonably sure it wasn't Richardson—not with James speaking at full volume, disclosing the kingpin's secrets. Unless this was all an elaborate ploy to turn me over to the most heinous criminal the Eastern Empire had ever known.

I shook my head and said, "Just tell me."

James ignored me and moved into the darkness.

I could stay with the traders—with the charming possibility that the guy on the porch might decide to take a break inside the house—or I could follow James to the second floor.

Rock, meet hard place.

I climbed.

The air was stifling upstairs, as if it hadn't stirred for centuries. A bathroom was carved into the space at the top of the stairs, but like the kitchen below, it had been gutted. A stained mattress lay where a bathtub used to rest. A pile of rags rested beneath the capped off faucet.

As I made the turn around the banister, ready to follow James down the hall, the rags moved.

A face peered out at me. Flat eyes stared without blinking, pupils dilated wide in the almost total darkness. The nose had been broken at least twice. Thin lips stretched over jagged teeth, with a single fang jutting off at an unlikely angle.

The woman—because that's what she was, or had been—reached toward me with a wrist like parchment over bone. Her throat worked, but she couldn't manage words. Instead, she hissed, long and low, like a tire crushed to death in a vise.

I backed away, only to find myself in front of another door. Another mattress. Another wasted, ruined vampire.

My legs were shaking. My knees threatened to buckle, reporting that they'd done enough work for one day and had absolutely no reason to carry me any farther.

But James waited at the end of the hall. I had to reach James. He was the only reason I made it to the last door.

"What are they doing here?" I asked, my voice a quaking whisper.

"They're livestock. They feed on humans. And the Impressed feed on them."

"They aren't Impressed?" I whirled to look back at the woman in the bathroom, but she'd disappeared into her pile of rags.

James shook his head, a single tight gesture.

"Then what in the name of Sekhmet keeps them there?"

"Where else would they go?"

"They have to have family. Friends."

"Richardson chooses carefully. No one will ever miss these women." He took a step back, gesturing so that I had to look inside the last room. "Girls," he said, correcting himself.

A child slept on the mattress there. Her eyes were sunken. Her lips were chapped. Her dark hair lay in tangles, but I could still make out her youth, the obvious beauty she'd enjoyed before she Turned. If I had to guess, I'd say she was thirteen. Maybe, possibly sixteen, but only if she was a late bloomer.

My gorge rose as I stared at her, at her nest of filthy rags, at her jagged, broken fingernails. I whirled, thinking I'd return to the bathroom, but there was no toilet there, no sink. I made it to the corner of the hall instead, emptying my stomach in the darkness.

Acid burned my throat. Tears stung my eyes and streamed down my cheeks. My nose ran. And still my belly convulsed, seizing over and over, as if it were the engine of James's decaying Ford Fiesta.

Finally, my stomach was empty. I started to wipe my face with the back of my hand, but I felt James behind me. He pressed something into my fingers, and I found myself staring at an impossibly white handkerchief.

I cleaned myself up as best I could, and then I followed him down the stairs. Not one of the women had spoken.

James led me to the front door. The vampire on the porch stirred, but he didn't manage a single proposition before we cleared the porch and regained the relative refuge of the Fiesta. James held my door for me, waiting until I nodded before he closed it and crossed in front of the car.

Taking his own seat, James turned the key in the ignition—once, twice, a third time before the emphysemic engine finally caught. He jerked the wheel hard, lurching out of the parking space, and part of my mind registered that gesture as the first awkward movement I'd ever seen him make. He left rubber on the street as he peeled away from the hellhouse.

I didn't speak until James pulled into the empty parking space in front of my apartment, the one created by the fire hydrant. Even then, I couldn't look at him, couldn't stare him in the face. Instead, I focused on the hydrant's neat metal caps, trying to forget the blood-like rusty stains I'd seen in front of Richardson's lair.

Questions spun through my mind, each more urgent than the one before. I finally settled on the most basic. I swallowed hard and asked, "Where the hell is Richardson?"

28

"Philadelphia."

"But you said I was going to meet——"

"I needed to get you there. I needed you to understand what's at stake."

When I'd first gotten involved with the insane world of vampires, I might have made a bad joke about stakes. Now, I merely grimaced and said, "You failed, then. Because I don't understand a thing. How the hell can you be working with a man who would do *that?*"

"I'm not working with him." James's flat denial was automatic.

"You have the right to come and go from his house. You aren't Impressed, when all those other men are. That creature on the porch called you *Chief!* What the hell is going on, James?"

His fingers clenched on the steering wheel. I didn't have the patience to let him debate whether he was going to tell me a lie, the truth, or some tortured half-truth.

"There's a child back there who needs our help," I said. "We need to get those women out of there."

"And do what with them?"

I clutched at straws. "We'll take them to the Den. The sphinxes can help."

"Ah," James said, his lips curling with bitter sarcasm. "The tender mercies of the Ancient Commission."

"No!" I said. "There are other options!"

Damn. Not two hours ago, I'd kept Chris from sharing his plan, and now I was trotting it out like some gold standard?

But James didn't give me a chance to explain. Instead, he said. "Forget the women." His voice was grim. "I'm going to destroy Richardson, once and for all. And I need your help to do it."

Vampires hated being indebted to people. But here James was, making an outright statement, asking me to give him something he desired. That fact sobered me more than anything I'd seen at the rowhouse.

I said, "The two of us can't possibly fight—"

"I'm not asking you to fight. Not physically anyway."

That answer chilled me. James's solution was always to fight. That's why he'd dragged me down to the Old Library when I'd first started working for him. Everything ended in a fight, and he wanted me to be properly prepared. But if he didn't intend to grapple with Richardson... "What, then? What do you want me to do?"

"Delete every case ever brought against Richardson in the Eastern Empire night court."

"Are you *insane?*" My response was immediate.

In the first place, someone was certain to notice as soon as the records disappeared. Dozens of cases had been filed against Richardson over the centuries. Even though he'd escaped imprisonment every single time, the old files were routinely reviewed by prosecutors trying to find some new way to block him, some novel approach to pen him in with the law.

In the second place, I was personally sworn to protect those records. That's why James had hired me two years ago. I'd invested countless hours organizing the files, bringing order to the chaos engendered by decades of haphazard clerks before me.

In the third place—

I didn't need a third place. James was simply asking too much.

And that was before I considered that I might have been wrong all along. James might really be working *for* Richardson. This entire field trip might have been orchestrated somehow, in some way, to make me cave. To make me eradicate the Empire's records on Richardson.

"What the hell are you doing, James? How can it possibly help for me to erase Richardson's record?"

"It's safer for you if you don't know."

"That's crap, and you know it. It's not *safer* for me to commit a felony on behalf of Maurice Richardson. Anyone with the computer skills of an eighth grader would know I'm the one who did it."

James stared straight ahead, as if the secrets of the universe were written on the bumper of the Camry parked in front of us. "I'm running out of time. He ordered me to procure another cow."

"Don't call them that." I protested automatically, even as my stomach threatened to reprise its star role in *The Exorcist* remake.

"*He* calls them that. He thinks of them that way. You don't get to forget that."

"I don't get to forget any of this!" I protested. "You made sure of that."

"She was eight years old."

This time, my stomach didn't rebel. It didn't have a chance to, because my heart was clenching tight enough that I gasped for mercy.

"It was a test," James said. "I knew that. When I failed, I did my best to make it look like an unavoidable mistake. I never could have predicted the girl would have an oak chair in her bedroom. I never could have planned that the mother would break the chair, would grab a leg, would have the presence of mind to stab me."

He pressed his hand against his chest, just south of his heart. How close had he come to dying, staging his injury?

"So what happens next?" I demanded. "Will he Impress you again?"

His jaw tightened. "He doesn't have the strength to do that. Not after I broke his hold, the first time."

After Judge DuBois saved him. "What then?" I asked.

"He'll have to kill me outright."

James was younger, both in vampire years and in human ones. He kept his body lean; he took advantage of every training tool in the Old Library. I asked, "You can beat him in a fair fight, can't you?"

"In a fair fight? Probably. But do you really think Richardson will fight fair?"

Of course Richardson would tilt the odds. He'd make sure that James fought with damaged weapons. Or he'd spike his own gear with silver, wash edged weapons with the corrosive metal or conceal a deadly stake. If he didn't salt the weaponry, he'd bring in extra men.

And even if James somehow managed to defeat an army, Richardson would gain some other advantage. He'd make the battle public, guaranteeing the Empire Bureau of Investigation would get involved. Worse, he'd bring in mundane authorities— see that James was locked up in a maximum-security prison or the proverbial padded room, forever.

Richardson had no scruples. And he'd had centuries to plot his takeover—of the Eastern Empire, of Washington DC, of the world.

I sighed in a futile effort to bleed off some of my despair. "I don't get it," I said. "What do you gain by my destroying court records?"

"Richardson's on to me. He can't prove I sent you the Bitcoins to meet his ransom demand, but he suspects I did. If I convince you to delete the files, he'll believe he still controls me. That will buy me all the time I need."

"Time for what?"

For the first time since we'd left the rowhouse, he looked at me. I knew his eyes were blue, but they looked black in the moonlight that streamed through the car's windshield.

He reached out, and I thought he was going to touch my face, but he wrapped his finger around a lock of hair that had escaped my ponytail. He tucked it behind my ear, as if he actually cared about keeping things neat, about restoring order. His hand dropped back to his lap.

"I'll tell you again. It's not safe for you to know more."

"Angelique Wilson hates me. She's just waiting for me to make one more mistake so she can fire me. Deleting those files will guarantee I never work at the court again."

"I wouldn't ask if there was any other way."

"It's not just Angelique. The Pride will pounce on me like I'm a wounded gazelle."

"The Pride threw you out of the Den. They don't get a say in your good behavior anymore."

"But Chris does. What would he think?"

He didn't have an answer for that. He'd never had an answer for Chris.

He shrugged. "You have to trust me."

That's what it all came down to. For the first time in my life, James had asked me outright for assistance. He'd violated every tenet of his vampire life to become indebted to another person. He wouldn't, maybe couldn't, tell me why. All I knew was that his request would cost me—my job, the tattered remnants of my status as a sphinx, my sorely tested relationship with Chris.

Trust him.

I didn't know if I could.

I let myself out of the car and headed down the stairs to my basement apartment. I half hoped James would follow. I half feared he would.

I entered my home alone.

29

I n the end, it was the child who convinced me.

Not the dark-haired girl in the last room of Richardson's prison—she'd already lost her safety and security, along with any hope she'd had of a normal life.

The child who haunted me was the girl who escaped. The one James spared.

Because he wouldn't be able to protect her the next time, or the time after that, or the time after *that*, forever and ever and ever.

And he had a plan to end that threat. A plan he wouldn't tell me, a plan that threatened me in ways I couldn't understand. A plan that required me to act.

In the middle of the afternoon, I helped myself to a boysenberry yogurt and an apple from the fridge. I took a shower, applying two coats of conditioner. I dressed in casual clothes, jeans and a green cashmere sweater I'd had since college.

I took the subway to the office, the same way I would on a typical workday. I greeted the weekend security guard with the same patient smile I spared for Bubba and Earl, and I cleared Security Level Orange.

In my office, I twitched everything into order, the way I

would any evening. I straightened the pens, putting all the blue ones with blue and the black ones with black. I returned my stapler to its customary place beside my monitor. I untangled the telephone cord, which had looped around itself three times.

It only took a minute for my computer to boot to life. At the login screen, I considered using the "Test" account I'd generated months earlier when I restructured the court's database.

It would only take a moment, though, for anyone to trace that login back to me. Besides, if I acted surreptitiously, I'd have zero chance of pleading my innocence.

Instead, I logged in under my standard credentials. I ran a search, collecting all the Richardson files. I double-checked the results, making sure I wasn't snagging extra files by mistake.

I tapped the *Delete* key.

A warning came up on my screen—black letters in a grey box, surrounded by a bright red border. Did I really want to delete those files? My action would be permanent.

My finger hovered over the *Delete* key.

I was a sphinx who created order. I couldn't do this. I couldn't destroy records.

But I wasn't a sphinx. I was something else. Something different. Something older and wilder, something wrapped in serpents, living in shadow.

I thought about the Impressed vampires, staring at the flickering computer screens on the ground floor of Richardson's house. I remembered the pile of rags huddled on the mattress at the top of the stairs. I remembered the girl at the end of the hall.

I pressed the *Delete* key, and I watched a progress bar measure out the destruction.

I should have felt an ache at overturning the hard-won order I'd constructed at the court. I should have triggered my sphinx compulsions, the desperate need to turn something, to straighten something, to bring order into a life hopelessly out of balance.

Instead, I felt a surge of energy, as powerful and purifying as a blast furnace.

I ran a single search, confirming that the name Maurice Richardson was expunged from imperial records. And then I left the courthouse, walking through the cool May night until I reached an open restaurant, an Indian curry house that I'd never eaten in before.

I ordered cauliflower vindaloo and phaal curry and Mumbai potatoes with chilies. And I finished every bite.

30

I knew I'd torpedoed the only job I'd ever loved.

I just didn't count on destroying the rest of my life.

Monday evening, I dressed like I was going to a funeral. I wore a black skirt, and a plain white blouse. I added a black blazer and sensible shoes. I pulled my hair back into a neat twist. I kept my makeup to a minimum.

I considered arriving early, as if I were atoning for my sins, but I discarded the idea almost immediately. Prompt appearance at the courthouse wasn't going to make a dent in the debt I owed.

Angelique met me at the security station, her lips pressed into a tight line. She marched me back to her office without saying a word. I didn't bother making any protest. There was nothing left for me to say.

The court bailiff, Eleanor Owens, stood beside James's old leather couch, her feet spread, her hands linked behind her back. She'd donned amethyst jewelry for the night, with sparkly purple eyeshadow to match.

Angelique didn't bother closing her office door.

"You're fired," she said, her eyes doing their best to burn a hole straight through my forehead.

I didn't respond. I'd been imagining those words since Angelique had put me on probation.

"I want your ID card on my desk. Now."

I complied.

Angelique turned to Eleanor and snapped, "Serve her."

The griffin produced a sheaf of papers that had been hidden behind her broad body. She brought them forward in a controlled sweep and touched the center of my chest. "Sarah Jane Anderson, you've been served."

I caught the document by reflex. It only took a moment to glance at the header on the front page. I was accused of trespass, destruction of property, aiding and abetting a known criminal in the evasion of legal process, and a dozen more counts.

I knew the gig. I wasn't going to get any Miranda warnings. If I wanted a lawyer, it was up to me to find one. I suspected that the only reason I wasn't being hauled in front of Judge Finch for an immediate arraignment was the fact that I was already under indictment for a laundry list of other crimes.

A crazed voice at the back of my head wondered who was going to log in the complaint, who was going to create a new file for the court.

Angelique snapped at Eleanor. "Get her out of here."

I let Eleanor take my elbow, because that seemed the fastest way to escape my cat-shifter boss. Ex-boss.

Eleanor speed-walked me to the imperial court's secret stairs and our hidden underground exit. Five minutes after arriving at work, I was out on the street, unemployed and under indictment.

I walked to Chris's house. I needed the time to clear my head.

My best possible scenario had included my being suspended temporarily, giving everyone a chance to calm down and letting James do whatever he planned on doing. Richardson would be destroyed, my misdeeds would blow over, and I could step back into my job when the coast was clear. Ideally, with Angelique

Wilson banished and James back as the court's actual Director of Security.

Those had been my *dreams*, but I'd expected to be shown the door.

I hadn't expected the criminal counts, though.

Chris hadn't either.

But the press had.

It rapidly became clear that *someone* had managed to docket the criminal complaint against me. And the courthouse reporters had pounced on the fresh story like tabbies on catnip. They hadn't wasted their time walking across town, the way I had. Instead, they'd arrived in force on Chris's doorstep. Half a dozen microphones were shoved into my face before I got to the front door.

For one long, horrible minute, I didn't think he'd answer my knock. I kept my face perfectly straight, fully aware that video cameras were capturing my every move, that within the next ten minutes my image was going to be slapped on the website of every one of those publications.

Just as I gave up hope, the door swung open. Chris kept himself hidden behind the door. He didn't want to be in the frame as I crossed over the threshold.

I couldn't say I blamed him.

At least he waited until the door was closed before he groaned, "What the hell were you thinking, coming here?"

Numbly, I reached inside my purse and pulled out the papers Eleanor had served on me. The corners were bent and one page was ripped from the binder clip, but Chris would still be able to make out the pertinent information.

"Here," I said, shoving the papers toward him. "We have to answer this."

He barely glanced at the cover page. "We?"

"You're my lawyer," I said, like that was the most basic truth in the world. Water was wet. Grass was green. Chris was my Sun Lion lawyer, the only one who'd dared to take my case when I was accused of murder. Who else was going to represent me with these new charges?

"I *was* your lawyer," he said.

"You can't—"

"Now, I've got a conflict of interest."

"What do you mean?"

"There's no way I can represent you when I'm on trial for the same charges."

"The same charges?" He wasn't making any sense. "But you didn't delete any files."

"Files? You think this is all about files?" Before I could answer, he pulled his phone from his pocket. He slashed at the screen to pull something up and then he shoved the phone at me, hard enough that I had to take a step back to keep my balance.

The Paranormal Post was displayed across the top of the screen. Below it, in letters twice the size of the masthead, three shouted word: SEPARATED AT BIRTH? The rest of the page was filled with three photos. Chris's formal headshot from his days as a *Banner* reporter sat next to my staff photo from the courthouse. Below them, filling the rest of the screen was a grainy black and white image. Clearly taken from the Natural History museum's security tape, the image caught both our faces —disheveled wigs, prosthetic noses, fake teeth, and all.

I scrolled down the screen. There was an image of the Sekhmet amulet, the very charm that was hidden in my sock drawer.

"I don't understand," I said. "How did they—"

"*The Banner* has the same security footage," Chris said. "They skip over the imperial angle, of course, but they're asking readers to help identify two 'persons of interest' in the theft of the amulet."

"That doesn't make sense." I skimmed the *Post* article. It stopped short of accusing Chris and me of stealing the amulet. Instead, it poked sly fun at the pair of us, speculating that we sphinxes might have liberated the artifact because we didn't approve of the museum's haphazard filing system. It ended, though, with ominous speculation that the Empire Bureau of Information would certainly want to question any imperials who were so *unfortunate* as to have their photos featured on the front page of any mundane newspaper.

Chris grimaced as I finished the piece. "The Pride is furious. They're holding a special session right now, to decide what to do."

"What *can* they do? They've already excommunicated me. And they're not about to endanger the Sun Lion."

Chris glared at my snide tone. "Don't be so sure. They have a remarkably low tolerance for being dragged through the mundane mud. Especially by someone they've taken action against once."

"Me?" I said, my voice shattering with incredulity. "You think *I* had anything to do with this?"

"How else would the story get out there? It's not like the museum takes inventory of every item, every night. Someone pointed them toward the missing amulet."

"Why the hell would I do that?"

Chris sighed. "I don't know, Sarah. According to the Pride, you'd do it for revenge. You'd drag me down. You'd take out every sphinx in the Eastern Empire, if that meant you could get back at us for expelling you."

"That's absurd, and you know it!"

"Do I?"

I couldn't believe he doubted me. Chris. The man who had helped me understand what it meant to be a sphinx, what it meant to be *Other* in the heart of the nation's capital. My voice cracked with accusation: "*You* were the one who suggested going to the museum in the first place! You wanted to find the Seal. You wanted to put a shiny bow on your glorious New Commission."

"You stole the amulet, Sarah. It isn't the Seal. It doesn't have anything to do with sphinx business. You could have planned this all along."

I gaped at him. "You think I'd do that to the Den? I'd do that to you?"

"I don't know what to think any more."

I stared at him in disbelief. We'd supported each other through so much. I'd killed Judge DuBois, and he'd stood by my side. He'd thrown me out of the Den, and I'd forgiven him. We'd fought together. We'd slept together. And he was drawing the line at *this*?

I reached for the court papers he still held. "Give me those," I said.

He snatched them away, as if he were only seeing them for the first time. It only took a moment for him to skim the allegations on the first page. "Sweet Sekhmet," he breathed. "What the hell were you thinking?" He flipped through the information, shaking his head faster at each allegation. "*Were* you even thinking? Did you stop for one single second to realize what would happen when you deleted those files?"

"Of course I thought about it!" I snapped. "James has a plan. He's—"

"You did this for James." Chris's voice went deadly still.

"He's going to—"

"James Morton," Chris said. "The vampire who's been missing for the past ten months. The vampire who's repeatedly been seen in the company of Maurice Richardson. The vampire who has every reason to want you dead. Or worse." He gestured to his phone, to the screen that held our photos. "I wouldn't put it past him to have fed that story to *The Post*. To *The Banner* too, for that matter."

A tsunami of doubt washed over me.

Maybe this had been James's plan all along. Maybe he'd spent the past ten months cooking up this revenge plot. He'd dragged me to Richardson's place to set the hook, but he didn't *have* any second act. He'd let me destroy myself, and now he was lurking somewhere on the sidelines.

No. He wouldn't do that. I'd seen the revulsion on his face as we'd watched Richardson's Impressed scions. I'd seen his pity and disgust at the imprisoned women.

James wanted to destroy Richardson. Not me. Richardson.

I stared at Chris. "This isn't about James. This is about me, trying to do the right thing. Trying to bring down Maurice Richardson once and for all. I saw what he's doing, Chris. I went to South East, and I saw his Impressed vampires, saw the women he's using as some sort of perverted blood herd. James isn't asking you for help. I am."

"I don't think I can help you anymore."

"Chris—"

He cut me off. "The Sarah Anderson I knew had a sphinx's love of order. She'd never intentionally destroy court records. She'd never take any action to help Maurice Richardson win."

He handed me the court document. My fingers grasped the paper without my issuing a conscious command. The pages blurred before my eyes as I said, "I *need* you."

"You should have thought about that before you did James Morton's dirty work."

That was it. There wasn't anything else I could say. There wasn't any other argument, anything that would change his mind, no matter how long I stood there, clutching my pitiful sheaf of papers.

"Can I leave through the back door?" I finally asked.

"Go," he said, dropping his head as if the single word cost more than running a marathon.

I flagged a cab the next street over, not daring to wait for an Uber. I gave the driver my address, but I asked him to drive around the block once. He probably thought the request was odd, but that was nothing compared to what he'd think if he recognized the sylph, the centaur, and the faun waiting by my front door. The imperial press had found me too.

My apartment didn't have an alley entrance. I couldn't sneak into my own home.

For a single heartbeat, I thought of going to James's sanctum. But I couldn't swear that I hadn't been followed from Chris's house.

I could always check rear-view mirrors for suspicious vehicles. I could change cabs a dozen times. I could wait in the darkness of Rock Creek Park, hoping the coast was clear.

But if I was wrong, James's sanctum would be disclosed. His life would be endangered. If I failed him, he would be vulnerable every second the sun was above the horizon.

I couldn't go to Allison either. She had a young daughter. She didn't know that the imperial world even existed. And there was a chance—a non-negligible one—that if she saw me next to the photo from the museum, she'd turn me in. After all, the authorities only wanted to question me. In her mind, she wouldn't be subjecting me to arrest.

I had limited options, but I had to do something. So I told the cab to stop in front of my house. I fished my key out of my purse, so I wouldn't have to dig for it on my doorstep. I paid off the driver, adding a generous tip. *He* hadn't done anything wrong, except pick up a crazy lady for his fare.

The reporters started baying like hounds the instant my foot touched the sidewalk. "No comment," I said as I strode toward my door.

They called my name, trying to get me turn around for a photo. "No comment," I said.

They asked me if I'd seen the cover of *The Post.* "No comment."

They told me I had a chance to tell my side of the story, to get it out there before anyone else told theirs.

Anyone else. They meant Chris. Chris who'd just thrown me out of his house.

"No comment."

I got the door open before they could come up with another

gambit, and I darted inside. I locked it, turning the deadbolt and sliding the security chain.

And I found James Morton sitting at my kitchen table.

His fangs were out. He'd stripped off his tie, dropping it into a tangled pile beside an array of papers. His palms were flat on the table, as if he were willing it to hold him in place, as if he were fighting the urge to slice open my jugular before I could speak.

I gazed down at the brochure from Empire General, the hospital pamphlet I'd taken from Chris: *Welcome the Night.*

Chris's sphinx-neat notes sprawled across the back cover. *All vampires,* he'd written for my edification. *Clearance program. License. Annual re-certification.* And in capital letters, underscored twice: *New Commission.*

"You're putting me in a goddamn prison."

"It's not a prison," I said, and then I recognized my mistake. "*I'm* not doing anything. This is just an idea Chris had. Something to help vampires."

"Chris Gardner." James's sneer echoed in my mind, and I realized he'd used the exact same tone that Chris had, not an hour earlier, when he'd dismissed the possibility of James's good intentions.

"He wants to help," I said.

"And you think enough of his idea that you kept this… garbage in your nightstand."

"You had no business—"

"Did you or did you not agree to help the Sun Lion create this prison program for all vampires?"

I had, but there were extenuating circumstances. I didn't have a choice. I only wanted to help James, help him and vampires like him.

The words caught in my throat. I knew them. I might even believe them. But I knew James would never understand, no matter what I said, no matter how I tried to explain.

"Those vampires we saw last night," I finally said. "The

ones in Richardson's lair. If they'd had a program like this, if
they had the New Commission to support them—"

"If they'd had a sphinx control them, instead of a vampire!"

"It's not like that! Mother Sekhmet—"

"So your *goddess* demands this."

"She told me I can save her children."

"You honestly believe—"

This time it was my turn to interrupt. "I just need to find the
Seal. Then Sekhmet says I'll be able to save everyone, the
vampires and the sphinxes."

James stared at me as if I were speaking in tongues. "You
honestly believe that crap?"

"It's not—"

But he wasn't listening. His hands moved faster than my eyes
could follow, ripping the brochure in half, in half again, one
more time. He threw the resulting confetti onto the table.

"Don't you *dare* hide behind some religious hocus-pocus,"
James spat.

"It's not—"

He threw back his chair and headed for the front door.

"James!" I shouted. "Wait! Don't go out there! There are
reporters—"

But it was too late. He'd thrown back the chain, slammed
back the deadbolt. And he bared his fangs for all to see as the
paparazzi converged.

I heard their panicked screams and the thunder of their feet
as they fled down the sidewalk. I waited for James to come back,
to curse me, to engage me in a physical fight.

But James was gone. The reporters too.

I closed my door and locked it, no longer bothering with the
chain.

And I sat, alone, at my kitchen table until the sun rose,
trying to figure out how I'd destroyed my life so completely.

I t took me about half an hour to realize I couldn't stay in my basement apartment. The paparazzi would return, or they'd be replaced by other reporters. The amulet story wasn't going away.

But more importantly, I was going to be hauled in front of the Eastern Empire court to answer the charges in the new complaint. Earlier that night, Eleanor had let me go because I was a citizen in relative good standing.

Now, I was an imperial who'd called mundane attention to my activities. *The Banner* had me on the front page, and it wouldn't take much for imperial legal eagles to conclude I'd dragged Chris into the mire.

Judge Finch would waste no time throwing me back into a cell beneath the courtroom. This time, I couldn't guarantee I'd have a lawyer to represent me in the courtroom. I couldn't be sure when I'd be released.

I ran into my bedroom and ransacked my closet, throwing random clothes into a backpack. I scared up a phone charger and the extra hundred dollars in cash that I kept at the back of my nightstand drawer.

At break-neck speed, I flew to my dresser. I shoved under-wear into my backpack, along with a couple of bras.

Only then did I force myself to slow down, to take a few deep breaths and steady my shaking hands. I reached back into the dresser and gently shifted my socks, selecting three pairs to add to my bug-out bag.

The only thing left to secure was the amulet. I lifted it care-fully from its improvised nest in my terry anklets. With trem-bling fingers, I wrapped it in a fleece sock. Then I planted it in the middle of the backpack, taking care to cushion it completely.

Standing at my front door, I realized I'd forgotten one thing. I dashed back to the bedroom and collected the photograph by my bed, the one of my mother holding me as a swaddled newborn. I slipped it into the backpack's front pocket. Then there was nothing left to do but grab my denim jacket from its hook by the door and head into the city streets.

As I hurried away from my home, I imagined Empire Bureau of Investigation cars screaming around the corner, complete with agents leaping out to kick in my door, to drag me off to justice. I quickened my pace, putting several blocks between me and my sage-painted walls.

Only as I reached the wide stretch of Massachusetts Avenue did I admit the truth to myself. I didn't have anywhere to go.

I couldn't bring my troubles to Allison—not when she had to protect Nora. Especially when I wasn't sure if we were even still friends.

Chris and James were both out. I'd careened from the potential of two—what? Boyfriends? Suitors? Lovers? I still didn't have a suitable word. But that problem hardly mattered now. I didn't have either man in my life, and I couldn't imagine I ever would again.

I couldn't sleep at the courthouse, in my office or in the Old Library. I couldn't set foot in the Den.

For one insane moment, I thought about breaking into the

National Museum of Natural History, about returning to the scene of my crime, stealing a blue apron, and finding a corner of the Smithsonian to hole up in. They didn't have my real face on film—only the disguised one. But surely *someone* would check to make sure the museum was empty at night. I'd only compound my problems with another charge of trespassing.

I didn't have enough cash for a hotel, and I was afraid to use my credit card, for fear of being traced by law enforcement authorities, imperial or mundane.

It was well past midnight now. A stiff breeze had picked up, amplified by the tall office buildings on either side of the city street. I shoved my hands into my pockets and hunched my shoulders to better settle the backpack.

My fingers brushed against cold metal.

Car keys. The keys to James's Prius, which I'd left on a street a few blocks from Chris's house.

If I circled around and approached the car from the north... If I avoided Chris's street entirely, stayed out of the way of any reporters or police who might be staking out his home...

Once I had the car, I could go anywhere. Anywhere I could reach on a hundred dollars of gas, anyway.

But I didn't have to spend my money on fuel. I could stash the car in one of the countless parking garages downtown. Garages only required payment upon exit. I could hide out until I'd built up a hundred dollars in parking fees—longer, if I was ready to flee pursuit the instant I used a credit card to get the car out of hock.

If I chose a garage near a hotel—one fancy enough to have an attached garage, but not so swank as to require valet parking—I could take advantage of public restrooms. I could probably snag a few free meals as well, helping myself to buffets set up for business meetings.

It was far from a perfect plan. But it was the best idea I had.

I headed toward the convention center, figuring I'd be more anonymous in the ever-changing crowds of conference attendees. Choosing the Grand Duke at random, I pulled into the garage. I slipped my white parking ticket under the sun visor, so I could find it easily if I ever got my life in order.

I drove down the ramp, circling three levels before I found a space in a conveniently ill-lit corner. I backed the car in, so I'd have a better view of anyone who approached. I turned off the engine and settled back in my seat.

Pulling my jacket close around my waist, I told myself everything was going to be all right. I was friendless, homeless, and practically broke. But I'd think of *something*.

I leaned my seat back and tried to relax. Every time I heard a car squeal as it rounded the ramp, though, I sat up and looked around.

No one was coming for me. No one had the faintest idea of where I was. I repeated those words like a mantra a few hundred times.

Finally, though, I gave up. I reached into the backpack, and I took out the amulet, cupping it in my hand as if I could keep it safe forever.

I wanted to commune with Mother Sekhmet; I wanted her to tell me what I should do. I longed for the tingle I'd felt in the museum, the flare of indescribable sensation that had told me Sheut was near.

Maybe the amulet was silent because I was forty-five feet underground. Maybe it held its counsel because I'd stolen it from its rightful home. Maybe I'd imagined all of it, my conversations with Sekhmet and my discovery of Sheut.

Maybe I was insane.

But I didn't have any better option. So I held my blue glass charm. And I reduced my prayer to two words: *Mother Sekhmet. Mother Sekhmet.* And I tried to believe that somewhere, somehow, some way, everything would be better in the morning.

I spent a week living in James's Prius.

 I didn't stay in the car the entire time. I ventured out a few times each day, haunting the conference floors of the hotel. Every afternoon, I moved the car to a different location in the garage. I figured if any staff was keeping an eye on the hybrid with Florida plates, they'd think I was a long-term tourist with a dedication to seeing every last site in the nation's capital.

 I'd grabbed my phone charger before I left my house, but after thinking things through, I was afraid to use my cell. I was fairly sure the EBI had the technological acumen to triangulate my location from any tower I accessed. I *knew* the mundane police could track me that way.

 Once, almost a year ago, I'd bought burner phones to avoid police detection. They'd allowed me to communicate with Chris and to coordinate an entire skirmish with James by my side.

 That time seemed like ancient history. Even if I'd been able to find burner phones in the strange, suspended world of the convention center hotel, I didn't have anyone to call.

 Left to my own devices, without a job to wake up to or friends to socialize with or real meals at specific times and places, I quickly lost track of day and night. My two years of working at the Night Court had conditioned me to sleep during the day and to be awake at night. Mostly, I kept to that schedule at the hotel, making suitable adjustments to raid conference meals.

When I had to, I spent some of my meager cash. I didn't dare leave the hotel, but there was a Starbucks in the lobby, along with a gift shop that charged criminal prices for candy bars. Stressful times called for desperate measures. I splurged on a Snickers. Or two. Or three.

Early on, I fished a discarded room key out of a trashcan in the lobby. It wouldn't get me into a guest room, or the luxe fitness center advertised in the elevators. It wouldn't even open the door to the business center. But I quickly discovered that other hotel guests held doors for me when they saw that piece of plastic nestled in my hand.

I used my ill-gained computer access to help pass the time, reading countless articles on topics as varied as spring planting schedules in colonial DC and the ongoing debate about whether Pluto was a planet. Along the way I slipped in searches for information on Sekhmet, on Sheut, on anything to do with the darkest, most distant days of ancient Egyptian civilization.

After a week, there wasn't much more for me to discover. Worse, I was starting to attract unwelcome attention from the front desk staff, who studied my comings and goings with a bit too much attention. Worst of all, I was losing the hygiene battle after my countless "cowboy baths" in the restroom. Even the Grand Duke's plush terry hand cloths weren't a substitute for a real shower. My scalp itched, and my hair was starting to look as bad as the wig I'd worn inside the natural history museum.

I had to face reality. It was time to move on. I had to blow my cover and use my credit card to get the car out of hock. While I was at it, I could use my ATM card to stock up on cash. The only question that remained was where I would go when I fled, and whether I'd be fast enough to get there ahead of the FBI and mundane law enforcement.

Eyeing the blind glass globe of a surveillance camera in the business center, I debated reading my personal email. On the one hand, I was about to surface to the mundane and the imperial world. On the other hand, I dared not give away a single second of my head start.

But I had to know the status of the imperial cases against me. The imperial press—*The Paranormal Post* and the *Imperial Inquirer* and all the other papers that had staked out my home and Chris's—were blocked from mundane browsers. I couldn't reach them from a public access computer.

I had another option, though. I could go directly to the source for my information. I could check the court's own records.

I wasn't brave enough to log in to any imperial network as myself. But I could pose as Angelique Wilson. I'd helped her to log in often enough when she first took on her job as Acting Director of Security.

Working fast, I typed in an IP address I'd memorized long ago, a numeric code that corresponded to the computer system humming beneath the courthouse. Once the screensaver showed up, the familiar image of a sword piercing a sheaf of parchment, I was prompted to enter a username.

Catching my lower lip between my teeth, I typed *angelique.wilson*. I tapped the *Return* key quickly, as if the speeding electrons would somehow minimize my invasion of Angelique's privacy.

The computer asked me for a password.

If James were still in charge, the password might have been changed. He'd issued orders on a regular basis, requiring all staff to update their security protocols.

Angelique, though, hadn't required password changes in all the time I'd worked for her. I crossed my fingers, hoping she'd maintained her lax stance for the past couple of weeks.

I picked out the letters and numbers I'd memorized in Angelique's service: *G3rm@nSh#ph3rdD0g*

The screen wavered for a moment, and then I had access.

"Ma'am?" The question came from the doorway of the business center. I swallowed a surprised gasp and looked into the earnest eyes of Samuel, the most worrisome of the front desk clerks. He took a step into the room, and the overhead light glinted off the lapel pins announcing which languages he spoke: German, French, Italian, and Spanish. Over-achiever.

"Yes?" I responded, pretending that I had every right to be sitting in front of the computer.

"Is there anything I can help you with?" Samuel's voice was sharp with fake concern.

"No thank you," I said. "I'm just finishing up some work for the office."

I could tell he didn't believe me. I thought he was going to insist on my leaving, but he merely nodded and backed out of the doorway.

My fingers flew as I dove into the court's filing system. I typed my own name and was immediately treated to three files, the names printed in scarlet. Bench warrants had been issued for my arrest. I was a fugitive from the Eastern Empire Night Court.

I should have expected as much, but actually seeing the words displayed on the screen felt like a punch to my solar plexus. That shock, that sense of unfairness and abandonment, was the only reason it took me so long to realize there were *three* cases. There should have been two—the murder charges regarding Judge DuBois and the trespassing charges from deleting Richardson's records.

My whole arm shook as the cursor hovered over the third case. I clicked and blinked twice before I could make sense of the words.

The Clans of the Empire Empire v. An Amulet in the Form of Two Egyptian Gods.

Without thinking, I slipped my hand into the pocket of my denim jacket, closing my fingers around the amulet. I carried it with me everywhere; I didn't dare leave it in the car, in case the Prius was towed away as an abandoned vehicle. In just a few days, the amulet had become my secret habit, my worry stone, helping diffuse some of the stress of my strange new life.

My thumb automatically surfed over the smooth shape of Sekhmet, coming up short at the jagged line where Sheut's head had once been attached. As I had every day since I'd huddled with Chris in the museum, I waited for a rush of power, for the secret flame that had nearly consumed me.

Nothing.

The amulet was dead.

Worrying at the glass with my thumb, I skimmed the documents that some substitute clerk had added to the database. Weeks ago, when I'd tried to track down information on Sekhmet's Seal, I'd searched for just this type of litigation, where a legal action was brought against an object.

It seemed that an overzealous prosecutor had initiated the case to lay the groundwork for a criminal action for Mundane Exposure, for displaying the paranormal world to humans. I was listed as a potential party, as was Chris. The only reason *he* hadn't been dragged into the courtroom already was that the amulet itself was owned by a human, by Mohammed Apep. The Eastern Empire Night Court had to tread carefully to avoid exposure.

It shouldn't have mattered—three cases against me or two. But seeing that new filing stripped something from my soul.

I really was an outsider. The Empire truly considered me a threat.

The wheels of justice were grinding forward, and I was going to be crushed.

And the awful irony was that the amulet no longer held magic. It no longer connected me to my past, to the father I'd never met, to my unknown imperial nature.

I longed for someone who could teach me, a guide who

knew more about the amulet than I did. The sphinxes weren't going to help me. Vampires kept lousy records.

But staring at the court files, my eyes were once again drawn to one name: Mohammed Apep.

Chris and I had already done research on the man. I'd read about his generous gifts, his love for his adopted country, his absolute refusal to be seen or photographed. Better investigative journalists than I had tried—and failed—to track down the elusive philanthropist.

Nevertheless, I started typing away. This time, I used court-specific databases, relying on the high-powered search engines of Westlaw. Without hesitating, I billed my searches to Angelique's administrative account.

The subterfuge was worthwhile. My screen was immediately filled with more articles than I'd been able to find by searching the Internet at large, and at first glance every one of them seemed relevant.

Before I could study the results, though, the business center door opened. This time, Samuel didn't surprise me with his "Ma'am." This time, he wasn't cautiously polite.

"Yes?" I asked, forcing myself to give him a neutral stare.

"I'm going to have to insist that you finish your work."

I looked pointedly at the empty workstations. "Does someone else need this computer?" I asked.

"The business center is a privilege we reserve for Grand Duke guests," Samuel said. "*Paying* guests."

"Which is precisely why I'm here," I said.

"If you could just give me your name, Ms...."

"Smith," I said levelly. "Susan Smith."

The exasperation on his face would have been perfectly clear in German, French, Italian, or Spanish. "And if you could show me your room key, Ms. Smith?"

I flashed him my decoy piece of plastic, adding a deadly smile. I was typing before the door closed as he went off to check Ms. Smith's mythical reservation.

I didn't have time to read articles about Apep's familiar gifts —his restoring the buildings on the Mall, the American University professorship focusing on the history of civilization. I flew through the databases, keeping one eye on the door. It wouldn't take Samuel long to discover that Susan Smith wasn't registered at the hotel.

I almost shouted out loud when I hit pay dirt.

The article wasn't in a newspaper or a glossy magazine. It wasn't an academic inquiry into the nature of war.

It was a school kid's class project, collected in an obscure journal about early childhood education. The article discussed the ongoing value of having children write essays about What I Did Last Summer.

Kayleigh Sanders had taken a trip to Washington DC. She had to visit the National Cathedral "because everybody in my family gets to choose a place, and that's what my sister wanted to see because the Cathedral looks like a castle in *The Lord of the Rings* or *Game of Thrones* or something like that, but I can't watch those shows because they're too violent."

Kayleigh was bored by "rows and rows of benches inside." But she warmed to the cathedral's gargoyles. And she was absolutely fascinated by the stained glass windows. "There's a moon rock in the center of one, and there's a scarab in another, which is a beetle that lived in Egypt centuries and centuries ago. It's in a window called *The History of Civilization*, and it was given by a really rich man named Mohammed Apep."

She included a picture of the scarab window. The tiny image wasn't very clear. But one thing stood out immediately: A dark oval shape, centered in the field of glass.

The fingers of my right hand drifted over my left wrist. I remembered the new insignia Sekhmet had shared with me, the oval, bisected by a solid line. If I squinted at Kayleigh's project, I could imagine that shape in her report. I could believe that Sekhmet had marked me with a scarab.

I glanced at the hotel front desk. Samuel was talking to a

man in a dark blue suit. Both of them were looking at the business center. Blue Suit raised a hand, waving over a uniformed security guard.

I plunged my hand into my jacket pocket, ready to fish out my bogus room key and try one last bluff. My fingers brushed against the amulet, though, and I felt a tingle.

The faience didn't ignite with the same power I'd felt in the museum. It didn't send energy coursing up my arm, threatening the very rhythm of my heart. But it did *hum*, just a little, just enough to let a hyper-vigilant woman on the verge of detection know that *something* was afoot.

I needed to see the National Cathedral's scarab window. Now.

The glass door opened. Samuel glared at me, his face flushed dark with victory as he let Blue Suit precede him into the business center. "Ms. Smith," Blue Suit said.

"Thank you," I answered, as if he'd offered me something of value. "I was just leaving."

Blue Suit gave a curt nod to the security guards, who fell in beside me. Neither one touched my body, but they force-walked me to the hotel's massive revolving door. I only had a moment to glance over my shoulder and see Samuel's gloating smile.

Then, I was out on the street. In the open. With less than a dollar to my name and a million-dollar price tag on my head.

I felt like a thoroughbred racehorse parading around the paddock before the start of the Kentucky Derby. For the moment, I was free to go anywhere. I could circle around. I could buck off my pursuers. I could take a power walk around the block.

But any minute now, I'd be forced into the tight confines of the starting block. And when the pistol fired and the gates opened—when I actually used my credit card—I'd be forced to run for my life.

These few minutes were the end of my life as a normal person. This was the moment for dramatic last words. If I'd smoked cigarettes, now was the time to light up.

I didn't smoke. I didn't have a family to receive my final words of wisdom. Here, at the end of the road, I didn't have anything to say to anyone, to the Den or to Chris or to James.

As I blinked in the late-afternoon sunlight, I realized that wasn't completely true. I *did* have someone to talk to. I had the friend who'd stood beside me before I ever discovered my paranormal life. I had Allison.

My cell phone had long-since died; it was entombed in

James's Prius three levels below ground. I couldn't remember the last time I'd seen a pay phone in DC.

But I was standing across the street from the Convention Center. Surely, a meeting place as large as that one would have pay phones. *Someone* who visited DC on business had to arrive without a cell.

I crossed at the light and sauntered up the ramp with a group of conventioneers. It looked as if the International Brotherhood of Amalgamated Associations was having their annual meeting. I slipped past the giant posters announcing a full week of panels and workshops.

It only took a minute to find the international symbol for *Telephone*, displayed next to directional signs for restrooms, escalators, and a nearby subway station. I descended to the Exhibit Hall and walked the length of the floor before I found a bank of four black-and-silver phones.

I dug in the pocket of my jeans and pulled out my last two quarters. They clanged as the phone ate them, and a loud dial tone demanded my attention.

It took me a moment to remember Allison's number; I was accustomed to tapping the icon next to her name. The phone rang four times, and then a recording answered—Allison's somewhat harried plea for me to leave a message, as Nora gabbled in the background.

"Hey," I said. "It's me. Sarah. I just wanted to call... I wanted to say..."

I thought about the last time I'd talked to Allison, about how I'd asked her for information, asked her to help me. It seemed like I was always asking for something, always taking. That wasn't the way things used to be. That wasn't the way our friendship had started.

"I just wanted to find out how you're doing. You and Nora. I think about you, both of you, a lot. I hope you're well. If we were getting together for dinner, I'd bring string cheese and baked sweet potato and a handful of Cheerios."

Those were all of Nora's favorites.

"And cupcakes!" I added quickly. Then I said, "I miss you. I hope I can see you soon."

I hung up before my throat constricted my words into a sob.

I settled my palm over the amulet. I could still feel something, a low-level, expectant hum. It was time to head to the National Cathedral.

The Convention Center offered a convenient entrance to my underground parking garage. I found the Prius without any problem, and I started the engine. When I slipped my credit card into the fare machine, I half expected alarms to go off, complete with flashing lights and a portcullis dropping across the garage entrance.

Instead, the machine spat out a receipt and wished me a mechanical good afternoon. I barely refrained from laying down rubber on the exit ramp.

Fighting the urge to run every red light in the city, I worked my way out of downtown. The cathedral sat on high ground north of Georgetown, allowing me to cruise past some luxurious neighborhoods. My route took me along Embassy Row, and I found myself studying the various official buildings and their brightly colored flags. I wondered which countries had no extradition treaty.

For that matter, I wondered which of the embassies had security cameras trained on the street, focused at an angle that would pick up my vehicle. I considered each major intersection, wondering if my presence was being monitored by traffic cameras.

My eyes shifted constantly to my rear-view mirror, and I strained my ears for sirens in the distance. The EBI's jurisdiction was limited; the Empire took most of its enforcement actions under the secrecy of night. But mundane authorities had no such scruples.

I ditched the car a few blocks from the cathedral. Technically, I needed a residence sticker to park in the neighborhood, but I was willing to risk a ticket. Only as I passed through the heavy iron gate to the cathedral grounds did I realize that any ticket would be billed to James. He'd be responsible, once again, for my shortcomings.

I should care. But every time I tried to muster a sense of guilt, I pictured the rage on his face as he shredded Chris's *Welcome the Night* brochure. A parking ticket was nothing, compared to the affront of the New Commission.

This time, though, my familiar twinge of guilt about Chris's plans melted into another emotion: Anger. I was angry that James had lurked in my home. I was furious that he'd raided my nightstand. I was enraged that he'd confronted me in my own kitchen without giving me a chance to explain, on the very night when I'd destroyed my professional and personal life for him.

He'd asked me to trust him, to destroy Richardson's court records because he, James, said that was necessary. Well, I *had* trusted him. But he hadn't trusted me, not enough to listen to an explanation of *Welcome the Night*.

For the past week, I'd believed my emotions didn't matter. I could force an orderly solution to the chaos my life had become. I'd thought there was a way for me to escape, to make things right with the Eastern Empire and the mundane authorities. I could believe my lie as long as I was hiding at the Grand Duke, as long as I was removed from the everyday world.

I'd even held on to the fiction that I was somehow still a sphinx. I'd had a child's naive confidence in the Empire, an Easter-Bunny-Tooth-Fairy-Santa-Claus certainty that the Den and the Sun Lion would somehow intervene to make my problems disappear.

Now that I was on the run, I had the clear-eyed certainty of prey. The Den and the Sun Lion were part of my past. James was out of my life forever.

But I still had the amulet. I still had Sekhmet. I still had the secret of Sheut, a secret that—judging from the increasing hum emanating from my pocket—was inextricably linked to the scarab window in the mighty cathedral before me.

Find the Seal, Sekhmet had said. *And save my children.*

Nothing else in my life had worked out as I'd planned. But I still had my charge from the goddess. I still had the goal she'd set for me. The amulet told me I was closer than ever to finding the Seal. Maybe I could still serve Sekhmet, still save her children, even though I was lost and outcast and alone.

I walked through a stone doorway, ready to face my destiny.

And I came up short, in front of a ticket window. The kiosk would have been perfectly in place outside a movie theater or a theme park. The woman behind the glass window was a dead ringer for Mrs. Claus, complete with twinkling eyes and spun-cotton hair.

"Are you here for a tour, dear?" she asked.

"Um, yes, please."

"Which one?" she asked with a laugh.

The one that goes to the scarab, I thought. But I didn't want to call attention to my quest, so I rephrased. "I'm interested in the stained glass windows."

My answer earned me another bell-like laugh. "You're in luck, then! Geordie McIntosh is leading a roof-top tour in fifteen minutes. That'll be twenty-seven dollars."

"Twenty-seven—" I cut myself short. The fee sounded exorbitant, especially for an unemployed former civil servant.

But my day-to-day expenses would plummet as soon as I was incarcerated. And I needed the ticket so I could track down an ancient Egyptian artifact that spoke to the very fiber of my soul.

Twenty-seven dollars was a small price for magic. I took out my credit card.

And then I had another moment of hesitation. It had been one thing to use the card as I left the parking garage. The EBI and the police might identify where I'd been, but they'd had no way of guessing my ultimate destination.

If I charged the ticket now, it would be like sending a flare from the cathedral's bell tower.

"Dear?" the woman asked, her apple-doll face starting to crumple into a frown.

As if in response, the amulet buzzed. Not like my cell phone, nothing that pronounced. Rather, I could feel the charm's...*presence*. Its expectation.

I handed over my credit card.

Geordie McIntosh turned out to be a spry man, dressed in wide-wale camel-colored corduroys and a bristly green-wool sweater. A flat tweed cap covered his greying red curls, and he had a Burberry scarf knotted around his throat. He looked overjoyed to be leading our group of eleven dedicated tourists.

"All right, then," he said, and I caught a whisper of a Scottish accent underneath his words. "We'll be climbing a few hundred stairs on this tour, and we'll work through some stone passageways that are a wee bit tight. We'll be on the roof too, where ye can look down on the courtyard, from the base of the bell chamber. Anyone here weak in the legs, or claustrophobic, or scared of heights?"

We all attested that we could handle the challenges ahead.

"Let's go, then!" Geordie exclaimed, leading the way into the cathedral's heart.

My fellow tourists followed close behind our guide, whipping out phones and taking countless photos as Geordie gave us an architectural overview of the magnificent stone building. Narthex, Geordie proclaimed with relish, pointing to the covered stone anteroom behind us. Nave. Transept. Apse.

I heard the words. I followed Geordie's pointing fingers, nodding as if the world around me was making sense for the first time in my life. I craned my neck to study the groin vaulting, with its load-bearing boss stones that weighed up to five tons.

As fascinating as the stonework was, though, I was focused

on the glass. Geordie obligingly told us that the Te Deum windows were sixty-five feet in height. They were cleaned and restored after the 2011 earthquake that had damaged the cathedral, sending stone finials to the ground and severely damaging a turret on the south side of the building.

Other windows had been removed after the earthquake. After much prayerful debate, stained glass depictions of Robert E. Lee and Stonewall Jackson had been taken down. The gaping holes were covered over until suitable replacements could be devised.

A moon rock was enshrined in the famous Space Window. The stone was sealed between two pieces of tempered glass, preserved in a nitrogen environment to keep it from deteriorating.

"Any questions before we begin our climb?" Geordie asked.

I raised my hand, the left one. My right fingers curled around the amulet in my pocket. In response to Geordie's gracious nod, I asked, "I heard there was a window about Civilization?"

"Aye," Geordie said. "The Scarab Set. We'll get a good view of it from the roof."

The amulet jerked beneath my palm, a single hard contraction that mimicked my upstart heart. I held the faience close and tried to wait patiently while the other people in the group asked their own questions. Or, to be more accurate, made their own comments, extensive explanations of which windows they liked the most, and when they'd first seen vaulted ceilings, and how they used to think the phrase was "flying butler" instead of "flying buttress."

Finally, mercifully, we began our climb to the cathedral roof.

The stairs rose in stages, taking us first to the clerestory aisles, then to a massive storage area that arched over the nave's ceiling. We passed a rehearsal room where the cathedral's musical staff could practice playing the carillon on a full-size keyboard that was not attached to actual bells. We saw mammoth statues, two times the height of a man, waiting to be cleaned and returned to the elements. And in one room, perched on a shelf high above the floor, we saw a row of dusty bottles, each labeled with a year, to celebrate another twelve months of labor from the expert stonemasons who had carved the building's gargoyles.

All of it was magnificent. All of it was magical. And I couldn't wait until we got out on the roof, until I could see Mohammed Apep's scarab, preserved in all its glory.

Geordie dropped back to walk with me before we climbed the last flight. "So ye've got a special interest in the Scarab Set?"

I didn't want to make small talk. I just wanted to see the window. But I managed to say, "My cousin saw it last year and said it was one of the most beautiful things she'd ever seen."

Geordie preened like a proud parent. "Ye'll be seeing it at the right time of day."

"When's that?"

"Right before sunset. Just before the sun disappears over the central roofline. It reflects off the red glass in the window. Strange effect—it seems like it's on fire."

Once again, the amulet leaped in my pocket. I barely managed to disguise the clench of my fist from Geordie's friendly gaze. "Th— that sounds amazing," I said.

"In medieval times, red was the rarest color of glass. They made it with gold."

I made polite sounds as we finished our climb. My mind was far from medieval gold. I was concentrating on the ancient Egyptian glass in my fist.

"Right!" Geordie called, as we reached the door that led onto the roof. "I'll lead the way, folks. Ye can take all the photos ye want, but make sure not to drop your phones. It's a long way down!" He laughed at his own joke, and a number of the tourists joined in uneasily.

One by one, we stepped over a high stone threshold onto an elevated walkway. On one side, the slate-tiled roof of the transept sloped up to its central line. On the other, a dead drop plummeted to the ground. A chest-high wall of stone blocks guaranteed that no one would accidentally slip overboard.

My fellow tourists exclaimed at the view. One by one they ventured onto the walkway, chattering nervously and taking hundreds of photos.

I hung back, closer to the bulk of the nave. Geordie had said I'd have a good view from the roof. That meant the window must be…just…about…there.

From the outside of the building, the window wasn't much to look at. The lead stripping between its panes was heavy. The colors were dark, too shadowed to distinguish a clear design. In the middle, framed in a rectangular space, was a single pane of clear glass.

The scarab sat in the middle of the glass.

The beetle was as long as my hand. It was fashioned out of faience, the same bright blue as the amulet in my pocket. The head was stylized, separated by a single incised line from the paired wings. The body was an oval, bisected by a straight line. Even from this distance, I could make out the indigo shadows that defined the shape. I knew they'd be the identical shade of the lines that creased my amulet.

Geordie had shepherded the group to the far end of the walkway. His hand was stretched out, pointing to an empty platform at the top of the nearest buttress. He was talking about the 2011 earthquake, making a pitch for donations to add to the cathedral's ongoing repair fund.

A woman said something in a voice too soft for me to hear, and the entire group laughed. A child spoke up, her voice ending in a question. Geordie's gruff drawl began a response.

And the sun shifted.

Not enough to change the world. Not enough for the group

to even register. But I saw it. I saw the moment the window ignited.

Geordie was right. The red glass burned. It wasn't the same gleam that people would see from inside the cathedral. It wasn't the transparent glow of light passing through colored glass.

Instead, I saw a reflection, as if all the gold ever used to fuse red glass in the Middle Ages had surfaced on the panes of this one window. It blazed up, too bright for mortal sight.

Catching my breath against the glare, I closed my eyes. Only then could I sense the true power in the glass. Only then could I feel the sacred force of the scarab.

I *knew* it, the same way I'd known the power of my amulet. I didn't see the charm, didn't hear it, didn't taste or smell or touch. Instead, the scarab in the glass spoke to the amulet in my hand. It whispered through the bones of my body, through the scaffold of my soul.

The scarab's power reverberated through the cathedral. It *pulled* me, and I was over the stone threshold that led back inside, halfway down the ladder before I knew I'd moved.

I was breaking the rules. I was supposed to stay with my group. It was dangerous on the ladder, in the attic, on the stairs that led to the ground floor.

I didn't care.

The scarab held me in its grasp. It built a bridge to the amulet in my pocket, keeping me safe. Holding me captive.

Emerging from the stairwell, I crossed the nave to look up at the scarab window. The sun had continued its movement across the evening sky. The glass still glowed—crimson, claret, ruby, red—but the fiery force that had gripped me on the rooftop was invisible now.

From this distance, I shouldn't be able to see the scarab itself. It was too far away. Too small to be anything more than a dark speck set in clear glass.

But my imperial eyes could make out the blue faience as if it were no more than a handspan from my face. And now, looking at the underside of the piece, I could see new indigo striations.

They were carved into the scarab's belly, sharp lines that formed the shape of hieroglyphics.

Sheut, I read first. Then: *Sekhmet.* And finally: *Together we shall rule the world.*

34

I t was patently impossible to make out the words at such a distance. I couldn't read ancient Egyptian. I had no way of translating the deep-carved shapes.

But I saw them, and I read them, and I knew what they meant. I knew the force that had drawn me to the cathedral floor. I understood that my mission had not ended yet; I'd only just begun.

The scarab compelled me to walk toward a chapel, the one dedicated to St. Joseph of Arimathea. No. Not *toward* it. Into it.

A sign stood beside a door: *West Crypt Columbarium.* In front of the door stood a stanchion, with another smaller announcement: *No Admittance Without Appointment.*

I didn't care about signs. I didn't care about rules. I was caught by the power of the scarab. I was bound by Sekhmet's Seal.

I walked down the stairs, determined to make my way to the crypt.

My footsteps echoed. The stone ceiling was low, close enough that I could almost touch the vaulting. Part of my mind gibbered, reminding me about the weight of the building above us, the thousands of tons of stone that could come crashing down in a single moment.

But part of my mind knew without a doubt that I was safe. Sekhmet's Seal had guided me here. Sekhmet's Seal would protect me.

I walked past walls covered with orderly plaques. Names. Birth dates. Death dates. I was surrounded by the ashes of the dead.

The amulet in my pocket had grown hot to the touch. There was no reason to keep it a secret any longer, not here, not when we were encircled by ghosts.

When I took it out, blue light shone between my fingers. The bones of my hands stood out like cobalt X-rays. My blood glowed lapis.

The amulet wasn't home yet. It wanted to move. Sekhmet's Seal called it, as loudly and clearly as the scarab had called me. I paced the length of the crypt, until I came up fast against the far wall.

The echo of my footsteps died. My eyes could see blank stone. I reached out with my left hand, the one without an azure glow, and I touched cold, solid marble.

But those senses lied. My ears and eyes and fingertips failed me. Somehow, in a language I couldn't reduce to words, the Seal drew me forward.

I needed to go farther. Deeper.

Chris had taught me how to move beyond my senses. He'd shown me how to focus on my insignia, how to forge a path with coral and hematite.

I didn't have any coral; my ring had been taken away. I didn't have any hematite; the court still held my bracelet.

But I had something more valuable than either of those jewels. I had the amulet.

I took a deep breath and held it for a count of five. I lifted the faience charm to my forehead. Its radiance suffused my flesh, warming me, turning me to light. I produced the word Chris had taught me, the word for thought: *Skepsi.*

I exhaled slowly, letting the dark poison of tension drain out of my skull, my temples, my jaw.

I lowered the amulet, settling it against my throat. I drew another breath, measuring another count of five. I felt the blue light spread across my larynx. I thought another word from Chris: *Phoni.*

I exhaled, offering my voice to the amulet. As my breath left my body, I felt like I was drifting. The air in the crypt was the same temperature as my skin. It was thick around me, like water, like a vast sea of sand.

My hand drifted to my heart. I could see the blue glow now. I watched the light filter through my flesh as I inhaled for another count of five. Chris had given me one last word, the word for passion. I thought it now: *Pathos.*

And when I exhaled, everything was different.

35

The flagstones dissolved beneath my feet. A flight of stairs beckoned me into the darkness below.

Something about the sight was familiar. The image nagged at my brain, whispering in a well-known voice. I'd been here before. I'd stood at the top of these stairs.

Before I could take the first step, my mind filled in the blank. The descent into darkness looked like the secret passage in Judge Finch's courtroom. I felt like I was entering the administrative offices of the Eastern Empire, the booking desk and holding cells and interrogation rooms.

But I wasn't in the courthouse. And these stairs led somewhere else. Somewhere unknown. I held the amulet high, and I descended.

I found myself in a good-size chamber, a room as large as Chris's study at the Den. This room, though, lacked windows and chairs. There was no overstuffed sofa, no desk with papers laid out in perfect precision. This room was absolutely, completely empty.

At first, I thought the walls were made of cobblestones. The nubbed surface stretched from floor to ceiling, catching the light and carving it into shadows. As I grew closer, though, I saw the walls weren't rock.

They were made of bones.

I was staring at the rounded ends of femurs, thousands and thousands of them, stacked on top of each other. But unlike ordinary human bone, these bones were black, as if they'd been scorched by a merciless fire.

I should have been terrified. I should have turned around and run up the shadowed stairs, crossed the crypt and caught up with Geordie and the tourists and any other normal human being I could find.

But bone was bone. People lived. People died. It didn't matter if they were imperial or mundane; when their days were over, they were stripped to bone. I had nothing to fear here.

Holding the amulet like a sacred offering, I moved into the next chamber.

This one was lined with spines, individual vertebrae marching from floor to ceiling, ladder after ladder after ladder. These bones were blackened as well, scorched just short of cracking.

Dark ribs formed the walls of the next room, delicate curves woven together like laths that had never seen plaster. Next were blackened shoulder blades, graceful plates fitted together like miniature shields to cover every vertical surface. After that were walls that looked like rough concrete, until I came close enough to recognize the short, sharp lines of burned fingers and toes, jumbled together until they'd set like some sort of sedimentary rock.

The last room was lined with skulls.

They alternated—rows of shiny pates, polished and rounded, set beside gaping noses and open, clacking jaws. Each was darker than the one before. They could have belonged to humans, to sphinxes, to vampires. Death made no distinction.

But this room was different from the others.

This room held a dais, also made of skulls. And on that platform was a chair. No. A throne. This room held a majestic throne fashioned of seared femurs and still more skulls, the entire thing backed with a glinting arch of jet-black arm-bones, like a photographic negative of the haloes surrounding medieval saints.

A man perched in the center of the throne.

It was hard to judge his height because he was sitting, but I suspected he didn't stand much taller than I. His head seemed large for his body, but maybe that was because he was completely bald. His narrow chest was covered by a white linen shirt, which hung loosely over the waistband of his wrinkled khaki pants. His hands rested on his knees, and his fingers were long and skinny, with unusually deep nail beds.

Welcome, he said.

Except he didn't *say* it. His lips didn't move. Instead, he set the word deep inside my mind, beneath the blue light of the amulet, past the haze of my worry about credit cards and Prius parking spots and when I could finally take a shower.

"Thank you," I said, because politeness seemed like an excellent option. I hesitated at the end of that familiar phrase, though, because I didn't know what I should call him. Sir? My lord? Your honor?

He seemed far older than I was, but maybe that was because of the baldness. His skin looked like tanned leather, tawny and smooth, without a single wrinkle.

You may call me Apep, he said, again placing the words deep inside my head.

Apep? Mohammed Apep? This was the man who'd donated millions to save beloved sites in Washington DC? The man who'd endowed the American University chair? Who'd given the amulet to the National Museum of Natural History?

But no ordinary man had the power to place words inside my mind. No everyday reclusive philanthropist huddled in a secret cave of bones beneath a marble crypt.

My confusion must have amused him, because he laughed.

The sound filled the room around us, bouncing off those gleaming skulls and rattling around in the gaping eye holes and nose holes and mouths.

Perhaps you'd prefer my true form?

Blue light surged from the amulet in my hand, coruscating off the skulls and the throne of bone. My eyes automatically squeezed closed, but I forced them open, unwilling to miss anything in this impossible magical space.

In that single heartbeat, Apep had changed. The leathery man was gone, and in his place was a snake.

Its body was as big around as my waist. Its scales glittered with iridescence, brown-blue-green-grey as the beast slithered around the throne. Its head was hooded, like a cobra, and its distant tail tapered to a sharp point. It opened its mouth wide, displaying rows of concentric teeth, like a shark.

As I gaped, the beast unhinged its jaw, and it swallowed the back of the throne, the sunburst of fire-blackened arm bones. Its mouth couldn't possibly be wide enough. There was no way the serpent could consume the sun.

But with a massive crack, the throne was destroyed. The seat —the part fashioned of femurs and skulls—shattered into its component bones, flying across the room with the force of bullets.

The snake's throat worked, convulsing on itself over and over and over again with a grinding noise that made my own bones ache. The beast shuddered, curving toward the ceiling in a beautiful, terrible arch. And when it crashed down to earth, the sun was destroyed.

The snake was monstrous. It was terrifying. Yet even as I watched it destroy the throne, I saw the beauty in the beast. Its muscles rippled beneath its skin, long and strong and supple. Its teeth gleamed in the amulet's blue light, each one tapered to a perfect needle point. Its eyes were flat, glinting like onyx in the chamber of bone.

Or perhaps you find this older form more pleasing? The snake's voice reached deeper inside my head than the man's had. It rooted me to the spot, as if I were a songbird or a mouse. I couldn't have moved if the cathedral collapsed around me.

As I watched, the snake transformed again. Its hood stretched into a crest along the back of its head. Long whiskers descended from its mouth. Legs budded from its body, four appendages that coalesced from long, sleek muscle. Two more buds spiked from the back, growing taller and thinner until they transformed into wings. The snake's scales grew thicker, hardening into armor. Its iridescence rippled, cascading from nose to tail until all the grey and brown was consumed, melted into swirls of blue and green.

I stared at the dragon, mesmerized by its sinuous gait. It slunk from the dais and made a circuit of the room, each jointed leg dancing an impossible ballet. Its wings opened and closed overhead, their fine skin stretched like cloth made of sky. Its tail lashed, and I realized I'd overlooked part of the transition from snake. Four spikes, each as long as my forearm, decorated the armored tip of the tail.

The dragon's dance brought it to the far side of the room, to the door where I'd entered. With its tail stretched back to the now-empty dais, the dragon filled its lungs. Its sides heaved outward, blue-green hillocks rippling with strength. A blast of frozen fire tore through the underground chambers beyond the throne room.

Even sheltered behind the dragon's body, I was driven to my knees. My hands clapped over my ears, trying to block the creature's roar. My eyes squinted shut at the brilliance of the icy flames. I finally understood how all those bones had been scorched to utter blackness—not by fire but by ice.

I was still kneeling when the dragon turned around. His whiskers trailed on the ground below his mouth, and his crest lay flat on top of his head.

Or you might prefer my oldest form.

The wings pulled into the dragon's body, sinking toward its

massive back at the same time that the spikes were absorbed by the tail. That tail grew shorter and stouter, feeding into the creature's jointed hind legs. The spine twisted, pulling the torso off the ground, and the front legs contorted into recognizable arms. I'd forgotten to watch the head, the crest, the whiskers; I didn't see the moment they took on human form.

The armored plates lost their green, melting away to perfect sapphire flesh. The man grew fingernails and eyebrows, lashes and lips. Once again, his head was perfectly shaved. The remnants of his wings twisted around his waist, weaving together to become a cyan linen skirt.

He shifted his weight, moving his left foot in front of his right. His arms hung straight at his sides, his fingers folding into fists beside his thighs.

For one timeless moment, he was the figure in the amulet, new-forged and complete. He was balance and strength. He was ancient and new. He was glass and stone, perfect and whole.

"Sheut?" I whispered, turning the ancient name into a question.

That one word broke the spell. Or maybe it completed the ancient working. All I knew was that the second my lips moved, the glorious lapis light faded from the man before me.

Darkness rose from within him, an obsidian sheen that gathered all the blue and scattered it, hardening and transforming into something older, stranger, *true*.

"Sheut," I said again, but this time I was certain. This time I knew.

Daughter, he said.

That one word filled me. It echoed inside my skull and twisted in my DNA. It filled gaps I'd never known I possessed, empty hollows that had ached for my entire life.

When I'd found Sekhmet, she'd flooded my mind with desert sun. She'd shown me a lioness's love for her cubs, a predator's thirst for blood. She'd brought me the shift of *agriotis*, the bloodlust I could never control. She was mighty and mysterious, mother of sphinxes and vampires. Mother of me.

Sheut was from the desert too. But he was the velvet night, the bottomless cave. He was secrets and shadows. He was desire and self, the urges we hid from others, sequestered from ourselves out of terror for our own gaping needs.

He stood before me in the classic pose of my people, one foot forward, hands clenched into fists at his sides. Rigid and aloof, he waited, waited, waited, having offered the one thing I longed for most, the title: *Daughter.*

I took a single step forward. I uncurled the fingers of my left hand, the empty one that didn't hold the amulet. I set my palm against his fist and I thought one word: *Father.*

Dark light flowed into me. Power and glory and strength and the will to decide who I was and who I would be and when and how and why.

For this day, I have waited, he said. And then, before I could answer, he showed me a vision of our city, a map of Washington. Gemstones glowed upon the surface, at the Botanic Gardens, at the base of the Capitol, the National Gallery of Art and the National Archives, in a dozen other spots.

For you, he said.

Me? Once again, I thought my response, the communication suddenly as natural as speaking.

Gifts in your honor, he said. *Because I knew you lived in this city. Because I hoped you would see what I had done and understand a father's love.*

Love. I basked in a sense of rightness, of belonging. For the first time ever, I felt truly protected. Complete.

But then Sheut said, *Time is short. You must choose.*

Choose?

Go on as you were. Or unlock your full potential.

Unlock me, I said, without hesitation.

I felt his laugh, a velvet ripple that rolled along the edges of my mind. *Not so hasty, brave daughter. The change will hurt.*

I'm not afraid of pain.

You should be.

He was my father. He'd donated millions to rebuild a city, in hopes I'd recognize his love from afar. He'd come to me, now, when I was utterly abandoned, completely separate from the mundane and imperial lives I'd known. I could bear whatever pain he offered.

I'm not afraid, I said again. But I was grateful that my larynx didn't need to vibrate in my throat. My lips didn't need to form around the words. I didn't have to keep my voice from shaking.

I felt his presence gather close. The shadows around me thickened. The velvet night of the room crushed me.

Yes? he asked, giving me one last chance to flee the shadowed mystery.

Yes, I answered.

Midnight wings folded around me. Darkness seized my body. Instinctively, I gripped the amulet tight.

For one glorious, perfect moment, Sheut flowed into the faience charm, feeding the statuette, completing the form. His head was restored, drawn in blue faience, distinguished by indigo lines. Sheut stood beside Sekhmet, passive and resolute. The god matched the goddess.

I held them in the palm of my hand. I *was* them in the core of my heart. My mother and my father were made whole, made perfect, in the amulet and in me.

But I blinked, and the faience melted. It dissolved in an acid torrent, flowing through my hand and into my bloodstream. Every cell of my body opened. I was consumed with agony, with frozen fire, with burning ice.

I couldn't speak.

Couldn't breathe.

Couldn't think.

And finally, in the wake of that scouring, I was born again.

My new self was healed. Perfect. Annealed.

I no longer mourned my physical mother, the creature who

had given birth to me, who had chosen to hide my worldly father.

I no longer mourned the sphinxes, the imperfect Den who had cast me out, rather than work to understand my execution of Judge DuBois.

I no longer mourned Chris—

Go, Sheut said.

I looked at him with dazed eyes, scarcely understanding the word.

I thought we'd have more time, he said. *Even a god can be mistaken.*

I formed a dozen questions inside my head, but I didn't have a chance to reduce any of them to words. Instead, I watched as Sheut spread his fingers wide. Shadow gathered between them, and a pool of darkness flowed across the room.

It twisted and it swirled, encircling my left wrist. At the same time, a wreath of the same shadows enveloped the ring-finger on my right hand.

I braced myself for another shock of pain, for the purifying ice that had seared me only minutes earlier. This time, though, the shadows cleared without a single physical sensation.

In their wake, my flesh was marked with perfect, shimmering tattoos. Glinting dragon scales, obsidian and lapis, circled my wrist and my fingers. They were patterned like tiny scarabs, like Sekhmet's Seal.

Go, Sheut said, as I marveled at his work. *He's here.*

Before I could protest, he pushed me past the rooms of bone, up the shadow stairs, through the crypt. Before I could ask who *he* was, Sheut delivered me into the heart of battle.

36

The cathedral was empty.

The world had continued to rotate on its axis while I'd communed with Sheut. Evening had slipped into night. Darkness pressed against stained glass windows, tamping down the color, siphoning away the designs. All the candles that had flickered in side chapels were extinguished.

A handful of work lights illuminated the church, soft white lamps that splashed against stone. They weren't enough to guide tourists, weren't even enough to provide a path for worshippers familiar with the space. But they lent a sense of safety and security as the cathedral slept through the night.

But the cathedral wasn't safe. It wasn't secure. Sheut had said, *He's here.*

I left the St. Joseph chapel and stepped over a brown velvet rope, striding to the base of the altar. I didn't have permission to invade the holy space, to stand upon the dais. But I wanted the protection of solid marble at my back before I faced my enemy.

I didn't have long to wait.

Maurice Richardson entered from the narthex. He paused for a moment, just inside the door. Maybe he was giving his eyes a chance to adjust to the dim light. Maybe he was giving his

troops the opportunity to form a phalanx behind him. Maybe
he just enjoyed making a dramatic entrance.

His hair was combed back from his forehead, more grey
than black. His face was jowly, and he narrowly avoided a
second chin. The first time I'd met him, I'd thought he was fat
and out of shape, but I'd found myself sadly mistaken.

The bulk of his belly was muscle, strong bands that encircled
his waist, swelling his chest and thickening his neck. I knew his
biceps were as hard as oak, and his forearms were knotted. His
wrists were thick with brawn.

I'd fought him before—twice. He'd drunk from my throat.
Against my will, my heart started to race as I remembered the
pain of his slashing fangs, the agony as my blood was drained.

Perhaps his vampire hearing let him detect my quickened
pulse. He smiled widely, his fangs already on full display. "Sarah
Anderson," he said, and his voice carried the length of the nave
in the deadly still building.

"Richardson," I responded.

He began the long walk down the stone aisle. I dared not
take my eyes off him. I knew how fast a vampire could pounce.
But I longed to know how many vampires huddled in the throng
that moved behind him. Had he brought his Impressed men?
Or did he have other vampires to do his bidding?

He fixed his gaze on my face. "I understand you visited my
home while I was away."

I didn't bother answering.

"I *smelled* you when I returned. Funny thing about the sense
of smell. Fear shows in a person's signature, no matter how
brave a face she paints."

He wanted me to know he smelled me now. He read my
fear, had known it from the moment I remembered his punc-
turing my jugular.

But I wasn't the same creature I'd been that night two years
ago. When Richardson had drunk from me, I'd thought I was

human. I hadn't learned about Sekhmet, about the sphinx blood I carried in my veins. I certainly hadn't dreamed I was a dragon.

Enough of this farce. I clenched my jaw and tightened my gut and willed my body to *shift* into my birthright from Sheut.

Nothing happened.

Blue ice didn't rise beneath the darkness in my soul. I didn't feel a hint of wings or tail. My arms and legs didn't sprout armor, didn't change from their ordinary configuration. I didn't even feel a whisper of a cobra's hood, swaying around my head.

Richardson came closer. "I punished James, you know. I told him he should have waited until I was home, to show you a proper welcome. We could have given you a room upstairs, to spend the night. Or longer. So much longer."

I shuddered. I couldn't squelch the reaction; the mere thought of those women, serving Richardson because they had nowhere else to turn...

At the same time, I cast a thought toward the St. Joseph chapel, toward the crypt and the hidden ossuary below. *Father!*

All my life, I'd longed to know my father. Now I'd met him. Now he'd transformed me, or so it had seemed when I'd frozen with fire.

But when I called upon him, when I needed him most, I heard nothing. For one terrifying second, I wondered if I'd imagined him, if I'd hallucinated the entire encounter.

But no. I could see the tattoos banding my finger and wrist, glinting faintly in the work lights.

Richardson was halfway down the nave. The crowd behind him was larger than I'd imagined. Maybe he had thirty vampires, forty even.

"James could only tolerate so much...discipline," Richardson said. "He begged me to forgive him. He offered something in exchange."

I ordered myself not to think of how James had been tortured. Richardson had too many tools in that bag. I bit my tongue, knowing I was supposed to ask what James had forfeited. Richardson wanted me to beg.

Sheut! I called. But still no one answered. I was as alone as I'd ever been, not human, not sphinx, not anything I could possibly understand.

Richardson had reached the velvet rope. I hadn't granted his desire. I hadn't pleaded for his story, but he gave it to me all the same. "The New Commission, Sarah. James told me all about it. He explained what your Sun Lion pimp came up with. Papers for all vampires? Certification before we're allowed to roam the night?"

Richardson might be a master at revelation, drawing out his attack. His soldiers, though, were far less practiced at holding rank. They hissed at the mention of Chris's plan. I heard fangs pop, and the entire dark clutch surged closer to their master.

He held up one meaty hand, and the vampire horde settled down. "You were just waiting for Sekhmet's Seal, right? You'd bring it to the Den, like the desperate whore you are, and then they'd launch their goddamn plan."

I'd told James I needed the Seal before the New Commission could move forward. He'd passed on that information, obviously casting me in the worst possible light.

Even as I fought despair, I focused on my reflexes, on the almost uncontrollable urge to look up at the Civilization window. I didn't want Richardson following my gaze. I didn't want his vampire eyes raking over the scarab-shaped Seal.

He went on: "You thought you were so clever, hiding away. No home. No email. But I have eyes where you never imagined. I've been reading Angelique Wilson's email for weeks."

I caught my breath. That was how he'd found me. I'd logged in as Angelique, then run a hundred searches about the National Cathedral, about the Civilization Window and the Seal.

Richardson's smile was wide. "A little Lethe was all it took," he said. "My man added a key tracker the night you caught him at the courthouse. That gave me Wilson's password. The rest was waiting, to see what the cat would drag in."

I wanted to curse. I wanted to scream. I'd brought this attack on myself, because I'd been so confident I could beat Angelique, so certain the incompetent shifter would never detect me masquerading as her online.

Richardson planted his fists on his hips. "Make this easy on yourself, Sarah. I know the Seal is here. Give it to me, and I'll spare you the attentions of my...pets."

The vampires behind him whined like beasts. They were excited, shifting from foot to foot. I wondered how long Richardson had starved them, how long he'd kept them from the women in his house, from a legitimate Source, even from a drugged and desperate blood herd.

"No?" Richardson said. "Not willing to talk? Well maybe you just need a little encouragement."

He raised his right hand far above his head. The seething horde behind him froze. He snapped his fingers, once, and the vampire ranks parted.

James glided to Richardson's side.

He looked rougher then I'd ever seen him. He'd abandoned his customary white dress shirt for a black turtleneck that only emphasized the pallor of his face. His cheeks were covered in stubble, as if he'd forgotten to shave. His eyes were bleary, and I wondered if Richardson had somehow kept him awake for days.

"Drain her," Richardson commanded. "Drain the feeder bitch dry."

"With pleasure," James said, his voice nearly as cold as the fire that had purged me in the ossuary.

I'd let myself believe he was a double agent. I'd accepted his explanation, that he'd embedded himself with Richardson's men, that he'd worked for the kingpin so that he could bring Richardson down, once and for all.

Lies. All of that was lies. James was really and truly an enemy.

His fingers flexed, and I remembered them ripping apart Chris's brochure. I remembered the spiked rage in James's voice, the raw fury when he thought I'd joined with the sphinxes against him. I hadn't been able to reason with him then. I hadn't been able to make him understand the truth.

What hope did I have now, when he was standing before the vampire who'd broken him so many years before? He'd been tortured. He'd been betrayed. He was powerless before Richardson.

As the gang of blood-crazed followers hissed and hooted, James sprang lightly onto the dais. Despite the black turtleneck, he still wore dress pants, as if he'd stopped by the cathedral on his way home from work.

But James didn't work any longer. He'd left the courthouse, left his job, left his source of honor and security, all to follow the most dangerous criminal the Eastern Empire had ever known.

He started to circle behind me, moving with slow, gliding steps. I matched him instantly, drawing on the countless hours we'd trained together in the Old Library.

"Rule one," James said. We both knew what he didn't bother to say: *Don't waste energy fighting a hopeless battle.*

Well, this battle was lost before I'd begun. Even if I succeeded in escaping James, I wasn't getting out of the cathedral alive. Richardson would simply send another one of his dogs. One, or two, or three. More. No creature on earth could fight off a dozen vampires at once.

I was dead. My body just didn't know it yet.

As if he could smell my resignation, Richardson took a full step forward. The motion distracted me. I almost missed James lunging toward my right side. At the last possible second, I spun to my left, ducking low.

Vampires are fast, that was the second rule.

But James never committed to attacking my right flank. Instead, he'd feinted. Before I could parse my mistake, he'd spun to my left, to where he knew my body would be.

I barely had time to throw my head forward, to protect the vulnerable curve of my throat. My cheek stung as he sliced it down to the bone.

Blood immediately soaked my blouse. The pack of vampires bayed their excitement. Richardson clenched his fists, barely limiting his excitement to taking another step closer to the altar.

I clamped a hand to my cheekbone, futilely trying to stop the flow of blood. James looked down at me with the aloof eyes of a statue. "Rule two," he said.

I wanted to punch the words out of his throat. I wanted to keep him from baiting me, from playing with me like a cat with a mouse. Instead, I said, "Rule three." *Vampires don't breathe.*

Richardson growled a command: "Kill the bitch."

As James spared a single glance for his master, I chose not to waste my last breath on reciting the fourth rule: *Humans are better off on the ground.*

I knew it. James knew it. I started to drop and roll and pray for a single chance to use James's vampire force against him before he finished me.

I was too slow. James was at my side before I could move. One hand clamped over my right biceps. The other grappled at my left hip.

"New rule," he said. And before I could understand his meaning, he was lifting me into the air. Leveraging my arm and leg, rotating from his waist, he tossed me onto the altar, where I landed hard enough to knock the wind out of me.

I wasn't a vampire. I had to breathe. I fought to sit upright, choking, gasping, trying to gather even half a breath.

James ignored me, letting his momentum carry him around to the place where I'd crouched only a second before. Richardson was there now, fangs bared, fingers stiffened into battering rams. He howled like a wild thing, clearly crazed by my spilled blood.

And James fell on his throat.

James wasn't Richardson's lapdog. James hadn't been

defeated. He was a free and independent vampire. He was *my* free and independent vampire, doing everything in his power to save me, when my death seemed long foregone.

He didn't have the right angle to rip open Richardson's jugular—not with the spin from having thrown me to safety. He opened a shallow gash, though, torn flesh that ran from chin to larynx.

Richardson bellowed a curse. The pack surged forward, fighting each other for the first chance to draw James's blood.

James staggered toward them. I knew what he was doing. He was trying to draw the vampires away from my perch on the altar. He was off-balance, though, after his run at Richardson. He didn't see the vampire closing from the transept, a man who must have separated from the pack before they ever started their death march down the nave.

I lowered my head. I tightened my ribs, as if I were lashing on a corset. I sucked in a breath and shouted as loudly as I could, "On your left!"

James dropped to one knee, stymieing his enraged attacker. Trembling, still trying to manage a full breath, I tried to climb down from the altar to join him, to fight with him.

"Stay out of this!" he roared at me. At the same time, he landed a kick on the rogue vampire's chest, sending him flying into the pack.

Two men took the place of their fallen comrade. From their dazed expressions, I assumed they were the Impressed workers, the ones who'd been staring at computer screens for Sekhmet knew how long.

James leveled one with a hasty jab to the eyes, two stiffened fingers that sent the creature screaming down the nave. The other hurtled forward without any clear plan of attack. James grabbed his wrist and elbow, twisting hard enough that I heard the cracked ulna from the altar.

Richardson had recovered now, at least enough to shout directions. He was deploying his men in teams, sending three at a time to attack James. They rolled across the transept in waves, too many and too fast for any one vampire to defeat.

I had to help. I had to fight. But as a human, I was a hopeless liability. I'd failed at becoming a dragon. That left nothing but reaching toward *agriotis*, toward the deadly shift I'd sworn never to use again.

Agriotis? Or death at the fangs of a dozen vampires? I couldn't let James die, not without trying to save him. To save us.

I wrapped my fingers over my tattooed insignia. I closed my eyes. I breathed a prayer to Mother Sekhmet, and I *shifted*.

I knew in a heartbeat that it hadn't worked. I didn't feel the transfer through time, the belly-swooping moment when I moved faster than human eye could see. I didn't slip into the bloodlust of my goddess.

I was lost without my insignia. The black designs that Sheut had left on my wrist and around my finger carried no power.

Another trio of vampires spun away from James, spraying blood and nursing broken limbs. There was a break in the action, a single path visible only to me, from my elevated vantage point.

"To me!" I called, trusting James to hear. "Follow me!" Even as I shouted, I hurled myself from the altar, sprinting toward St. Mary's Chapel.

He tried. He fought like a trapped bear, throwing attackers left and right. He lifted a chest-high vase of flowers and sent it crashing down on an opponent's head. He brained another with a candlestick. He passed the velvet rope with a pair of vampires wrapped around his legs.

But for every man he threw aside, three more sprang to take his place. James reached my hand once, but he was ripped away before our fingers could lock. As I stood in the relative safety of the chapel's iron doorway, James was dragged back to the nave.

I couldn't stay there. I couldn't watch him die beneath a tidal wave of vampires. I searched the chapel for a weapon and found nothing but an iron stand for votive candles. It was too heavy to make a decent mace, but the spikes would work some damage before Richardson's forces took me out.

I hefted the candle stand and whirled for the doorway. But before I could fight my way to James's side, everything changed.

Lights snapped on, hundreds of them, flooding the space with a blinding glare. The transept was awash in white, blocks of marble gleaming.

At the same time, warriors flooded the nave, screaming ancient battle cries. Sphinxes filled the aisle, scores of them. Some wore hardened leather armor, the ancient battle gear of our people. Others wore modern equipment—Kevlar vests and ballistic helmets, with combat boots laced tight.

No matter their attire, every sphinx bore weapons. There were spears made of silver. Swords made of silver. Hammers and maces and fine balanced throwing stars, each and every edge glinting with deadly metal.

One sphinx stood at the front of the army. He wore a Kevlar vest strapped tightly over his blue Oxford-cloth shirt. His khaki pants were neatly creased. His fingers wrapped around an oak stake, a length of polished wood capped with a shining tip of silver.

Chris found me across the throng. His eyes locked with mine, and he raised his weapon. He nodded once, and then he shouted Mother Sekhmet's name, leading his force into battle.

Vampires howled. They wailed in agony as their chests were pierced with silver spears. They screamed as silver swords found bloody sheaths.

But once the moment of surprise was past, the vampires regrouped. They used the pews to their advantage, guarding their flanks before they leaped at attacking sphinxes.

A pair of vampires ambushed a sphinx wearing a full suit of boiled leather armor. One gripped his hair, stretching his neck to an impossible angle, and the other lanced his carotid, sending arterial blood spraying. Only as I glimpsed the dead man's face did I realize it had been Liam, the young guard who had so ably protected the Den's front door.

As chaos spread, I searched for James. He'd been dragged half-way to the altar, but he had his feet under himself and he was shaking off an attacker who had straddled his back.

A sphinx burst down the nave's right aisle, screaming as he ran. His stork-like legs carried him faster than his fellow soldiers. He used his massive wingspan to slice a silver sword through the air, driving back half a dozen vampires who wisely chose to seek easier prey.

Ronald Mortenson, leader of the Pride, seemed determined to gain the altar. He dispatched one of James's attackers. He terrified another into fleeing. Before I could shout anything, before James could, Ronald slashed at James's waist, barely pausing to pull his bloody blade free.

James collapsed to his knees. I couldn't see him above the wooden pews between us.

Sphinxes were dying. Vampires were dying. Good men and women all, who'd done nothing more than follow a leader into a battle far larger than they.

I had to do something. Anything. I had to stop this fight before everyone was dead.

I clutched my right fingers around my left wrist, taking care that my newly tattooed ring crossed over my tattooed bracelet. I touched the obsidian band to my forehead and shouted, *Skepsi!*

I lowered my hands to my throat, twisting them to press the tattoos against my voice box. *Phoni!* I cried.

I tugged at my blouse and twisted my wrists, contorting my arms to press the tattoos against the flesh over my heart. *Pathos!*

My body shattered.

My spine arched high, scraping against the chapel's iron gateway. Barely conscious amid the pain of transition, I staggered forward, dragging my feet into the clear.

Those feet curled in, ripping my shoes to shreds as razor claws emerged. Wings sprouted from my shoulder blades, reducing my blouse to a worthless white flag. The spikes on my tail destroyed my pants.

My body echoed with the pain I'd felt when Sheut seared my soul. My form was breaking down, tearing itself asunder. I was rebuilding myself into something new and magnificent and terrible.

I tossed my head, and I realized my crest had risen. Whiskers curled from my jaw, pulling my lips back from my eyeteeth.

I raised one hand, intending to feel the limits of my snout, but my fingers had curled into claws. I twisted my wrist, the better to view my knife-like talons, and light cascaded off the scales on my forearm.

My skin had hardened to armor, a carapace that looked more durable than steel. Each individual scale seemed black, but as I twisted in the blazing overhead lights, I saw glints of lapis blue.

I planted my hand on the ground, recognizing the rightness of moving on all fours. I lashed my tail for balance, accidentally taking out a pew with my spikes. I surged forward, into the central aisle of the nave.

The battle had frozen around me. Sphinxes and vampires alike gaped in disbelief. Weapons drooped toward the floor.

I could smell vampire blood and sphinx blood and bodies that had fouled themselves in death. Stronger than that stench, though, was the rank stink of terror.

Lowering my head, I unfurled my wings, testing their limits in this glorious stone cavern. Half a dozen imperials bellowed in new terror, sphinxes and vampires alike scrambling for the doors.

But one sphinx stood his ground.

Chris.

My dragon senses measured the fear in his body, the stiffness of his muscles, the wariness of his stance. But his face was tilted up toward mine. And when I looked into his eyes, I saw the essence of his being—his logic, his calm, his trust.

Slowly, as if *he* feared spooking *me*, he raised one hand. He curled his fingers, stretching for a spot I knew was tender, where my crest met my skull.

If I hadn't lowered my head for his touch, I never would have seen it: Maurice Richardson, wrapping his fingers around a shard of shattered vase. He raised the porcelain like a dagger and darted forward, shouting to his vampires, "To me, you fools! Rise and fight for me!"

I thought he was aiming for my heart. He couldn't harm me. His pottery blade would bounce off my scales like water droplets on a hot skillet. I swiveled my head toward him, opened my mouth, and roared.

But Richardson wasn't aiming for my chest. He hurtled past me, arm extended, driving straight for Chris's throat.

I didn't think. I didn't measure. I simply slipped a latch in my throat, a flap of skin I hadn't even known I possessed.

This time, when I roared, fire poured out—a great blue gout of ice, narrow and focused like an acetylene torch. I tracked Richardson for one step, two, and then he burst into flames, clothes exploding with his hair and teeth and flesh.

His Impressed vampires collapsed as his corpse hit the floor. Each body lay where it fell, regardless of bleeding wounds, of broken bones. I could smell that they were dead before the sphinxes knew. Richardson's pack would never harry another innocent again.

But one vampire still lived in the cathedral, a vampire who wasn't Impressed, who'd been scythed with a sword and burned with silver. A vampire who'd crashed to his knees, from shock or pain or blood loss. A vampire who'd saved my life when all the odds in the world said he'd die for the effort.

I didn't know how to reverse my transformation. As a dragon, I had no insignia. I couldn't offer my thoughts, my voice, my passion.

But I needed to change. I needed hands. I needed arms. And in the end, it was sufficient to *think* my way back to my human form.

This transition was easier. Maybe it didn't hurt because I was going from a larger body to a smaller one. Or maybe my cells were accustomed to my human shape. Maybe becoming a dragon would become less painful with practice.

I didn't know. I didn't care. Because by the time I opened my human eyes, I could see James fighting to gain his feet between the pews.

I stumbled toward him, awkward on my narrow human feet. I hadn't considered how much energy the transition took. Every cell in my body was exhausted. I could barely think enough to move.

But I had to reach James, had to stand beside him before any sphinx decided to be a hero and finish the job Ronald had begun, eliminating the last of their enemies in the monstrous battle.

My fingers closed around James's wrist. His eyes met mine, as dazed and confused as I expected mine were.

I heard someone move behind me, and a cloud of white settled over my shoulders. *Shirt,* my stunned brain finally supplied. I was trying to remember how to work buttons, trying to remember what buttons *were,* when my very human nose recognized Chris's familiar scent.

"Sarah," James croaked. Chris said my name at the exact same moment.

Before I could answer either of them, a clap of thunder knocked me to my knees.

37

The thunder rolled on, longer and louder and lower than any thunderclap I'd ever heard. I thought I felt it in my bones, but then I realized the stones were moving beneath my feet, rising and falling as if they floated on a stormy sea.

This wasn't thunder.

It was an earthquake.

I thought of Geordie McIntosh, with his tour of the cathedral's earlier earthquake damage. I pictured towers plummeting to earth and shattering into millions of pebble-sized stones. I considered fleeing to the outdoors, but the ground shook too much; I'd never make it.

I thought about changing back to a dragon, but I didn't have the strength.

Powerful arms closed around me. Broad hands spread over my head, firm and still, as if they could ward off a million pounds of stone. My face was pressed against a wall of pine and snow, against James.

A sharp crack sounded above the rumble of the earthquake, followed by the sound of a million goblets shattering. I looked up, prepared to see the end.

I was just in time to catch a cascade of glass and lead, showering onto the cathedral floor. Bits of red and blue and gold caught the brilliant light in the nave as they tumbled to their final resting place.

The thunder stopped. The ground stilled. A dozen voices cried out, sphinxes checking with each other about who was hurt and who required aid.

All the windows stood above us—the Te Deum planes of glass, the Space Window, the plywood hole where Lee and Jackson had once reigned. The only window that had shattered was the Civilization Window.

I moved before anyone else could reach the debris. I waded through the glass and lead, even though my feet were bare.

The scarab glowed as if it were lit from within. Its blue faience stood out in the spray of stained glass, blazing like a beacon.

It faded, though, the instant my fingers lifted it from the ground.

Instantly, I realized the temblor had been sent by Sekhmet and Sheut. My mother and father had worked together to give me a gift. They'd made it possible for me to gather up the Seal, so I could stay true to the promise I'd made the goddess.

The faience scarab felt heavy for its size. It was warm to the touch, as if it had basked in sunlight for hours. It sent a tingle up my arm, a buzz that centered in my shoulder blades, in the place where I grew wings.

James reached out to help me cross the sea of glass, concern carved into his face. I couldn't believe he was standing. In the midst of the melée, I must have misjudged Ronald's attack. James must have spun away before the silver sword actually hit him.

"Sarah," he said, his voice as broken as the Civilization window. His hand reached for me, and I realized all over again that he had protected me from the shattered glass. He had kept me safe.

"Just a minute," I said, softening my words with a smile.

Before I could see how he'd master his congenital lack of patience, I beckoned to Chris, pulling the sphinx into the privacy of the St. Mary's chapel.

I knew the gap between his two front teeth. I knew the quizzical look in his eyes that were more gold than brown. I knew the shape of his collarbones, of the chest he had bared to give me the literal shirt off his back.

"It can't be safe here," he said, glancing around the chapel. "We have to get everyone outside."

"We're safe enough," I said. "Until the EBI gets here."

He glanced over his shoulder, automatically noting the sphinxes gathering their wounded, stacking the dead. His people thrived on order. They'd minimize the work the EBI had to do to hide our battle from mundanes.

And the Bureau *would* be arriving soon. I suspected they'd moved into action the instant I purchased my twenty-seven dollar ticket to tour the cathedral. That seemed like a century ago.

We had a moment, though. A minute for normal conversation. Chris needed it, before... I wasn't ready, myself.

"How did you know I was here?" I asked. "What made you bring an army?"

He thought he didn't want to talk. He thought other things more important. Reluctantly, he said, "I couldn't leave things where they were after..." After our fight. "The next day, I hired a pair of griffins to guard you, but by the time they got to your place, you'd already left."

"I left that night." There was no reason to torture him. No reason to tell him about my fight with James.

"I looked all the places I thought you might be hiding. The whole time I was searching, I kept thinking about what you told me, about Richardson, about that house."

I nodded. It took some willpower not to look past Chris, not to see the corpses of the men and women who'd labored there.

"James said it was in South East. It didn't take a mastermind to divide up the territory. I sent out sphinxes in teams of two, going block by block. They found Richardson on the fourth night."

My lips quirked. Chris's search had been as orderly as everything else about him. It was like stirring his coffee ten times. Like organizing his pens by color.

"I posted a lookout on the street," he said. "The entire Den slept during the day. We knew Richardson could only make his move at night."

"So you followed him here…"

"It took an hour for us to mobilize. Almost too long, in retrospect. You know sphinxes. Not one of them was going to speed to get here."

"And they all had to find legal parking spaces after they arrived."

We both grinned. For just a moment I wondered how James's Prius had fared during the night, whether it was ticketed or towed. I should have known I was something other than sphinx when I'd left the car to its fate.

Chris's mood shifted. The skin tightened beside his eyes. He shot a glance over his shoulder at James, who looked like he was contemplating throwing me over his shoulder and carrying me out of the cathedral, whether I was willing to go or not.

Chris's brain understood this conversation, even if his heart was slow in catching up.

Reaching forward with my right fist, I revealed the Seal on my open palm.

"What's that?"

"Sekhmet's Seal."

"How did you know—"

I cut him off. We really *didn't* have enough time for all of that. "Apep told me. He's imperial. He's Sheut."

He made the connections faster than I'd thought he would. "And Sekhmet's Seal was in that window?"

I nodded and then I folded my fingers over the charm. "I'll use it. I'll follow Sekhmet's command to save her children."

"The New Commission—"

"No." I cut him off, because nothing he could say would make me agree again to his proposal. I'd known it was wrong when I'd accepted it the first time.

"Sphinxes have to—" He tried.

"Sphinxes *had* too," I interrupted. "You were the elders, charged with protecting our younger siblings. But that was millennia ago. After all these generations, vampires and sphinxes are equal."

He wanted to trust me. He wanted to believe. But he was the Sun Lion. He'd run the sphinxes' archive since he was fourteen years old. He'd spent a lifetime solving equations with the reliable, steady rules of mathematics. I was about to shove him into the ungoverned wilds of quantum mechanics.

"Besides," I said. "You built your argument on a single false assumption. For all these years, you've believed that sphinxes were the first born. But Sekhmet had another child. Someone who was actually first."

I gestured with my clenched fist, taking in the full absurdity of my standing in his white shirt, my bare legs, my bare feet.

His throat worked. He couldn't deny what he'd seen in the cathedral. He couldn't ignore that I was *Other.*

"I only wanted to help," he said.

I believed him. "You will. You'll help me. And the Den will help me. And we'll get together a group of vampires as well. We'll build a new solution, and we'll base it on equality. On justice for sphinxes and for vampires alike."

He wanted to argue. I saw it in his eyes and in the determined set of his mouth. But he wasn't a foolish man. He knew I was right. I was offering him order and logic and structure and peace.

Finally, he nodded. "All right," he said.

That was the instant I knew for sure. It seemed like years

had passed since Chris first said he loved me. He'd loved me when he'd shifted me into my first battle, awakening *agriotis* and my ancient memories of Sekhmet. He'd loved me when he'd tested me for membership in the Den. He'd loved me when he'd cast me out, and when I'd stolen the amulet, and when he'd come to the cathedral, willing to fight Maurice Richardson to the death.

And I loved him too, for all of that and more.

But it wasn't enough. It could never be enough.

He closed his eyes and took a deep breath. Held it for five. Exhaled. And when he looked at me again, I knew he'd forged some fragile shell of acceptance.

I wanted to kiss him, to tell him goodbye. I thought about brushing my lips against his cheek. But I didn't want to hurt him, not ever again.

I raised the Seal between us, letting it be the pledge he needed. "Soon," I said. "We'll get to work soon."

He nodded once, and then he strode to the nearest of his sphinxes and started issuing orders.

Before he could get a word out, though, the cathedral doors crashed open. Two dozen imperials flooded the nave, each one dressed in the crisp blue uniform of the Empire Bureau of Investigation.

James's fingers clamped on my wrist. "Let's go," he said.

"I don't think they're going to let us just walk out of here."

"They will if they don't get a chance to ask questions."

He pulled me down a narrow aisle between a pair of pews. A vampire body lay in a heap in the middle of the row. He nudged the corpse with his toe, as if checking to see if it was really dead.

The body rolled over. It was the strung-out foot soldier from the lair's front porch, the vampire who'd invaded the Old Library and Enfolded Angelique. His mouth was stretched in a rictus of agony. His arms were curled in front of his chest. A length of silver chain was wrapped around his wrists. His flesh had blistered and blackened before he died.

"Take that," James said, kicking at the end of the chain.

"What?" I didn't want anything to do with the creature who'd once strangled me.

"Loop the chains around your hands. I can't do it. Now."

I pulled the links free. The man's body was lighter than I expected it to be. I wrapped the chain around my wrists.

"Tighter," James said. "Tuck in the end."

Awkwardly, I followed his orders. He frowned, but he didn't risk self-immolation to correct me. Instead he closed his fingers over my elbow and marched me toward the front of the building.

I thought he'd try for one of the side doors, maybe double back to the transept. Instead, he headed directly for the main entrance. I realized why when I saw a single kitsune guard manning the egress. The fox spirit looked like she was ten years old.

"Excuse me, sir," the fox spirit said. She sounded like she was ten years old too.

James had us half-way out the door before he stopped. "Me?" he asked, with the privileged belligerence of a man called to heel on his own territory.

"No one's supposed to leave or enter the premises, sir. We have to account for every one of the casualties."

"Do either of us look like a sphinx?"

With his dangerous stubble and his rumpled black clothes, no one was likely to confuse him with a member of the Den. Me either, for that matter, with my bare feet and a shirt that hardly reached the middle of my thighs.

"Well no, sir. But I'm under strict orders—"

"I'm under orders, too." With his free hand, James slapped at his pockets, as if he were trying to produce a pen and a note-book. "What's your name, officer? Who should I report is obstructing my investigation?"

"I'm not obstructing, sir!"

"Excellent," James said, looming close enough to make the poor kitsune take a step back. "I'll add insubordination to my report as well."

She squirmed, clearly unhappy with her options.

"Does it look like I'm going very far with an imperial dressed like this?" James demanded, nodding curtly toward me. "The Bureau's job is to hide the Empire from mundanes, not to advertise it."

"You're from the Bureau, sir?"

"Who the hell else would I be? Do you see a living vampire on the floor in there?"

The kitsune crumpled under the pressure. "I'm sorry, sir. I didn't realize, sir. This is my first time at an actual crime scene, sir."

She was still making her excuses when James pulled me past the ticket booth and into the cool night air. I stared up at the dark sky. How many hours had passed since Sheut had transformed me?

I staggered, losing my footing with my head thrown back. James steadied me by pressing his palm to the small of my back.

"Easy," he growled. "I'm having a hard enough time keeping my own feet."

"You *are* hurt." I reached toward his side, where I'd seen Ronald's blade slash.

He hissed, and pulled away. "That Bureau flunky is going to realize her mistake any second. We should be far away from here when she calls in reinforcements."

It was faster not to argue. I wriggled free of the silver chain and dropped it behind a nearby bush, taking care that the metal didn't glint in the moonlight. "I don't suppose you've got a phone on you?" I asked, figuring Uber was our fastest way to flee.

"Never bring a knife to a gun fight," he said. "Or a phone to a highly illegal criminal pursuit."

"And I'm pretty sure a wallet's right out."

"Got it in one."

"Well, I'm not carrying either." I gestured at my scanty attire. "I had the car key in my pocket, before my clothes were destroyed. I suppose that means it's *somewhere* on the floor in there." I nodded toward the cathedral.

"Which car key?" he asked.

I blushed. Given my current state of semi-undress, I probably had better reasons to be embarrassed, but I was oddly reluctant to admit I'd been joy-riding around town at his expense. "The Prius."

"*My* Prius?"

I nodded. "I drove it up here. It's parked around the corner."

"Let's go," he said.

"But—"

A chatter of voices spilled out from the cathedral entrance. There was no mistaking the kitsune's little-girl whine. James grabbed my hand and pulled me toward the main road.

I was limping before we cleared the cathedral grounds. Each step I took in my bare feet found another sharp-edged stone. James threw his arm around my waist, but I felt his body spasm the instant I leaned against him.

"How bad is it?" I asked, hobbling forward another couple of steps.

"Bad enough," he said.

That meant a mundane would be gibbering in agony. I squirmed beneath his grip until he rested his arm around my shoulders. The fact that he gave in lit a spark of terror beneath my heart.

Pulling each other forward, we speed-walked down the sidewalk. A car whizzed by, honking in an apparent salute to my bare legs. I barely resisted the urge to signal my appreciation with my middle finger.

We turned onto the side street where I'd left the car. I was thinking furiously, trying to remember if it was even possible to hot-wire a hybrid. James was grunting a little with each step, leaning more and more heavily on my shoulders.

By the time we reached the Prius, I could feel blood soaking through my shirt. James ignored my increasingly frantic solicitude, though, shrugging free from my support as we arrived at the vehicle. He tried to kneel by the rear door on the driver's side.

"You can't—" I said.

He planted his palm on the side of the car. I was terrified he'd leave a bloody handprint. "So *you* get it," he hissed, nodding toward the wheel well.

I crouched down, following his labored instructions. Up further. To the right. Back more.

My fingers finally closed over a lump of metal. I twisted sharply and a magnetic box came away in my hand. At James's jutted chin, I slid the container open and removed a key.

"Not very safe, Mr. Director of Security."

"So sue me. I'm a vampire who lives alone, without anyone to call if I lock my keys in the car."

"It's a Prius with an electronic key fob. Is it even *possible* to lock your keys in your car?"

"I'm not taking any chances."

I laughed and let us into the car.

James was in no shape to drive. He was alert enough to hiss, though, as I ran three consecutive yellow lights. And he wasn't at all satisfied with my parallel parking, even after I accepted his demand to block the fire hydrant in front of my house.

I had to dig my extra front door key out of the planter on the top step.

"Not very safe, Ms. Clerk of Court."

I snorted. "That's Ms. Former Clerk of Court, to you."

He didn't get a chance to retort. He was concentrating too hard at making his way down the stairs to my front door. I had to help him over the threshold and down the hall to my bedroom.

"Wait!" I said, before he could collapse on the bed. "I don't want blood all over my comforter."

He grimaced, but he supported himself on the doorframe while I grabbed a stack of towels from the bathroom. Once the linens were protected, he collapsed onto the bed with a wince.

"Let's see," I said, tugging at his shirt.

He shoved away my hand.

"Don't be a baby!"

My heart lurched as he sank back on my pillows. He should have fought me more than that.

I thought I was prepared. I'd watched Ronald deliver the blow. I'd gauged James's failing strength as we staggered home. But I hadn't taken into account his stoic resistance to pain.

The sword had severed skin and muscle, leaving a gaping, bloody mess. But Ronald had clearly stopped short of reaching anything vital. If James's bowels had been split or his liver sliced, he never would have made it to my bed.

The blade had done plenty of damage. But the silver had done even more. The edges of the wound were charred black. The cut muscles were an angry red. White blisters multiplied around the wound.

"Sweet Sekhmet," I whispered. "How the hell did you walk to the car?"

"What else was I going to do?" he asked. "Accept a ride from the EBI?"

I gathered my hair into a loose ponytail, pulling it to one side of my throat. "Go ahead," I said, leaning closer.

He turned his head to the side. "I can't."

"Of course you can. You need to drink. You'll take weeks to heal without fresh blood."

His fingers were gentle on my chin as he made me meet his eyes. "Sarah," he said. "I saw what happened in that church. I saw what you became."

Until he said the words, I hadn't realized I was avoiding a conversation. But now, staring into his unwavering gaze, I forced myself to say the words, because I knew he'd never let me go until I did. "I turned into a dragon."

"No," he said, shaking his head just a little. "You *are* a dragon."

He was right, of course. It didn't matter that I had a human form. I was like a shifter—wolf or cat or bear. Certainly, I was wholly *other* when I took my alternative form, but that potential lived inside me with every breath I took.

It wasn't like agriotis. It wasn't a choice, or even an instinct. It was something I *was*, woven into every fiber of my being. And the destruction I'd wrought in the cathedral, the death I'd delivered to Richardson, was part and parcel of who I truly was. I had to accept that I carried within me the power of ultimate ruin. But I could—I *had*—used that power for good.

In other words, James was right. But he was also bleeding through my towels onto my bed. "I'm a dragon," I said. "But I was a dragon the first time you drank from me. My blood didn't hurt you then."

"I'm not worried about me!" he said, exasperation sharpening his tone. "You transformed today, for the very first time. And you killed Richardson. You have every right to be too exhausted for me to feed."

I sighed in exasperation. "Then I have every right to decide what I'll offer. And to whom."

I leaned close again. I knew he could smell my blood, and he had to hear my heart pounding.

His lips were cold on my throat. His chilled tongue made me shiver as he traced the scar from the night he'd cornered in his foyer. I pressed closer to his too-still body.

"Please," I whispered.

I felt his fangs express, hard against my flesh. He angled his head and made one short thrust. I tried to keep from jerking.

"Sorry," he murmured, but then his mouth was pressed against my skin. He worked the wound with his frozen lips, swallowing once before he pulled away.

"James," I warned. He needed more if he was ever going to heal himself.

"That's enough."

"The hell it is."

He refused to meet my eyes. "That's all I deserve."

"What the—"

"I went to Maurice Richardson," he said, his voice like shards of stone. "I purposely joined forces with the worst criminal in the Eastern Empire. I didn't care if I died. I just thought I could bring Richardson down too. In Robert's honor…"

His voice trailed off, and I fought a flutter of panic. A healthy James would never make such a maudlin confession. He was too far gone to manage what he was saying.

"You weren't yourself," I said gently. He needed to drink. Now.

"I wasn't strong enough. I did bad things, Sarah."

"You—"

He barely had enough strength to cut me off. "I had to make him believe he had me. Believe I was lost."

I spread my hand across his chest. "But you drew a line. That girl, the one he wanted to bring into the house."

He didn't have the energy to pull away. "Too little…" His eyes drifted closed. "Too late…"

I didn't know what to do with this James, how to handle this man who thought he didn't deserve to live. I was losing him—to silver and blood loss and regret.

I raised my hand to my throat, to the tiny trickle of blood that flowed from his incision. Swiping my neck clean, I brought my wet index finger to his mouth. His lips felt like ice when I smeared them with my blood.

For a moment, I thought he was too far gone. He'd fainted, or slipped into a coma, or worse. He was a vampire; he didn't have a pulse for me to find. I could never watch the rise and fall of his chest.

But then the tip of his tongue ventured over his lips. He swallowed the little nourishment he found.

I wiped more blood from my neck, bringing my fingers close enough for him to suckle. He tried to turn away, but I insisted, collecting twice more before I dared sit back.

James turned his face away. "I needed help," he whispered. "That day… At the rowhouse…"

Annoyed that he'd rather talk than heal himself, I leaned over his body. I purposely cocked my head, making sure my fresh blood was directly in front of his mouth. No vampire could resist his instinct to drink—not when he was exhausted and wounded and morally defeated.

James drank. His lips were still chilled. His tongue barely moved. But I leaned into him until he swallowed—once, twice, three times, four.

I was shifting for a better position when his hand closed over my wrist. His grip wasn't iron—more like soggy cardboard. But he opened his eyes, holding me close enough that I could see his pupils adjust to the light.

"I should have told you then," he said.

"Told me what?" He was so close I barely breathed the words.

"I should have told you that I needed you. That I wanted you. That I loved the courage you showed, agreeing to delete Richardson's files. I loved your strength. Your faithfulness. I love you."

My belly twisted, and my heart started pumping as if I were running a marathon. I felt James twitch, and I knew the wound on my throat was weeping fresh blood. But he didn't attack. He didn't even take what I had offered.

"You can't mean that," I said. "I killed Judge DuBois."

"You were given an impossible situation, and you did your best to make it right." His lips quirked, offering just a hint of a shattered smile. "If you'd known you were a dragon that night…"

I suddenly felt shy. He'd seen me in my animal form. He'd seen my whiskers and wings, my talons and the spikes on my tail. He knew that I was as large as a house, and as deadly as a napalm bomb.

"Sarah," he said. He dropped my wrist, and I thought he was going to pull away forever. Instead, I felt his palm against my cheek, warm now with the help of my blood. "I under-stand," he said.

"Understand what? That I'm a murderer? Or just a monster?"

His fingers shifted, keeping me from turning away. His cobalt eyes were earnest as he said, "I know what it's like to have two forms. I live a life no mundane can begin to comprehend. Let me help you with this. Let's learn together."

I'd already made my choice, back in the cathedral. I knew it. James knew it. So the only thing left to do now was to pull my hair back over my shoulder. I tilted my neck again, offering myself, leaving myself open, exposed.

He licked his lips, then rolled them over his teeth, taking care not to catch his fangs. And then he returned to the wound on my throat.

This time, his mouth was warm. His tongue was supple, rolling my vein with a slow rhythm that made my breath come short. His lips were firm, demanding, making something inside me melt.

I moaned and pressed my body closer to his. There was magic between us, the blood magic of giving life, of taking life.

He cupped the back of my neck and shifted his mouth, drinking even deeper. Now, I felt my heartbeat as he pulled, faster and faster as urgency built within both of us.

I shifted my weight, longing to throw my leg over his body, to straddle him. When I looked down, I was astonished to see how fast his wound was healing. The rent in his side had already knit together. The charred flesh had faded to crimson. The blisters had disappeared.

He might have a vampire's miraculous power of healing, but his body *had* been through the wringer. Daylight was only a few hours off. He should rest, get a full day's sleep to heal all the sword's damage. I leaned back with a rueful smile.

He caught my hands before I could pull away. "I have every right to decide what I'll offer," he said, throwing my words back at me. "And to whom."

And then his fingers were working the buttons on my shirt.

And my hands were returning the favor, unfastening his belt. We both laughed as we shifted for better angles, and I wasn't sure whose clothes hit the floor first. I kicked the bloody towels away, consciously squelching my compulsion to fold everything neatly.

He must have seen my struggle to focus, because he used both hands to pull me back to the bed. We lay beside each other, face to face. He spread a possessive hand on my hip, giving a lazy grin when I shivered.

His eyes burned fiercely, and I realized he'd reabsorbed his fangs. "Sarah," he said. "We don't have to do this. I know you wanted to wait."

I *had* wanted to wait. Chris had terrified me with his talk of the imperial birds and the bees. He'd made me fear creating a half-breed like myself, a creature not quite a sphinx, not quite another.

For just a moment, I remembered my vision with Sekhmet, when I'd caught her toddler son straying from his pride. I'd collected his toy for him. I'd held the doll in my arms like a baby, and it had felt good and sweet and right.

I wasn't a sphinx. I never had been. I was a dragon, with whatever powers and secrets and abilities—including fertility— that identity brought. The inferno banked inside my imperial body could keep me safe from any harm.

Still, a human woman would have taken a break. She would have reached inside her nightstand. She would have produced a condom and guaranteed that she and her lover did the responsible thing.

But that was something else I'd never been—a human woman. Besides, everyone knew vampires couldn't breed.

I pulled James's face close to mine, and delivered my answer with a kiss.

T *wo weeks later.*
 I shifted the white paperboard box to the right, making it align perfectly with the keyboard on my desk. I'd already twitched my stapler back to where it belonged. Pens were in the proper holders. The phone cord hung straight.

Before I could docket the first case in my inbox, I slipped my finger under the flap of the white box. Earlier that evening, it had contained thirteen miniature cupcakes from the Cake Walk bakery. I'd already sacrificed the Berry Jumble and the Caramel Castle to my unusually sharp hunger pangs.

Two cupcakes down. Why not go for three?

I chose the White Hot Chili Pepper. Before I peeled off its decorative paper, I looked again at the card that had been taped to the top of the box. "Happy second first day at the new job!" Allison's perfect handwriting made me smile.

The previous Sunday, I'd entertained her at brunch, offering a highly edited version of how I'd been fired and hired again. This coming weekend, she and I were supposed to take Nora on an adventure. I'd told Allison I was game for anything but the National Museum of Natural History.

My phone rang before I could take a bite of the third cupcake. "Yes?" I asked, feeling unreasonably guilty.

"Could you come back to my office for a moment?"

I typed a quick code to lock my computer screen and headed through the door that said *Staff Only*. It still felt strange to be back in the office. I half-expected Eleanor Owens to be waiting in the hallway, ready to haul me back to the booking desk.

I sighed in exasperation as I reached the sign that said *Director of Security*. Once again, it hung crooked. I edged it back into place with a fingernail and stepped into my boss's office.

If only it were that easy to organize the kaleidoscope of papers inside said office. Stacks covered the desk and the credenza. Three different piles spread across the couch.

"I don't know how you make such a mess!" I said.

"Vampires aren't very good with paperwork," James retorted.

"You've only been back for a week," I pointed out. "You haven't had *time* to generate this much chaos."

"Do I have to remind you that Angelique Wilson was fired for cause? Maybe this mess is *her* fault."

"Angelique Wilson was railroaded." I didn't like the woman, but I had to speak the truth. "She was dosed with Lethe when an outside force took control of her computer."

James shrugged. "She wasn't fired for giving up computer access. She was fired for lying about it, when she was questioned. And maybe she kept her files in worse shape than you thought."

I shook my head, letting him win. "You want some help straightening things up?"

"Later," he said. "I just received something you need to see. It's from Judge Finch."

My stomach dropped. I'd told him it was a bad idea for him to hire me back as clerk of court. The man had spent every day for the past two weeks in my basement apartment.

Someone had to shout *nepotism,* and the results wouldn't be pretty.

He'd told me it wasn't nepotism if I was the best person for the job. I wasn't sure about that. But I'd had a lot of fun letting him convince me.

But now, something from Judge Finch. A vampire who had plenty of good reasons to tell James he had to find another clerk. I was still awaiting trial on multiple criminal counts.

James passed me a piece of paper. Automatically, I noted the heading at the top. *Clans of the Eastern Empire v. Sarah Jane Anderson.*

I reached behind me blindly, fumbling until I found a chair. Safely seated, I glanced at the case number. There were actually two—my murder case and the action for trespass.

I read the title below the heading: *Dismissal of Prosecution.*

"What?" I asked James, as if he'd said the words aloud. He merely gestured for me to read on.

There was the usual mumbo-jumbo, the legalese that indicated the court was issuing an official order. I skimmed through a recitation of the facts, how I'd allegedly murdered Judge DuBois, how I'd allegedly destroyed files concerning legal actions against Maurice Richardson, vampire, deceased.

And then I got to the heart of the matter:

Therefore, with all evidence files missing in both of the above-referenced cases, this Court has no choice but to dismiss all charges against Defendant.

My fingers numb, I let the papers drop into my lap. "All evidence files missing?" I asked.

James shook his head. "I don't know what happened around this courthouse while I was gone."

I had a pretty good idea. I'd become a reluctant expert on exactly how evidence went missing when James Morton got a notion to work behind the scenes.

"What if those files reappear?" I asked.

"They won't," he said flatly.

"James—"

"That's a legal document you're holding, Sarah." He spoke with all the authority of the Eastern Empire Night Court Director of Security. "Can you see that it gets filed on the appropriate dockets?"

I nodded and climbed to my feet, heading back to the front office.

"Oh, and Sarah?" A smile twisted the corners of his mouth. "One more thing." He pushed back his chair and walked around the corner of his desk. "Could you close my office door for a moment?"

"Yes, sir," I said, unable to keep a matching grin from spreading across my lips.

The files on the couch got a lot more disorganized before I managed to return to my desk.

MORE MAGICAL WASHINGTON

Sarah and James are finally together, but there are more magical adventures afoot in Washington DC. Check out these other books in the Magical Washington universe!

∼

Girl's Guide to Witchcraft

Jane Madison has a problem. Or two. Or three. She's working as a librarian, trapped in a job that can't pay what she's worth. She has a desperate crush on her Imaginary Boyfriend. Her grandmother wants to reunite her with her long-absent mother. And then, she finds out she's a witch! Will magic solve Jane's problems? Or only bring her more disasters?

The Library, the Witch, and the Warder

David Montrose has a problem. Or two. Or three. Fired from protecting Washington's witches, he's stuck in a dead-end clerical job. His father says he's disgraced the family name. And instead of sympathizing, his best friend is dragging him into an all-out supernatural war. When David is summoned back to warder status, he must figure out how to juggle work, warfare, and warding—or all of magical Washington will pay the price!

The Witch Doctor Is In

Dr. Ashley McDonnell, a witch, has lost her magical powers and the supernatural hospital she manages is threatened with being shut down. Life becomes even more complicated when Secret Service agent and newly turned vampire Nick Raines appears in the ER. Can Ash regain her magic when the vampire making her hormones hum may be the man sabotaging her career?

ABOUT THE AUTHOR

Mindy Klasky learned to read when her parents shoved a book in her hands and told her she could travel anywhere in the world through stories. She never forgot that advice.

Mindy's travels took her through multiple careers—from litigator to librarian to full-time writer. Mindy's travels have also taken her through various literary genres, including cozy paranormal, hot contemporary romance, and traditional fantasy. She is a *USA Today* bestselling author, and she has received the Career Achievement Award from the Washington Romance Writers.

In her spare time, Mindy knits, quilts, and tries to tame her endless to-be-read shelf. Her husband and cats do their best to fill the left-over minutes.

ABOUT BOOK VIEW CAFÉ

Book View Café Publishing Cooperative (BVC) is an author-owned cooperative of over fifty professional writers, publishing in a variety of genres including fantasy, romance, mystery, and science fiction.

BVC authors include *New York Times* and *USA Today* best-sellers along with winners and nominees of many prestigious publishing awards.

Since its debut in 2008, BVC has gained a reputation for producing high-quality ebooks. BVC's ebooks are DRM-free and are distributed around the world. The cooperative is now bringing that same quality to its print editions.

Sign up for BVC's newsletter to find out about sales, promotions, and new books!

www.bookviewcafe.com

Made in the USA
Las Vegas, NV
26 December 2020

14755551R00187